HIGHEST PRAISE FOR DIAMOND HOMESPUN ROMANCES:

"In all of the Homespuns I've read and reviewed I've been very taken with the loving rendering of colorful small town people doing small town things and bringing 5 STAR and GOLD 5 STAR rankings to the readers. This series should be selling off the bookshelves within hours! Never have I given a series an overall review, but I feel this one, thus far, deserves it! Continue the excellent choices in authors and editors! It's working for this reviewer!"
— *Heartland Critiques*

We at Diamond Books are thrilled by the enthusiastic critical acclaim that the Homespun Romances are receiving. We would like to thank you, the readers and fans of this wonderful series, for making it the success that it is. It is our pleasure to bring you the highest quality of romance writing in these breathtaking tales of love and family in the Heartland of America.

And now, sit back and enjoy this delightful new Homespun Romance . . .

Something Borrowed

by ▮▮▮▮▮▮▮▮▮▮ author

D1026204

Praise for ▮▮▮▮▮▮▮▮▮▮▮▮▮▮ ▮un Romances, *Harvest Moon* and the award-winning *Golden Chances*:

"Delightful, warm, well-written . . . [A] 'don't miss' read!" — *Romantic Times*

"A clever plot, true-to-life characters . . . a story that will touch your heart." — *Rendezvous*

"The characters are vibrant and so alive that I feel they could walk right off the pages." — *Heartland Critiques*

Also by Rebecca Hagan Lee

GOLDEN CHANCES
HARVEST MOON

Something Borrowed

Rebecca Hagan Lee

DIAMOND BOOKS, NEW YORK

This book is a Diamond original edition,
and has never been previously published.

SOMETHING BORROWED

A Diamond Book / published by arrangement with
the author

PRINTING HISTORY
Diamond edition / February 1995

ISBN: 0-7865-0073-5

Diamond Books are published by The Berkley Publishing Group,
200 Madison Avenue, New York, New York 10016.
DIAMOND and the "D" design are trademarks
belonging to Charter Communications, Inc.

PRINTED IN THE UNITED STATES OF AMERICA

10 9 8 7 6 5 4 3 2 1

Dedication

For women of vision and courage everywhere.

Especially my women of vision and courage.

And, ladies, you all know who you are.

With love.

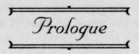

Prologue

Peaceable, Wyoming Territory
December 1872

Tessa Roarke Alexander snuggled closer to her husband, David, and burrowed farther beneath the stack of thick quilts until only her face remained uncovered. She listened to the clock chiming on the chest of drawers and realized they had been married a whole eight hours.

"David?"

"Hmm?"

"I can't stop thinking about the wedding. And I can't help thinking it was a shame Liam Kincaid couldn't stay a bit longer after the ceremony."

"I don't recall anyone missing him very much after he left the reception." David leaned over and kissed her. Lee Kincaid was one of David's oldest and dearest friends—one of the first friends he had made after being recruited by Allan Pinkerton to work as a spy for General McClellan and the Union army. But as recently as three days ago, Lee Kincaid had publicly announced his intentions to marry Tessa, and although Tessa hadn't taken Lee's proposal seriously, David wasn't quite ready to forgive and forget . . . yet.

Tessa pulled her left hand from underneath the covers,

making sure that the thin gold band that had joined the sapphire and diamond engagement ring she wore was still there. Tessa smiled to herself and said, "I think Mary did."

"Mary what?"

"Missed Liam." Only Tessa called Lee Kincaid by his Irish given name.

"My sister, Mary?" David laughed. "The same Mary who, three days ago, demanded that I break Lee's too-perfect nose?"

"The same. And I think Mary is really glad you didn't break Liam's nose," Tessa told him. "You should have seen how disappointed she seemed when I told her Liam had left for Baltimore on a mission for me. I could have sworn she was jealous, until I explained that I had hired him to locate the little girl who was supposed to be yours and Caroline Millen's." She paused for a moment and stared at her husband, suddenly not quite certain she had done the right thing in hiring Liam to try to find the child whose conception had ruined David's Washington career—the illegitimate granddaughter of the powerful Senator Warner Millen. "David, tell me the truth, did I do the right thing? If you don't want Lily Catherine to become part of our family, I'll tell Liam to forget about the search. I mean, you told me you'd had people looking for her, so I assumed that meant you wanted us to adopt her. Maybe I should have asked you first. Maybe I shouldn't have jumped to conclusions and involved Liam in your private affairs. Maybe I should have—"

David stopped Tessa's flow of words with another kiss. "You did exactly the right thing," he told her. "I do want Lily Catherine to be a part of our family. It isn't right for Senator Millen to hide her. She's an innocent. Her mother made a mistake, but that doesn't mean that Lily Catherine and I have to continue to pay for it. I want to right this wrong, and I don't *care* what other people think. I don't care who fathered Lily Catherine, or why her mother chose to name me. I only care about finding her. Senator Millen doesn't want anyone to know about his granddaughter, and while he might have cared about his daughter, as far as he's concerned, the scandal died along with Caroline. But I know Lily Catherine exists. And I know that whatever her reason, Caroline Millen gave her child my family name—Alexander. I barely knew Caroline, and I certainly didn't love her. I couldn't let the senator force me into marrying his daughter just because he *thought* I had seduced her. I couldn't be the father of Caroline's child, and I refused to marry her and be her husband. But I *can* be a father to Lily Catherine now . . . I *want* to be a father to her. And"—he smiled at Tessa—"I want you to be her mother. We want her, Tessa. Nobody else does. That's what important."

Tessa hugged her husband tightly. "Then, I'll pray Liam finds her soon."

"Me, too," David admitted.

"And I'll be sure to ask him for frequent reports."

"Lee won't always have anything to report," David warned. "You'll be disappointed."

"Maybe so," Tessa said. "But Mary won't be. Not as long as Liam stays in contact with us and the Trail T."

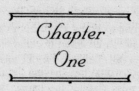

Chapter One

Trail T Ranch, Wyoming Territory
April 1873

"Mary, Mrs. Russo is here for your fitting."

Mary Alexander turned from the simple fractions she was copying on the blackboard to find her mother, Sarah, standing at the back entrance to the small one-room schoolhouse. "I'll be there shortly. Let me finish this assignment and dismiss the children."

Sarah nodded, then turned and walked back down the path around Mary's cabin to the main house of the ranch.

The Trail T ranch had been purchased and the main house built by Mary's uncle, Benjamin Jordan, her cousin Reese's father, back in 1862. Reese, his wife, Faith, and their girls, Joy and Hope, lived in the main house now. Legally, Reese was the owner of the huge spread, having inherited the vast acreage and a fortune to operate it, from his father, but the Trail T was a family operation. Cabins around the main ranch housed Mary, her parents, Charlie & Sarah, and her younger brother Sam along with Mary and Reese's mutual grandparents, Duncan and Elizabeth Alexander. The Trail T was also home to Joe, a cousin by marriage, his children, Jimmy and Kate, and his second wife, Ruth, and her son, Daniel. Mary's older brother, David, lived with his bride of

4

four months, Tessa, and their adopted son, nine-year-old Coalie, several miles away in the small railroad town of Peaceable, Wyoming, where David practiced law.

She finished copying the last fraction, then walked to the open door and watched as her mother made her way back to the big house. Mary would miss having family nearby all the time. She would miss sharing the happy, noisy communal family meals with her parents and grandparents, and Reese and Faith—miss the ranch talk and Reese's discussions of business. But she would miss teaching the children most of all.

Mary walked back into the classroom and faced her pupils—Joy, Jimmy, Kate, Daniel, and Coalie, who was spending the week at the ranch along with Tessa and David.

She lifted a wooden ruler from the top of her desk and gripped it tightly for strength. "Class," she addressed her students, "as all of you know, I'll be getting married Tuesday morning. This is my last day as your teacher."

The children groaned.

Kate raised her hand. "Aren't you coming back after you get married?"

"No," Mary answered. "I'll be living in Cheyenne. Faith will continue your lessons until the end of the term."

"Can't you come back to the ranch to teach us?" Kate's fifteen-year-old twin brother, Jimmy, asked. "We're not that far from Cheyenne."

"I'd like to," Mary admitted. "But my husband doesn't want me to continue my teaching."

"Why not?" nine-year-old Joy demanded. "Doesn't your husband want you to be happy?"

Out of the mouths of babes. Mary stared at Joy, marvelling at the little girl's perception. "Of course Mr. Cosgrove wants me to be happy, Joy. What makes you think he doesn't?"

Joy shrugged. "Reese says that we should encourage the people we care about to do the things they love so they'll be happy. And you always tell us how much you love teaching us. So I thought Mr. Cosgrove would want you to keep on doing what you love to do."

"Ideally," Mary agreed, "that would be the case, but Mr. Cosgrove is a banker at the Cheyenne Stockholders' Bank, and his position in society demands quite a bit of entertaining. He needs his wife to be free to socialize—to serve on women's committees and host teas and receptions for prospective customers. Mr. Cosgrove feels that, in order for me to be the kind of partner he needs, I'll have to devote the majority of my day to those kinds of things. He doesn't think I'll have the time to entertain *and* continue to come to the ranch and teach." Mary did her best to explain the situation without casting a bad light on her future husband. The children wouldn't understand the fact that Mr. Pelham Everhardt Cosgrove III felt that teaching the children on the ranch paled in comparison to being his wife.

"I don't understand," Coalie told her. "Tessa is learning to read and write so she can clerk in David's law office, and David's real proud of her. We both are," he added.

"And Faith runs the ranch house, orders all the supplies, helps Reese with the business accounts, and still has time to take care of Hope and Reese and me," Joy reminded Mary. "And she's real happy."

"My mother gets paid for cleaning the main house and doing the washing for everybody on the ranch," Daniel contributed. "She earns money just like Joe does. She's proud that she can work and still to be a good wife to Joe and a mother to Jimmy, Kate, and me."

"And Aunt Sarah cooks for all of us," Kate said.

"And she and Faith and Tessa serve on almost every women's committee in Cheyenne," Jimmy added. "Why can't you keep teaching us?"

"I'd like to," Mary told them, trying hard to keep from crying. "I really would. But sometimes we have to compromise. Sometimes we have to give up things we'd rather not give up for the sake of the people we care about."

"But this is Wyoming," Coalie announced. "This is a territory where women have just as many rights as men. David says so."

"My future husband doesn't want me to work and, well, in spite of the rights that the territory of Wyoming gives me, I feel I have a personal, marital, and moral duty to try to please my new husband . . ." She let her words trail off. *At least in the beginning,* she promised herself, *until she could convince Pelham that she would be a better, happier wife if she continued to teach.*

"Why don't you marry someone else?" Joy asked. "Someone who wouldn't mind your coming out to the ranch to teach us."

"Yeah," Daniel agreed.

Mary managed a small smile. "I can't marry anyone else. I've given my promise to Mr. Cosgrove. And even if I hadn't promised Mr. Cosgrove," she reminded them, "I couldn't marry anyone here on the ranch, and I don't know any other eligible gentlemen."

"What about Detective Kincaid?" Coalie asked.

Mary stopped suddenly and felt the blood rush to her face at the mention of Pinkerton detective Lee Kincaid. Her voice came out in a high-pitched squeak when she focused her attention on Coalie. "What about him?"

Coalie ran a hand through his hair, then shrugged his shoulders in a nonchalant gesture. "He seemed to like you back in Peaceable."

Four months earlier, Mary had come face to face with the devilishly handsome detective in her brother David's law office. She remembered his thick blond hair, his broad shoulders, the way his mustache framed his sensuous mouth, and the humor sparkling in the depths of his deep gray eyes. There had been a definite spark of something between them, but it hadn't been *like.* It was more *dislike—Intense* dislike. She and Lee Kincaid simply rubbed each other the wrong way. And it was a shame really, when Mary thought about it, because Detective Lee Kincaid was definitely the most handsome and exciting man she had ever met.

She shook her head and faced Coalie's intense green-eyed gaze. "Oh, no, Coalie, you're mistaken. Detective Kincaid isn't interested in me. And even if he were," she paused, her expression wistful. "He leads such an adventurous life, he would probably be bored to tears with the slow pace of life on the Trail T."

"Mr. Kincaid didn't dance with anyone except you at David and Tessa's wedding party," Kate pointed out. "I thought it most romantic."

Mary frowned. At fifteen, Kate found everything romantic. "Mr. Kincaid only danced one dance because he left for Baltimore on business immediately after he danced with me. He simply couldn't spare the time for further dances."

"But still, he danced with you," Kate persisted.

"Nevertheless," Mary struggled to dismiss the foolish romantic notions Kate brought to mind. "It's all neither here nor there. I'm engaged to marry Mr. Cosgrove on Tuesday, and that's the end of it."

"So you don't really want to continue teaching us?" Joy asked, on the verge of tears.

"Oh, no, Joy. It's not that I don't want to continue to teach you. I love you all." Mary rushed to console her favorite pupil. "It's just that . . ." She gripped the ruler tighter and felt its sharp edge dig into the tender flesh of her palm as she fought to keep the tears burning in her eyes at bay.

"She loves Mr. Cosgrove," Kate tried to explain.

"No, I—" Mary hesitated as she stared down at the two halves of the ruler that had snapped in her hands. She hid the pieces of the ruler in the folds of her skirt. "I'm sorry to disappoint you. I had hoped to be your teacher at the end-of-term celebration. I'll miss you all." She cleared her throat and took a deep breath before continuing in her most professional schoolteacher voice. "It has been my pleasure and my privilege to teach you. Thank you all. Class dismissed."

Minutes later, Mary Alexander stood on a box in the bedroom of her tiny cabin near the schoolhouse and gazed at her reflection in the full-length mirror. The face staring back at her showed the strain of the last few days and the look in her brown eyes expressed her sense of foreboding. Several times during the last few days, she had been tempted to cry off. But her cowardice stopped her. Pelham Cosgrove was the only man who had ever thought to offer her marriage, and Mary was very much afraid no one else ever would because she was part Cherokee Indian. She knew it wasn't the best reason to marry, but it was reason enough. After all, Pelham didn't love her any more than she loved him.

That was the problem, she told herself over and over. They didn't love each other. That was why she was plagued with uneasy feelings and doubts. She was about to exchange her safe, secure, well-loved existence and walk into the unknown with a man she hardly knew. And not for love—but for the sake of her cowardice and his convenience. Mary bit her bottom lip and stared at her reflection. Marriage was a lifelong pledge, and suddenly Mary wasn't completely sure she wanted to tie herself to Pelham Everhardt Cosgrove III for even a day—much less the rest of her life.

She sighed. Her daydreams of marriage had been so much more pleasant than the reality. In her daydreams, she fell in love and married a man who loved her—one who also loved the ranch as much as she did. In her daydreams, her husband moved into her cabin with her and they lived and loved and worked and raised their family on the Trail T. But her intended had other plans. He wanted to live in Cheyenne, and soon Mary would be legally and spiritually bound to follow him into the city—leaving behind her job, her family home, her parents, grandparents, brothers, cousins, nieces and nephews, and everyone else who lived on the ranch.

Mary frowned at her image in the silvered glass as she thought of all the upcoming changes. She would miss her loved ones, and the familiar confines of her cabin, but she would miss her job as schoolmistress to the ranch's children most of all. Pelham didn't want her to work, and had flatly refused to discuss the possibility of her riding the five miles out to the ranch every day to continue teaching. Nor would he consider allowing her to teach in Cheyenne. Mary sighed. So Pelham Everhardt Cosgrove III was a bit rigid and set in his ways. So what? He was punctual, reliable, and hardworking. He would go far with the Cheyenne Stockholders' Bank. So what if his kisses didn't set her heart racing? Mary reached up and thoughtfully traced the line of her bottom lip with one finger. Hadn't Pelham told her that the reason he didn't want her to continue teaching was that he wanted to start a family right away? Soon she would have children of her own to teach, and wasn't that what she really wanted? She should count herself lucky that Pelham was, in his words, willing to overlook her unfortunate lineage. If only she could convince herself of that before the wedding.

"Are you sure this is what you want?"

Mary looked around and caught Tessa's worried expression. "Of course. Why do you ask?"

"Maybe because you don't look very happy," Tessa Alexander answered bluntly.

Mary turned back to the mirror. "What gives you that idea? I think the dress is splendid. Mrs. Russo has outdone herself." She fingered the white lace and satin folds of her wedding dress, twisting this way and that, viewing the gown from different angles. "It's turned out very well. I'm pleased with my choice."

Tessa took a deep breath. At times Mary reacted just like her older brother, David, hiding her feelings with meaningless conversation. But in the four months since she had married Mary's brother, Tessa had learned to get straight to the heart of David's concerns, and she was equally confident she could do the same with Mary. "We're not questioning your taste in clothes," she said. "We're questioning your choice of a husband."

"We?"

"Yes."

Mary whirled around at the sound of another voice answering and came face to face with Faith. "You too?"

Faith nodded. She had come west as Reese Jordan's bride nearly four years ago and now made her home with Reese and the girls—Faith's eight-year-old sister Joy, and their three-year-old daughter, Hope—on the Trail T Ranch. Although the ranch was technically owned by the Jordans, Reese's father had followed Cherokee tradition and welcomed his wife's family onto his land and the Trail T had become home to all the members of the Jordan-Alexander clan.

Tessa Roarke had joined the family just four months ago when she married David Alexander, and Faith and Tessa had become the sisters Mary had never had—her dearest friends, staunchest supporters, and closest allies . . . until now.

Faith spoke up first. "I'm sorry, Mary, we don't mean to hurt you, but somebody had to come out and say what we've all been thinking." She watched as Mary gave Tessa an accusatory glance. "There's no call for you to be upset with Tessa. She speaks for all of us. We love you."

"I see," Mary replied dryly. "You question my judgment because you love me."

"Yes," Faith answered. "Because we're worried about you."

"Are you?" Mary arched an eyebrow and turned to Tessa.

Tessa recognized the gesture. She'd seen David raise his eyebrow that way at witnesses in the courtroom when he doubted their sincerity. "You know we are. Why shouldn't we be worried? This is all so sudden. How long have you known Pelham Cosgrove III?"

"Long enough."

"How long?" Tessa demanded. "Two weeks? Three?"

"Longer than you knew David before you married him," Mary countered.

"Our situation was different," Tessa protested.

Mary arched her eyebrow once again. "Was it?"

"You know it was," Tessa answered gently. "David and I married because we loved each other." She met Mary's brown-eyed gaze, refusing to be intimidated. "I don't think you can say the same about you and Mr. Cosgrove."

"Stop right there," Mary warned as a rush of tears brimmed in her eyes, threatening to overflow. She looked to Faith for support.

"Tell us you love him," Faith whispered.

Mary looked at Faith and Tessa and saw the concern in Faith's solemn gray eyes and Tessa's bright green ones, and the identical worry lines wrinkling their foreheads. "You two are the sisters I never had. Why can't you trust me? Why can't you and David," Mary glanced at Tessa, then focused her attention on Faith, "and you and Reese just wish me well?"

"We do, Mary." Faith was merciless. "That's the problem. We do wish you well. We want you to be loved and to be happy."

"I am."

"Then reassure us," Tessa probed. "Tell us you love the man you're going to marry. Tell us he loves you."

Mary bit her lip as the tears she had been struggling to hold in check suddenly began to roll down her cheeks. "I can't."

Tessa stepped closer, put her arms around her, and hugged her tightly. "Then help us, Mary. Please. Help us to understand why you are so determined to tie yourself to a man you don't love."

Faith produced a delicate lace-edged handkerchief from

the pocket of her housedress and reached up to wipe away Mary's tears. "It's all right," Faith said, patting Mary on the shoulder as she choked back another sob. "Take your time."

Mary took the handkerchief from Faith and dried her eyes. "There isn't much to tell," she said. "It's very simple. I agreed to marry Pelham Cosgrove because he feels it's time he started a family. And I met his requirements for a wife."

"His requirements?" Faith bristled. "What requirements?"

"Looks, education, fine manners, and a certain amount of breeding." Mary smiled sadly.

"A certain amount of breeding? What does that mean?" Tessa demanded.

"It means he's the first gentleman I've met who has looked me in the eye, took note of my obvious Indian heritage, and still considered me enough of a lady to offer marriage instead of an affair."

"Oh, Mary, I can't believe your Cherokee blood makes any difference," Faith said. "He must really care for you."

"He really cares about our family's bank account," Mary told her.

"And you're willing to settle for that?" Tessa couldn't believe her ears.

"Yes," Mary answered fiercely. "I'm a twenty-eight-year-old spinster schoolteacher, and a half-breed to boot. Yes, I'm willing to settle for a husband, a home, and children of my own. I know the price is high, but I'm willing to pay it."

"But Mary . . ." Faith began.

"Look at me," Mary ordered, "and listen carefully. I need to marry Pelham. And although I'll miss it, I need to get away from the ranch. I need to get out from under Mother's wing and your shadows. I need to start living my own life. I love the two of you like sisters. I love your children and I enjoy teaching them, but I envy you. I want what you have.

I want a family of my own. I feel as if I'm missing so much. And every day I seem to die a little bit inside. I'm afraid that if I wait too long, I won't have anything to offer a husband. I'll be too old and too set in my ways and too bitter—always thinking about what might have been. I can't be a hanger-on anymore." Mary caught her breath as she began to cry once again. "I don't like what it does to me. Don't you see? I'm afraid of what I'll become. I have to seize this opportunity."

"But Pelham Cosgrove . . ." Tessa protested.

"Please," Mary struggled to maintain her dignity. "try to understand. I know he's not what you wanted for me. He's not what I planned for me either, but"—she managed a wry smile—"as a half-breed Cherokee woman, I'm not likely to be overwhelmed by marriage offers, no matter how attractive or educated I am." She shrugged her shoulders. "Whether I like it or not, I'm too Indian for most white men, and too white for most Cherokee. I've discovered that life—at least *my* life—isn't like a fairy tale. Prince Charming isn't going to ride up on a white horse and sweep me off my feet." But even as she said it, an unbidden image sprang to mind—that of a blond-haired rogue with sparkling gray eyes, a voice that could melt butter, and a thick blond mustache that framed a most intriguing mouth. A blond-haired rogue who had, during each of their brief encounters, made her feel like the most desirable woman in the world.

Mary closed her eyes in an attempt to blank out the picture in her mind, and when her feeble effort failed, she tried a different tack. Fixing her gaze on the heavy pearl-encrusted ring on her left hand, she began to methodically replace her mental image of her Prince Charming, feature for feature, with a picture of Pelham Everhardt Cosgrove III, and prayed it would last a lifetime.

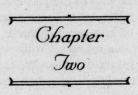

Chapter Two

Chicago, Illinois
April 1873

Lately it seemed to Lee Kincaid that even his most meticulous plans had been derailed by unexpected events. And what was worse, he decided as he finished slapping the soot and cinders from his hat and stepped through the front door of the Pinkerton National Detective Agency on Washington Street, was that there didn't seem to be a damned thing he could do about it.

He dropped his leather satchel on the floor and looked up to find Allan Pinkerton's oldest son, William, sitting behind his desk. Lee took a deep breath, then let it out, and ran a hand through his hair, smoothing out the place where his hatband had molded it to his forehead. His trip to Washington had been plagued with problems, including the suicide of Senator Millen—the man he had gone to investigate. His scheduled return had been delayed by the state funeral.

Lee muttered a curse beneath his breath. His holiday would just have to wait a little longer. If he had learned one thing after twelve years of working for the Pinkertons— first with Allan, and now with his sons, William and Robert—Lee Kincaid knew the Agency would demand an immediate recounting of the status of the Millen case. He knew he wouldn't be allowed a respite until the Agency was satisfied with his report, but he hadn't expected William to be waiting in his office to get it firsthand.

"It's about time you got back," William greeted him.

"I just stepped off the train from Washington."

"You were expected back three days ago."

Lee shrugged out of his long canvas duster and draped it across the wrought iron hat and umbrella stand beside the door. Such was the life of a Pinkerton detective; always on the road traveling from one place to another, and always with unexpected delays and daily reports to file. He tossed his hat atop the duster. "I stayed for Senator Millen's funeral."

"I heard," William told him. "The death of a United States senator usually means problems—especially when it's rumored that he died of unnatural causes."

Lee snorted.

"Was it a suicide?"

"Mrs. Millen is saying her husband died of heart failure. That's the official story."

"What's your story?"

"If he had a heart." Lee hooked the toe of his boot under the rung of a chair, pulled it to him, and straddled it. He propped his arms on the back of the chair and fingered one corner of his mustache. "I'd say it stopped beating after he put a gun to his head and pulled the trigger." He folded his arms across the back of the chair.

"You think it had anything to do with Tessa Alexander hiring you to locate the senator's illegitimate granddaughter?"

Lee met his boss's intense gaze. "I don't think that my asking questions about the senator's personal life or his business dealings helped the situation. Senator Warner Millen definitely had family skeletons in his closet. But if you're asking whether I personally had anything to do with the senator's death, rest assured that the Agency isn't responsible." Lee smiled. "I might have wanted to put a gun to the old bastard's head, but I didn't."

Pinkerton nodded once. "That's what I wanted to hear." He managed a grim smile. "Any luck?"

"Not yet. But there's going to be a senate investigation and I'm pretty sure they'll find that Millen was being blackmailed by his former clerk."

"Reason?"

Lee grinned and his gray eyes sparkled. "Now that's where my investigation comes in. The senator's former clerk knew the whole story of how Senator Millen railroaded David Alexander out of Washington for refusing to marry his daughter—of how the old man falsely accused David of seducing and abandoning Caroline Millen, leaving her alone and in the family way. And it seems"—Lee paused for effect—"that the senator's clerk also knew that Senator Millen, a man who prided himself on his loyalty to his family and friends, disowned Caroline when her daughter, Lily Catherine, was born. He sent the infant to live with strangers when Caroline died just hours after giving birth. The clerk apparently demanded money for his silence, and the senator had no choice but to pay."

William shook his head. "Nasty business, blackmail. Have you located the clerk?"

"Not yet," Lee told him. "But we will. I left Willis working on it. I couldn't telegraph a report that included the blackmail of a U.S. senator, so I figured you would want me to come back and report to you in person."

"It's a good thing you did."

"Why?" Lee asked. "What's up?"

"I'm not sure," William admitted. "But you've got a stack of telegrams waiting for you and all of them are marked urgent." William picked up the small pile of papers and thumbed through the messages. "There's four from Tessa

Roarke Alexander in Cheyenne and"—he counted—"one, two, three from McLeary."

Lee reached for the telegrams. "Who's McLeary?"

"Tom McLeary," William explained as he handed them over. "He's the man who took your place in Denver."

"Denver?" Lee frowned. "I don't know McLeary and I haven't been to Denver in"—he thought for a moment—"over three years. Not since—" He broke off abruptly. "What business could your man in Denver have with me?" He quickly scanned the three telegrams from Tom McLeary. "He says someone has left something for me there and he wants me to come and claim it. He says it's urgent."

William nodded.

"Any idea what it is?" Lee asked.

"None. But McLeary's not a man to exaggerate. If he says there's an urgent situation waiting for you in Denver, then I think you should take care of it. Immediately."

Knowing William Pinkerton had already read all the telegrams, Lee asked, "What about Tessa? What does she want?"

"She's ordering you to report to the Trail T ranch." William smiled his first genuine smile of the afternoon. "As soon as possible. She says it's very important."

Lee scratched his chin. "She knew I was going to be in Washington," he told Pinkerton. "She's probably eager to find out what I learned there."

"That's my conclusion as well," William agreed.

"And?"

"Go pack another bag," William said, "I'll send someone down to purchase your tickets and to telegraph McLeary that Mr.—" He paused, glanced over at Lee, then asked, "Smith or Jones?"

"Jones," Lee answered, a flash of amusement lighting the depths of his gray eyes. Assumed names were another part of detective life. "I was Smith on the last trip."

"Mr. Jones is on his way."

"Do I have time to shave and change shirts?"

Pinkerton glanced down at the copy of the train schedule spread out across his desk. "If you hurry. The next Chicago and North Western train leaves in forty-five minutes."

Detective Liam Kincaid arrived at Union Station in Denver some thirty hours later, exhausted, bone-weary, and heartily sick of traveling. He stretched his tired muscles as he stepped from the train onto the platform, eyed the hired hacks waiting at the depot, and decided to walk the few blocks up Sixteenth Street to Larimer. Pausing at the corner of Sixteenth and Larimer, Lee set his satchel on the ground beside him. He reached in his jacket pocket and took out a slip of paper with Tom McLeary's address. He scanned the signs painted on the false-fronted buildings and hanging from signposts until he located the Talbotton Hotel, across the street and four doors down. Lee stuffed the address back into his pocket and picked up his satchel once again.

"I'm looking for Mr. McLeary," Lee said as soon as he stepped through the etched glass door of the hotel. "I'm supposed to meet him here."

The desk clerk, a slight balding man, responded immediately. "Yes, sir. Mr. McLeary's been expecting you. He's in the Silver Suite. Up the stairs, last door on the right. Here's your room key. Now, if you'll please sign the register." The clerk turned the guest book around to face Lee and offered him a pen and a key on a silver chain.

Lee frowned. "I didn't ask for a room."

"Mr. McLeary booked the Silver Suite for you, sir, and your guests," the man explained.

"My guests?"

"They arrived a week ago, sir. They're waiting upstairs in your suite. Now, if you'll please sign."

Lee took the pen. He paused for a moment, gathering his

thoughts, forcing his weary mind to function, then scrawled a name across two lines of the book in bold, black letters. L. K. Jones. Lee shoved the pen and the register back across the polished surface, grabbed the key in one hand, picked up his bag in the other, and took the stairs two at a time.

He stood in the carpeted hallway outside the door to the Silver Suite for several minutes before he raised his hand to knock. He was getting too old for this. God, he was tired. Tired of traveling, of sleeping in hard chairs in stuffy trains surrounded by equally tired strangers with cranky children and crying babies. He was tired of the long list of aliases he used, the variety of personalities he assumed, the endless blur of towns, the relentless trailing, and the never-ending hunt. It was at times like this, when his brain was numb and his body beyond exhaustion, that he longed for the comforts of home. Lee toyed with the idea of settling down—of finding a nice woman to marry and a maybe a ranch to run. He grimaced at the idea. He had toyed with the idea of running for president, too, upon occasion, but that didn't mean he was the man for the job. Lee shook his head, then pinched the bridge of his nose and rubbed his eyes. He knocked once on the wooden door. He needed a thick beefsteak, a hot bath, and clean bed. He had to get this business with Tom McLeary out of the way. Leaning against the door frame, Lee raised his hand a second time.

But the door opened before he could knock.

A middle-aged man dressed in a dark suit stood in the entrance to the suite eyeing him warily.

"Are you McLeary?"

"That's right," McLeary answered. "And you must be Mr. Jones."

Lee managed a tired smile. "I see you got the telegram from our friend in Chicago." He offered his hand. "I'm Lee Kincaid."

"Thank God, you're finally here." The wary look on

McLeary's face changed instantly into an expression of complete relief. He reached out and took Lee's hand, then stepped back and motioned Lee into the sitting room. "Make yourself at home." McLeary kept his voice low. "I've been trying to reach you for a week." He reached for Lee's leather bag and set it on a walnut desk while Lee removed his hat and duster.

"I was in Washington," Lee answered automatically, as he placed his garments atop the satchel. "Your telegram mentioned you had something for me. What is it? And what the devil is this all about?"

"Old debts."

Lee turned at the sound of the voice.

An elderly man sat on a horsehair sofa. Lee watched as he leaned heavily on a sturdy black cane to raise himself from the depths of his seat. He, too, was dressed in a black suit—an old fashioned black suit, with a loose, thin striped chambray shirt, and a plaid waistcoat. He wore slippers on his feet instead of shoes. Lee studied the old man from the top of his white head to his slippered feet. Something wasn't quite right about his appearance, but Lee was too tired to figure it out. He continued to watch as the old man limped painfully over and held out his hand. His knuckles were gnarled and swollen with age and arthritis, and his skin was dry and parchment thin.

Lee gently shook his hand. "Do I know you?"

"No." The elderly gentleman spoke slowly and carefully. His words sounded rehearsed. "My name is Judah Crane. I'm an attorney. I represent the estate of Tabitha Gray."

Lee reacted as if he'd been punched in the gut. He let go of the lawyer's hand and stepped back as the air seemed to rush from his lungs and his knees began to wobble. Tabitha, dead? Six months ago, his partner Eamon Roarke had been killed, and now Tabitha. Lee tried to take a breath. His friends and former partners were dropping like flies. Swaying on his feet, he groped for the nearest chair. "Tabby Gray?" Lee glanced at McLeary, then at the lawyer, seeking confirmation.

McLeary nodded. "She died eight days ago."

Lee sank onto the chair. "Where? How?"

"At her home in Utopia," McLeary answered. "A little town about fifteen miles north of here."

"I know where it is," Lee snapped, suddenly irritated by Tom McLeary's matter-of-fact tone. "I passed through it on the way here. What happened to Tabby?"

"She caught a chill," Judah Crane blurted out. "She caught a chill and couldn't shake it." Crane's big brown eyes filled with tears as he looked at Lee. "I drafted her last will and testament," he said. "I drafted Tabitha's will and I did exactly as she asked. I was careful. You won't find any mistakes in it. No loopholes. It's ironclad."

"How did you know how to contact me?" Lee asked the lawyer.

"She gave me a letter," Judah answered simply. "And made me promise to remember to mail it." He limped back to the sofa and sat down.

Watching Judah limp back to the sofa, Lee noticed the old man's shirttail hung down beneath the hem of his coat. "I didn't get a letter," he said.

"The letter came to me," McLeary interrupted, "at the Highland Company post office box."

Lee squeezed his eyes shut. Of course he hadn't gotten the letter. Tabby didn't know where he was, but she had known how to contact him. They had worked together once, here in Denver. She'd been his partner. She knew to use the Agency post office box, knew that any mail sent to the Highland Company would eventually reach him. There was no Highland Company. It was simply a rented post office box—a means of collecting information and sending information to the Agency or to other agents.

McLeary continued. "She asked whoever received the letter to contact you through the Agency in the event of her death. And she asked that an Agent be sent to Utopia"— McLeary cleared his throat—"to oversee arrangements. She also left a letter for you." He walked over to the desk, unlocked the top drawer, and removed a letter. McLeary handed the envelope to Lee, then walked over to stand by the sofa. "We can leave the room if you'd like some privacy," he offered.

Lee stared at the envelope addressed to him. "No," he murmured, "I'd rather you stayed." He took a deep breath to steady himself, then ripped open the letter and read:

April 3, 1873
Utopia, Colorado Territory

Dearest Lee,

If you read this, my worst fears have been realized. I have pneumonia and the doctor doesn't offer much hope for me. He's recommended that I put my affairs in order.

I've never cared much for loose ends and I certainly don't intend to leave any for someone else to tie up. As you so often reminded me, I do like things wrapped up in neat tidy packages. And that, my dear, is where you come in.

I've taken the liberty of making you the executor and chief beneficiary of my estate. I don't own very much property, but there is a house and a silver mine in Utopia, a legacy from my late uncle, Arthur Ettinger. The mine doesn't bring in a great deal of income. The current silver veins are nearly played out, but I'm told there might be other larger, more productive veins. I haven't pursued that possibility simply because I lack the necessary capital to do so. I tell you all this because I'm leaving the mine and the house to you. The property is yours to do with as you see fit so long as you agree to meet the terms of my will.

(1) You must agree to keep the property for a term of no less than twenty years.

(2) You must agree to resign from the Pinkerton National Detective Agency within ninety days from the date of my death.

(3) You must agree to refrain from working in any area of law enforcement.

(4) You must marry and settle in Utopia within thirty days of my death. And you must allow Judah Crane, my attorney, to witness the marriage.

I want you to know, dearest Lee, that none of this is meant to cause you pain or harm. Quite the opposite, I'm afraid, for you see, I want you to live a long and happy life. That's part of the reason I'm asking you to make what I know you will see as impossible sacrifices.

"Dammit, Tabitha!" Lee jumped up from his chair and began to pace the confines of the sitting room. He stared up at the ceiling, focusing his gaze on the plaster medallion surrounding the brass chandelier, while he railed at Tabitha. "How can you ask me to do this? Why?" Lee wanted to crumple the letter and toss it aside. He wanted to forget about her demands or the reasons behind them. "I won't do it," he glared at Tabby's lawyer. "I don't give a damn about a silver mine or a house in Utopia, Colorado. I'm not quitting the Agency for Tabby Gray or anyone else!" He walked over to the old man. "I don't need this! You keep the silver mine and the house and whatever else she left behind."

"That's the problem, young man," Judah answered. "I can't keep what Tabitha left behind. I'm too old. My mind and my eyesight are failing me. I can't remember things. And I don't see well enough to look after her."

"Her?" Lee stopped in his tracks and stared at the old man. "What the devil are you talking about?"

Judah Crane pushed himself to his feet. "Come here, young man," he grabbed Lee by the elbow, "and I'll show you." Leaning heavily against Lee, Judah limped to one of the suite's two bedrooms and quietly opened the door. "You look at that," he nodded toward the bed, "and finish reading Tabitha's letter before you say what you are or are not going to do."

Lee stared at the little girl on the narrow bed. She lay sprawled on her stomach at the head of the bed. She'd flung the covers aside and her pillow lay on the floor. One plump arm was wrapped firmly around a doll with dark brown hair and an exquisitely painted porcelain face with a red bow-shaped mouth and big brown eyes—a doll that bore a striking resemblance to Tabitha Gray.

Lee edged inside the room, moving closer to the bed to kneel beside it. Her hair was dark brown, almost black, damp with sweat, and tangled around her face. Her long eyelashes fanned against her pink cheeks. She slept with her lips pursed around her right thumb, her index finger curved across the tip of her nose. Smiling, Lee gently brushed her damp curls away from her face, looped the strands behind her ear, then traced the line of her jaw with the tips of his fingers. He pulled the sheet up around the child's shoulders and over the doll in the dirty wedding dress, then pulled the sheet tight and tucked it beneath the mattress. "Sweet dreams, little one." Lee touched her cheek, marvelling at the baby-soft feel of her skin as she gave a small restless sigh and opened her eyes.

He sucked in a breath. He had expected her eyes to be the soft doe-brown color of her mother's. Or maybe a different shade of brown, lighter or darker—even green or hazel, but he never imagined the brilliant sapphire blue staring back at him.

She smiled shyly, yawned widely, then closed her eyes and returned to her dreams.

Lee straightened, then carefully backed out of the bedroom. He didn't speak. He simply returned to his chair, gathered the scattered pages of Tabitha's letter from the floor, and finished reading:

If I know you as well as I think, I expect you'll be ready to throw this letter and my will back in Judah's face once you've seen the terms. But remember, dearest Lee, I never asked anything of you in life, and never expected more than you could give. And I only ask these things of you because I can't see to details myself. Don't think badly of me for making demands now when you can't refuse me in person and please don't disappoint me. I believe I have every right to make demands. It's only fair when I'm about to give you my most precious gift.

Her name is Madeline. She's two and a half, and I want you and the bride of your choice to adopt her and raise her as your own. . . .

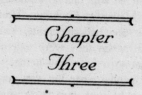

Chapter Three

"What happens to the little girl if I refuse?" Lee glanced toward the bedroom door as he folded Tabitha's letter and returned it to the envelope.

"She'll be sent to a Methodist Foundling Home in St. Louis," Judah answered matter-of-factly.

"Christ, Tabitha!" Lee swore, raked his fingers through his hair and glanced up at the ceiling once again. "Doesn't she have any relatives?"

"She doesn't have any kin that I know of. None that Tabitha mentioned," Judah answered.

Lee muttered another curse under his breath. "Well, she *must* have a father." He turned to the old lawyer in frustration. "Where the hell is he?"

"Tabitha didn't happen to mention a name," Judah replied, as he stared closely at Lee, his gaze intense and very acute. "I assumed you knew."

"How could I," Lee demanded, "when I didn't even know Madeline existed?"

"My mistake," Judah said softly. "I thought you might be the man we were waiting for."

Though Judah's words were phrased as an apology, Lee heard the silent indictment. "Aw, hell." He shoved his hands in the front pockets of his trousers and began to pace around the room. Tabby had known him too well. She had known, when she dictated her will, that he wouldn't let her daughter grow up in the Methodist Foundling Home or any other foundling home. She had apparently remembered Lee's mentioning once, when they were together, how he had feared being sent to a foundling home when his mother died and his great relief when his army sergeant father had decided to keep Lee with him in Washington. And Lee remembered being appalled when he learned that Tabitha hadn't been so lucky—that she had, in fact, spent several terrible years in the Methodist Foundling Home in St. Louis when her parents died in a wagon train cholera epidemic.

"What have you done?" Lee railed at the ceiling as if he could see Tabby looking down at him from a cloud on high. *Damn* Tabby and her penchant for trying to arrange his life. "You always had to have the last word, always had to have things your way. Well, you sure as hell didn't leave me much room to maneuver this time!"

"She didn't leave any room for you to maneuver, young man," Judah informed him. "Her will is ironclad. I saw to that," he added proudly.

"I thought you were losing your faculties. I thought that was why you can't take the little girl." Lee glared at the lawyer.

"I'm seventy-seven years old, young man," Judah answered. "Some days everything is there," he tapped the side of his head with his index finger, "and some days everything is blank. The day I wrote Tabitha's will, everything was there."

"And today you're wearing your nightshirt with your suit," Lee muttered beneath his breath, finally realizing what was wrong with Judah's appearance. "Just my luck."

"Well, what are you going to do, young man?" Judah demanded. "Do you want the house and the mine or not? I need an answer."

"I told you I don't give a damn about owning a house in

Utopia, Colorado, or a silver mine." Fighting a creeping sense of desperation, knowing there was nothing he could do to change the terms of Tabby's will or the demands she'd made of him, Lee glanced over at Tom McLeary. "What about you, McLeary? You're based here in Colorado. Wouldn't you like to get out of living in hotels? Wouldn't you like to own a big house and a silver mine?"

"No thanks." McLeary smiled.

"Why not?" Lee demanded.

"I've seen the house and the town. I'm not in the market."

"What about the little girl?" Lee tried again, "You wouldn't want her to be sent to an orphanage, would you? Why don't you take her?"

"I'm in the same line of work you're in," McLeary reminded him. "And I'm not ready to retire—or get married."

"Well, neither am I," Lee shot back.

"Tabitha Gray wasn't my partner," McLeary answered, "I didn't know her. Besides, I've been looking after Mr. Crane and Madeline for a week now. It's your turn. I've got my own business to see to." McLeary walked into the other bedroom to gather his hat, overcoat, and his carpetbag. Lee followed him and stood blocking the doorway.

"Yes or no, young man?" Judah asked, coming to stand behind Lee.

"It's not as simple as that," Lee hedged, searching for a way out of the situation. "How am I supposed to meet her demands?"

"I suppose you should start by finding a bride," Judah answered thoughtfully.

"In twenty-two days? You're asking the impossible!" Lee snorted in disgust.

"Tabitha didn't seem to think you would have trouble finding a suitable bride in the time required," Judah replied.

"Yeah, Kincaid," McLeary added as he bumped his heavy

carpetbag against Lee's leg, forcing him to step aside. "Denver's a big town, full of beautiful women. I'll bet you could get one to the altar in three weeks."

"If I *had* three weeks," Lee answered sarcastically, stepping back—right into the old lawyer. "But I have to be in Cheyenne tomorrow morning on more urgent business." He turned to Judah. "Can't you stay with Madeline for a couple of days until I get back?"

"No. Not me." Judah backed away, shaking his head. "You can't leave me here alone with that precious baby. I don't actively practice law anymore because I accidentally burned down my office. I forgot to bank the coals in the stove. Another time I left my door wide open all night. And I'm always forgetting what I'm doing or where I put things." He turned to Lee. "What if I forgot to keep an eye on her? What if something happened to her?" He took out a handkerchief and wiped his face. "I'm too old to be left in charge of a two-and-a-half-year-old child. I can't be trusted. That's why Tabitha didn't leave her to me. My mind's all here right now." Judah tapped his finger against his right temple. "But what if it's gone an hour after you leave?"

Lee reached over and awkwardly patted Judah's shoulder. "Don't worry about it. I'll think of something else." He eyed McLeary speculatively. "Be a pal, McLeary, and stay here for another couple of days and keep an eye on Judah and the little girl."

"I've been a pal," McLeary said as he passed Lee and headed for the door. "I'd never even met you, but I've been here for a week keeping an eye on your new family because you have a reputation as being a good man and a hell of a detective. I've got an investigation of my own to continue and I'm a week behind as it is. But if you're going to Cheyenne on Agency business, I might be able to go in your place."

Lee shook his head. "I appreciate the offer, but I've got to go report to an Agency client. And she'll have my head on a platter if I don't show up."

"Then it looks like you have two choices: either stay here, or take the old man and the little girl with you." McLeary chuckled as he opened the door and stepped out into the hall.

"No," Lee disagreed, "it looks as if I don't have a choice at all."

"Cheer up," McLeary said, "if your client's a woman, maybe you'll get lucky. Maybe she'll agree to marry you."

"Nope. She's already married. . . ." Lee stopped abruptly and slowly repeated his thought aloud. "Married. *Mary*. By God, that's it!" He slapped his open palm against his forehead. "Mary Alexander. She's perfect—beautiful, intelligent, honest, practical, and loyal. Very loyal." Her strong sense of loyalty would work to his advantage. She would understand why he had to accept the terms of Tabby's will—why he couldn't allow little Madeline Gray to grow up in the Methodist Foundling Home.

And she lived in Cheyenne at the Trail T ranch—the place to which he'd been ordered to report. She was part of the family. Lee smiled. Mary Alexander was the sister of one and the first cousin of the other of his closest friends, David Alexander and Reese Jordan. She was a perfect choice. Hell, he and David and Reese were as close as any three men could be. He was practically part of the Jordan-Alexander family himself. Marrying Mary would make it official.

Lee thought back to the first time he met Mary Alexander. He had known Reese Jordan and David Alexander since the early days of the war, when the three of them had worked as spies for the Union under Allan Pinkerton. He hadn't met David's younger sister, Mary, until the morning he walked into David's law office in Peaceable, Wyoming, and been unexpectedly attacked. It hadn't been funny at the time, but

Lee could now smile at the memory of Tessa Roarke swinging a pot of hot coffee at his head while Mary Alexander backed him out the front door of the law office with a loaded two-shot derringer in her hand. Just thinking about that made him grin. Mary—slender, elegant woman that she was—had been able to do what few men had ever accomplished. She had taken him by surprise and gotten the drop on him.

She was the only woman he had ever met who hadn't fallen for his easy charm and Irish blarney. On their first meeting, Lee had stared down the short barrel of her silver pocket pistol and decided death could very easily come in the form of a beautiful woman. At their second meeting, he'd been facing her brother's fists while Mary leaned out a two-story window and loudly encouraged David to break his perfect nose. Lee traced the contours of his mustache with his index finger. And the last time he saw Mary, at David and Tessa's wedding, she had threatened to break his nose herself—or shoot him full of holes—if he didn't watch his wandering hands and quit trying to kiss her every few minutes. And damned if he hadn't thought the pleasure of kissing her might be worth a couple of holes.

Mary Alexander had matched him move for move every time he'd met her. She had enough courage to sustain an army, a fierce love of home and family, an unshakable definition of right and wrong, and an incredible sense of loyalty. As far as Lee was concerned, she had all the immediate qualities he required in a wife: she understood family loyalty and she was available. And she was beautiful.

Very beautiful. Just looking at her set his pulse racing. And the thought of holding, of kissing her. . . . Lee grinned, supremely confident now that he'd made his decision. "Mary will agree with me. She'll understand." Yeah, the more he thought about it, the more he liked the idea. Mary was the perfect woman for him to marry. The only woman.

He grabbed McLeary's right hand and began to pump it. "Thanks, Tom. You're a genius." His mind began to whirl with the list of things he needed to do before he reached Cheyenne. "Look McLeary, I hate to impose on you further, but would you please stay with them for a couple of hours while I run some errands?" Lee hurried to the table and grabbed his hat and coat.

"You're not going to leave us?" Judah asked, an edge of panic in his quavery voice.

"Only for a couple of hours," he answered, "and only if you'll agree to stay here until I get back." He turned to McLeary.

McLeary nodded. "I'll stay for an hour. No longer. Agreed?"

"Okay," Lee agreed. "But if I've only got an hour, you'd better tell me where I can find the nearest jewelry store."

"Jewelry store?"

"Yeah. Since I don't have time to court the 'bride of my choice,' " he quoted Tabby's phrase, "then I sure as hell better have a nice ring in my pocket when I propose."

"Are you going to take us with you when you go?" Judah asked.

"I suppose so," Lee told him, staring at the striped chambray nightshirt Judah wore beneath his waistcoat, wondering what Mary would say when she saw them. "I can't leave you alone here in Denver, any more than I can let that little girl grow up in some damned St. Louis orphanage."

"You're going through with it?" McLeary was amazed.

"What choice do I have?"

"None. You want me to telegraph our friend in Chicago for you?" McLeary offered, carefully referring to William Pinkerton.

"You might as well," Lee said. "He'll find out soon enough anyway."

"What should I tell him?"

"Tell him congratulations are in order. Tell him I'm getting married."

Lee couldn't disguise his sigh of relief as the train rolled to a stop at the station in Cheyenne at seven-thirty the following morning. He stuffed Maddy's doll into the deep pocket of his duster and gently lifted the little girl from her place on the seat beside him back into his arms. During the past few hours, he'd learned quite a bit more than he ever wanted to know about the needs and demands of a two-and-a-half-year-old child and added a couple of very important "Maddy-talk" translations to his vocabulary.

Lee sighed and raked his fingers through his hair. He wasn't thinking straight. He was tired and irritable from an *another* long train ride and another sleepless night, and his right arm was numb from holding Madeline most of the night. He wanted to hand the little girl to Judah for a while, but one look at the elderly attorney told Lee that Judah was not at his best. Shifting Maddy to his left side, Lee ushered a sleepy, disoriented Judah into the crowded aisle as the passengers began to disembark from the train. A hired porter followed behind them with Lee's leather satchel and the heavy trunk containing Judah and Maddy's belongings.

"Mama," Madeline whined, turning and twisting against Lee's chest.

"Easy now, sweetheart," Lee soothed, "we'll be at the ranch in less than an hour and I promise you a nice big breakfast and plenty of nice ladies to take care of you."

It was a promise Lee couldn't keep. As he drove up the circle drive leading to the two-story log and stone main house of the Trail T, the first thing Lee noticed was the quiet. There were no people about the place: no ranch hands, no children, and no chatter of women going about their chores. Handing the buggy reins to Judah, Lee jumped down from hack, bounded up the stone steps of the front porch, and pounded on the front door. He slipped his hand beneath his duster and rested it against the comforting grip of his Colt. He pulled the gun free of its holster as the front door swung open, then re-holstered it just as quickly. "Ruth," he breathed at the startled Indian woman standing in the doorway. "Thank goodness you're here."

"We were looking for you to get here sooner, Mr. Kincaid," Ruth told him. "They left without you. Tessa said they didn't dare wait any longer."

"Who left without me?" Lee asked.

"The whole family."

"Where did they go?"

"To the church in Cheyenne. Tessa said that if you got here I was to tell you to hurry."

Lee thought for a moment, mentally counting the days. "Today isn't Sunday, it's Tuesday. What's everybody doing at church?"

"They're at Mary's wedding."

"What did you say?" The blood seemed to roar through Lee's brain.

"Everybody is at Mary's wedding except those of us who stayed to prepare the wedding breakfast and a couple of the older boys."

"Mary? Mary Alexander?" He managed to get her name out.

"Yes."

"Christ!" Lee swore, glancing over his shoulder at Judah and Maddy in the hired buggy. "What time is the wedding?"

"Nine-thirty."

He pulled out his pocket watch and flicked open the lid. If he hurried, he could make it to the church in time, but not in the buggy. He turned back to Ruth. "I need the fastest horse on the place and somebody to drive the buggy for the old man."

Ruth looked over at the elderly man and the child. The little girl was crying, while the gentleman tried awkwardly to comfort her. "They can stay here until you get back."

Lee shook his head. "They have to go with me."

Ruth shrugged. "My son, Daniel, is in the stables. He can drive the buggy. I'll get some sweet bread for the little girl."

Lee leaned over, placed his hands on either side of Ruth's face, and kissed her. "Thanks, Ruth," he said as he sprinted toward the stables.

"The fastest horse on the ranch is Reese's white stallion, Pegasus," Ruth called after him.

As he galloped toward Cheyenne on Pegasus' back, Lee called himself ten kinds of a fool for even considering doing what he was about to do. It was a crazy idea. And Lee knew he would never had thought of it if he hadn't been desperate and suffering from the effects of too little sleep.

He couldn't really be riding into Cheyenne for the sole purpose of asking Mary Alexander to marry him. He didn't want to marry again. He had been married once before for a few idyllic months before the war had intervened—before the war had cost him his beloved wife.

And although he occasionally toyed with the idea of marrying again and settling down, of raising a family of tow-headed children, when the demands of his job had become too much to tolerate, Lee knew he wasn't ready for the responsibility. It had taken him years to come to terms with his wife's senseless death. It had taken him years to recover from the heartache. Jeannie's death had nearly killed him. And Lee knew he couldn't withstand another loss like Jeannie.

He'd be better off to keep to himself, and to his bachelor ways. He didn't need a wife or a little girl. He couldn't risk losing his heart again. And Lee was very much afraid that

Mary Alexander and little Madeline Gray might work their way inside that vulnerable organ before he had a chance to stop them.

It was crazy. He was crazy. He ought to turn Pegasus around and head back to the Trail T. He ought to wait for Tessa and David there. He had no business riding hell-bent for leather toward the Catholic church in Cheyenne . . . no business at all. But, Lee reminded himself, lately all his plans had been derailed by unexpected events. What was one more?

He gripped the reins tightly, then squeezed his eyes shut, muttered a heartfelt expletive, loosened his grips on the reins, and let the white stallion have his head, praying all the while that he'd make it in time to stop the wedding.

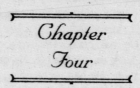

"Do you, Mary Amanda, take this man to be your lawfully wedded husband?"

"No, she doesn't!" Lee flung open the doors of the church.

"What?!" The couple at the altar, along with the entire congregation, turned to stare at the intruder.

"May I ask the meaning of this interruption?" the priest demanded.

Mary Alexander paled beneath her bridal veil and clutched the nosegay of white roses and orange blossoms in a death grip. She couldn't see the face of the man standing just inside the church entrance but she recognized the voice—the faint, but familiar Irish lilt that belonged to Pinkerton detective Liam Kincaid. Her pulse seemed to flutter. It was as if by thinking about him the other day, she had conjured him up today. Mary swayed on her feet, suddenly dizzy, and was afraid she might swoon. Her groom gripped her elbow to keep her upright. She closed her eyes, counted to ten, then opened them again to see if the Irish rogue was real or a figment of her imagination.

"I told you, I object to this wedding," Lee announced, stepping out of the dark foyer and into the light. He fixed his gaze on Mary and started down the aisle.

A loud murmur echoed through the church as the wedding guests realized that a strange man was intervening in the marriage of Mary Alexander to Pelham Cosgrove III. Somewhere close behind her, Mary heard Reese say, "What's he doing? We can't let him do this." And heard her brother David answer, "Stay out of it. Mary can handle him without our interfering."

And suddenly she realized he was real. If Reese and David could see and hear him he had to be real, very real, and about to ruin her last chance of marrying a respectable gentleman while she was still young enough and pretty enough to get one. "Stop right there!" Mary ordered, holding out her hand to ward him off, even as she feasted on the sight of him—his expressive gray eyes, the intriguing mustache, the calf-length canvas duster covering his suit, lending him an air of mystery. "Don't come any closer." Her knees were quaking with nerves. It was one thing to wish, in an abstract way, for Prince Charming to come and save her but it was quite another thing to have him actually try to do it, especially just as she was about to become another man's wife. "You can't object."

"But I do," Lee said softly, continuing to move closer.

"We've already done that part," Mary protested, nodding toward the priest. "He's already asked if anyone objected. Nobody did."

"I may be a little late, but I'm in time to object," Lee told her.

"All right, then," Mary challenged him. "Why?"

"Why what?" Lee paused for a moment, stunned. He hadn't expected her to demand a reason.

"Why do you object to my getting married?" She handed her mangled nosegay to her sister-in-law and chief bridesmaid, Tessa, and placed her hands at her sides, bracing herself for a showdown with Liam Kincaid.

"I don't object to you getting married," Lee told her, "I just object to your marrying him." He eyed Mary's tenderfoot groom, staring as Pelham Cosgrove III sucked in a deep breath, then let it out. Lee noticed that Cosgrove's nostrils flared with the effort. Lee continued to stare. Something about Mary's bridegroom looked familiar—as if he'd seen him before.

"Why?" Mary asked again. "What business is it of yours who I marry?"

Dammit, Lee thought, she *would* have to make him explain things in front of God and everybody. He took a deep breath. "You can't marry him. Not when . . ."

Mary held her breath, waiting for Liam Kincaid to admit he had feelings for her, and had had feelings for her from the moment they met in David's office four months ago. "Go on."

"Not when," he searched furiously for the correct phrase. "Not when I have a prior claim."

"Prior claim?" Mary's voice rose an octave. "Since when have you had a prior claim on me?"

"I've known you longer."

"How do you know?" she challenged him again. "How do you know Pelham's not a long-standing family friend?"

Lee turned his fierce gaze on Pelham Cosgrove III. "How long have you known her?"

"A-almost three months," Pelham stammered, as Lee reached the altar and stood towering over him.

Lee grinned in satisfaction. "There. I've known you much longer."

A whole thirty days longer, and that was in calendar days, not in time spent together. Mary opened her mouth to point out the fact that one month did not equal much longer, but Pelham interrupted her.

"Is that true?" Pelham Cosgrove III turned to his bride. "Does he have a prior claim on you?"

"He . . ." Mary began.

"Yes, it's true," Lee answered. "We've known each other

for quite a while. One might even say she knows me intimately, since we've been together in a few very interesting"—he drawled the word, giving it a different meaning—"situations."

Mary thought she heard someone chuckle nearby. It sounded like a man—it sounded like her brother, David! Her face colored a deep angry shade of red. She had been alone with Lee Kincaid only once, when they danced together at the celebration following her brother David's marriage to Tessa Roarke four months ago. Lee had tried to charm her with his Irish blarney and steal a kiss or two, and he hadn't been successful on either account. Mary turned to Pelham, "You must believe me when I say I've never heard such outrageous lies and insinuations."

Pelham Cosgrove pushed Mary out of the way and stepped forward in front of Lee. "What kind of situations?"

"Pelham—" Mary reached for her intended's arm and turned to the priest. "Father, go on with the ceremony."

"Not until he explains what he means," Pelham balked.

"Liam Kincaid, I'm warning you . . ."

Lee watched as Mary shoved her right hand into her skirt pocket. He'd seen her make a move to her skirt pocket twice before—and both times she'd withdrawn a deadly little silver two-shot derringer and aimed it at him.

"Not this time, Mary Two-shot!" Lee reacted like a flash. He grabbed hold of Mary's arm and pulled her to his side. He held her around the waist with one arm, in a firm but gentle grip, as he patted her right skirt pocket, searching for the little silver weapon.

"Let go of me," she hissed at him as he moved on to her left side. "I didn't bring it into the church."

Lee pretended to be shocked when in fact, he was more than a bit relieved. "What?" he asked. "Nothing old, nothing new, nothing silver, nothing blue for your wedding?"

"It's at home with my other personal belongings," Mary

informed him. "And the rhyme is: something old, something new, something borrowed, something blue."

"What did you do? Pack it in your luggage as a little wedding night surprise for your groom?" Lee asked sarcastically.

"Not at all," she replied sweetly, kicking him in the shin as hard as she could. "I put it in a safe place. You might say I was saving it for a special meeting with a charming rogue like you." Mary hadn't felt it right to bring her gun into church on her wedding day, but after carrying it for protection since she was a girl, she wasn't accustomed to being without it for any length of time either, and had carefully slipped it into the skirt pocket of the traveling suit she intended to wear on her honeymoon.

Lee had sucked in a breath when her foot connected with his leg. He tightened his grip around her waist, ducked his head, and whispered, "So you do find me charming. Oh, Mary-girl, I love it when you whisper sweet nothings in my ear."

Mary shivered at the touch of his warm breath against her neck. She let out a low gasp at the sound of his voice—as smooth and slow and sweet as warm honey—so close to her ear. She leaned back against him, forgetting for the moment everything but the pleasure of simply enjoying the wonderful feel of the strong, warm chest and arms that surrounded her.

"Unhand my bride," Pelham Cosgrove ordered.

As Mary jerked out of his embrace, Lee studied her bridegroom. He supposed the man was handsome in slicked-back, neat and tidy, buttoned-down sort of way. And under other circumstances, he might even have liked him. But not now; not today. He had a mission to complete, and Mary's bridegroom was standing squarely in the way of his objective. "Stay out of it," Lee growled.

"*I* stay out of it?" Pelham sputtered. "I'm Pelham Everhardt Cosgrove III, and this is my wife."

"Not yet, she isn't," Lee muttered, swinging Mary up into his arms.

"I demand an explanation!" Pelham shouted.

But before Pelham could get his explanation, the front door of the church opened and every head in the church turned to watch Judah Crane limp into the sanctuary with Maddy at his side.

Lee groaned.

"Young man." Judah's voice was thin and reedy as he called to Lee, but strong enough for the sound to reach every nook and cranny of the church's quiet interior. "Did we miss the wedding?"

"No, Judah," Lee answered gently, in spite of the sinking feeling in the pit of his stomach. He had arrived at the church some minutes before the slow-moving buggy and had expected Judah and Maddy to wait with Daniel in the vehicle outside the church. "I thought you and Maddy were going to wait in the buggy until I came to get you."

"But we wanted to witness the ceremony. Have we missed it?"

"Not yet. Now, why don't you take Maddy back outside until I come and get you?"

"No!" Maddy's objection was instantaneous. "Want Mama." She pulled her hand out of Judah's, spotted Lee holding Mary in his arms at the end of the center aisle, and ran clumsily toward them. "Mama!"

Mary could only stare in disbelief as the precious little girl toddled up to Lee and grabbed hold of his duster. "Mama! Mama!"

"Do something!" Mary ordered.

Lee all but dropped Mary on the floor in his haste to set her on her feet and reach for the distraught child. "There, there." He wiped at Maddy's tears with the sleeve of his coat. "It's all right now, Maddy darling. Mama's here." He reached into his coat pocket and pulled out the porcelain-faced doll he had stuffed in there during the train ride from Denver and handed it to the little girl.

"Mine." Madeline grabbed the doll and hugged it close to her body, then reached out for Mary. "Mine," she repeated.

Every pair of eyes in the church turned to stare at Mary. She glanced around at faces of her wedding guests and stepped away from Lee and the child he was holding.

It didn't take a genius to figure out that Maddy's actions had been misinterpreted by just about everybody in the church. Even those people who knew better. But Lee didn't care about the wedding guests or their reactions to Maddy. All he cared about was Mary's reaction, and the reaction of her groom. Lee hadn't intended to use Madeline to sway Mary—unless, of course, there was no other way. But, he decided, little Maddy's arrival was timely and effective. He could look at the faces of the wedding guests and tell that. Lee glanced over at Pelham Cosgrove III. Unless he missed his guess, Mary's groom was about to bow out of the wedding, and that was just fine and dandy as far as Lee was concerned. He was more than ready to step in and relieve him. What wasn't fine was the expression on Mary's face. Lee knew he'd never forget her look of pain, and he was very much afraid he might never get over the feeling of guilt that slammed into his gut when he saw it. Lee knew he ought to try to explain the situation to Cosgrove and try to make things right for Mary. A true gentleman would explain and apologize. A true gentleman would make his excuses and walk out of her life. But Lee held his tongue.

Mary turned to face her husband-to-be and saw the accusatory look in his light brown eyes. "Pelham, I don't know what's going on here, but it isn't what you think."

"Really?" Pelham sneered at her. "Because I'm thinking

that maybe she's"—he jerked his head in Madeline's direction—"the prior claim he has on you."

Mary gasped. "That's not true! I've never seen her before. And I've only know this man for four months. I couldn't possibly . . ." She let her words trail off as she caught a glimpse of the skeptical expression on Pelham's face, then impulsively reached out to touch his arm.

But Pelham brushed her hand aside. "Oh, come on, Mary, do you take me for a complete fool? She ran to you and called you her mama. And even I can look at her and see that she's related, with that black hair and those big blue eyes. She looks just like your cousin Reese's little girl."

Mary focused her attention on the child in Lee's arms. Pelham was right. She did look like Hope, so much so that they could almost be twins. She turned to Pelham and tried again. "There's a definite resemblance, but Pelham, that doesn't mean you're correct in what you're thinking."

"I'm thinking I made a terrible mistake in thinking you would make a suitable wife for me," Pelham told her. "I've ignored the advice of my friends and colleagues and generously overlooked your unfortunate heritage. I was willing to marry you and make you Mrs. Pelham Everhardt Cosgrove III because I thought you were different. I thought you were a lady."

"I am a lady!" Mary protested, reaching out to him as huge sparkling tears clung to her lashes and rolled down her face.

"No, you're not."

"Pelham, you don't understand . . ."

"I understand all I need to understand. You're not a lady, you're a—"

"One more word," Lee spoke to Pelham through tightly clenched teeth. "Say one more word, insult her one more time and, mister, you'll be swallowing your pretty white teeth."

Pelham drew himself up to his full height and puffed out his chest. "I don't have to stay here and listen to this." He held his hand out to Mary palm up. "My ring, if you please."

"Pelham, please don't do this." Mary saw her dreams for the future rapidly turning to dust. She made no attempt to stop the flood of tears. But she had to try once again to salvage the situation. "Listen to me."

"My ring," Pelham demanded.

Mary removed the heavy pearl-encrusted gold ring and dropped it into Pelham's hand, then watched as her former bridegroom pocketed her betrothal ring, turned his back on her, and walked down the aisle.

"Pelham . . ." Mary started down the aisle after him but Lee blocked her path.

"Let him go," he said.

She looked up at Lee. "I need to talk to him. I know I can make him understand."

"No, you can't." Lee stared down at Mary. He saw the shimmer of unshed tears and traces of the tears she'd already cried on this, her wedding day. He reached down and caught one shiny droplet on his fingertip and prayed he could make everything up to her.

"I don't know what the devil is going on here but you'd better have a good explanation for staging this . . . this . . . little melodrama." David Alexander pointed a finger at his friend, Lee Kincaid.

The wedding party, now minus the groom, had retired to Father's Joseph's office away from the prying eyes of the congregation while they attempted to console the bride. David had stayed outside the office to discuss the situation with Lee in private.

"I didn't *stage* this melodrama," Lee told him.

David raised an eyebrow at that. "Oh no? I thought your

appearance at the church rivaled that of Edwin Booth on stage."

"All right," Lee admitted, "I did intend to stop the wedding, but I didn't plan the rest."

David was skeptical. He glanced over at Judah and Madeline sitting quietly on a bench down the hall. "I suppose the old man and the little girl materialized out of thin air?"

Lee raked his fingers through his hair. "They were supposed to wait outside in the buggy until I came to get them."

"But you didn't stage anything?"

"Look David, I know you're upset. And you've got a right to be."

"You're damn . . . dead right I'm upset." David began to pace. "I ought to shoot you full of holes, or better yet, give Mary her little gun and let her do it."

Lee nodded, "I'd feel the same way if I were in your shoes. But you've got to believe me when I tell you I didn't come here to hurt your sister."

"Well, if you didn't come here to hurt her by breaking up her wedding, why the hell are you here?" David demanded.

"I came to marry her myself."

David stopped pacing and turned to look at his friend. "I don't believe you."

"It's true," Lee swore. "See?" He reached into his suit pocket and brought out a jeweler's box. He snapped it open so David could see the ruby and diamond engagement ring and the thin gold band.

Lee's admission took David by complete surprise. He staggered backward. "You and Mary? When? How?"

"It's a long story." Lee stroked the corner of his mustache.

"I've got plenty of time." David crossed his arms over his chest and waited.

"Look, David, I think it might be better if I explained all this to Mary," Lee began.

"You're not going to get a chance to so much as catch another glimpse of Mary until I find out what this is all about."

"Okay," Lee agreed as he closed the ring box. "Maybe you should take a look at this." He pulled out the envelope containing Tabitha Gray's letter and handed it to David.

David quickly scanned the letter and the copy of her will folded with it. He finished reading, folded the papers, and gave them back to Lee. He didn't insult Lee by asking if the silver mine and the house were Lee's main motivation: David knew his friend well enough to know they weren't. As an attorney, he had handled numerous business transactions for Lee Kincaid over the years. David was one of a handful of people who knew Lee didn't need the property or the income, so he asked the most intriguing question and the one closest to his heart: "Why did you pick Mary?"

Lee thought about telling David he had fallen madly in love with Mary but settled on the truth instead. "She was the only woman who came to mind—the only woman I trust enough to marry."

David smiled. "Are we talking about the same girl? You know, my sister, Mary? The woman who never misses the opportunity to pull her gun on you?"

"I know it sounds crazy," Lee admitted. "And in spite of the fact that she tends to brandish her gun whenever she feels threatened, Mary's the only woman I'll even consider."

David stood up. "I don't like this, Lee. I don't approve of your reason for wanting to marry my sister. It seems so cold-blooded, so businesslike"—he waved his arms in the air—"and I certainly can't condone your method. But Tessa's been . . ." David stopped abruptly as understanding dawned. He glanced over at Lee. "What are you doing in Cheyenne?"

"I told you."

"No," David said, "I mean, why did you come? How did you know about Mary's wedding plans?"

"I didn't know about Mary or her intended. My arriving in Cheyenne on her wedding day was purely coincidental." And too damn close to think about, Lee admitted to himself. A few minutes later and . . .

"Maybe we'd better clarify this," David suggested as his quick mind began to put the pieces of the puzzle together. "I thought you were supposed to be in Washington working on our behalf."

Lee glanced over at David, not quite sure how he should answer. After all, Tessa had hired him, not David.

Lee had, in the past, followed Tessa Roarke from Chicago to Peaceable, Wyoming, in an attempt to keep his promise to her dying brother to look after her. Her brother, Eamon Roarke, was Lee's Pinkerton partner. He had done his best, but Tessa wound up facing a murder charge and the hangman's noose, once in Peaceable. David Alexander had been hired to defend her, and Lee had helped his longtime friend find the evidence that convinced the jury that Tessa hadn't killed Arnie Mason for murdering her brother, Eamon. Tessa had married David, then promptly hired Lee to help her find Lily Catherine, not just to find out the truth surrounding the child's birth, or to help clear David's name, but so she and David could adopt her as their own. Tessa meant to give David the child whose birth had changed his life and brought the two of them together.

But until this moment, Lee wasn't sure if David knew of his work for Tessa.

"It's all right," David told him. "I know Tessa hired you to find Lily Catherine for us. She told me on our honeymoon. I know all about it and I know you were supposed to be in Washington looking into the situation."

"I was in Washington working on the case until . . . I don't know," Lee rubbed his tired eyes. "A few days ago." He managed a lopsided grin. "I can't remember exactly. My days are all running together."

David took pity on him. "How long has it been since you've had a full night's sleep?"

"Over a week."

David nodded in understanding. "We'll take it slowly. What happened after you left Washington?"

"What is this, counselor?" Lee raised one blond eyebrow as he recognized his friend's courtroom tactics. "I'm not on trial."

"If you want to talk to Mary," David informed him, "you'll answer my questions. And if you consider answering a few pertinent questions for an old friend a trial, then so be it." David shot Lee a stern, unyielding look. "But I will have my answers."

It was Lee's turn to nod in mute understanding.

"So what happened after you left Washington?" David asked again.

"I reported to William Pinkerton in Chicago. He listened to my report, then handed me a stack of telegrams requiring my urgent attention." Lee paused a moment, then added, "Three telegrams were from Operative Tom McLeary requesting my immediate presence in Denver, and four of them were from Tessa."

"My Tessa?" David asked the question, though he already knew the answer.

"Yeah." Lee grinned suddenly. "And I bet you live to regret teaching her how to read and write. Boyo, that's one woman who believes in the power of the written word."

David smiled in agreement. Tessa also believed with all her heart that Liam Kincaid and Mary were meant for each other. Matchmaking. David smiled. His red-headed Irish beauty was definitely matchmaking. "Did Tessa invite you to Mary's wedding?"

Lee shook his head. "She didn't mention the wedding. She just instructed me to come to the ranch as soon as possible. And when I failed to respond to the first telegram, she sent three others to back it up." He glanced at David. "You don't think she wanted me to . . ."

"Of course she did," David told him, clapping Lee on the back in a brotherly gesture. "Congratulations, old friend, you just floundered into Tessa's baited trap. And because my darling wife went to such trouble and expense to get you here, and because I trust Tessa's instincts as much as my own, I'm going to let you speak to my sister." David grinned in mischievous glee.

Lee was suddenly at a loss. "What do I say to her?"

"What you say to Mary is up to you. And if you can talk her into agreeing to marry you, I'll give you my sincere blessings, but if you hurt her, I'll finish what I started a few months back in Peaceable," David warned, reminding Lee of their brawl on the main street when David had done his best to break Lee's perfect nose after Lee had issued his well-meant, but halfhearted, proposal to Tessa.

"I understand," Lee replied solemnly.

"Good." David smiled. "I'd hate to have to break your nose. You're going to need your handsome profile. And you're going to have to be your most eloquent and persuasive." He paused for effect. "Because after what happened this morning, you're going to need that silver tongue of yours to talk Mary into considering you."

Chapter Five

Mary looked up as Lee entered the office. "Who let you in?"

Ignoring her hostile tone, Lee crossed the room to stand in front of Mary's father. He leaned over and quietly spoke to the older man.

Charlie Alexander nodded, then stood up. "We'll wait outside. Call me when my daughter makes a decision." He ushered the priest and the other members of the family out of the office.

"What did you say to make my father agree to leave the room?" Mary could have bitten out her tongue. She didn't want to admit to being curious about anything Lee Kincaid did. She was furious with him for upsetting her carefully laid plans for her future, and for ruining the calm resolution she had fought so hard to gain. She hadn't seen the rogue in four long months—not since the day of David and Tessa's wedding—and today he had turned up unexpectedly like the proverbial bad penny, just in time to ruin her wedding. But as she stood there looking at him, Mary found it almost impossible to maintain her anger. A part of her was furious with Lee for barging into her life and for manipulating Pelham, while another part of her was thrilled by the idea that Lee Kincaid had ridden to her rescue and had saved her from her own stupid, headstrong decision to marry a man she didn't love. But Mary knew it wouldn't do to let Lee think she wasn't angry.

"I told him I wanted to talk to you alone."

"I don't want to talk to you. Alone or otherwise."

"Fair enough," Lee agreed, stroking his chin thoughtfully. "I'll talk, you listen."

"I don't want to listen to anything you have to say, either."

"Maybe not, but you will," he told her. "Because I'm about to offer you a way out of this fiasco."

"Fiasco? You mean the one that just took place? The one *you* created?" Mary lashed out at him with her sharp tongue. "In case you haven't noticed, I've been deserted by my fiancé—left standing at the altar."

"It could be that everything will turn out for the best," Lee replied. "When the going got rough, your fiancé took off. Better to find out before the wedding than after it."

"Oh, please, spare me," Mary answered sarcastically.

"I think maybe I did," Lee told her.

"Only you would have the gall to say that to me." Mary exclaimed. "Only you would stand there and tell me how lucky I am to find out that the man who should have been my husband didn't trust me enough to listen. Especially after you arranged things so he was sure not to listen! I will never forgive you for this."

"He didn't even put up an argument," Lee pointed out. "He wasn't the right man for you, Mary."

"Pelham might not have been perfect," she said, "but he was willing to marry me until you showed up."

"Lots of men would be willing to marry you."

"That just goes to show how much you know." Mary gave a derisive, unladylike snort. "Name one."

Lee sucked in a deep breath, then slowly let it out. "Me."

Mary plopped down on the sofa, lifted her wedding veil, and stared at him. "Tell me this is your idea of a joke."

"I'm afraid not."

"You mean to tell me you hurried to Cheyenne from God knows where to keep me from marrying Pelham?" Her tone of voice made it perfectly clear to Lee that she didn't believe a word of what he'd said.

Lee would have mixed the truth with a few well chosen sugar-coated lies for any other woman, but he knew that wouldn't work with Mary. She had an uncanny ability to see through his blarney, and he respected that ability enough not to lie to her. "I didn't know anything about Pelham Cosgrove III. I rushed here from Chicago to Denver to Cheyenne"—he didn't think it would hurt to let her know how far he had traveled on her behalf—"because I happen to be in the market for a wife."

Mary raised her eyebrow in a gesture identical to her brother, David's. "I don't believe you."

"I came here to ask you to marry me." He raised his right hand. "I swear it."

"Be careful that God doesn't strike you dead, Lee," she warned. "Remember where you are."

"God doesn't strike men down for telling the truth."

He had the angelic, innocent look of a choirboy on his face and Mary found herself struggling not to smile. "Well, if you are telling the truth, it ought to be a unique experience for you."

"I can tell you don't believe me—" he began.

"Really? Am I that transparent?"

"But I can prove it to you." For the second time in less than an hour, Lee reached inside his coat pocket for the jeweler's box. He knelt in front of the sofa, at Mary's feet, and opened the lid.

The betrothal ring came as a complete surprise. She had never credited Liam Kincaid with having taste, but Mary had to admit his selection of engagement rings was impeccable—much better than Pelham's. If the truth were known, she hadn't been upset at forfeiting Pelham's pearl-encrusted gold ring or the matching pearl-encrusted wedding band, only at losing what it represented. Although she had kept her opinion to herself, Mary considered the pearl monstrosity overdone and gaudy, whereas the ruby and diamond ring and plain gold band Lee held in his hand were marvels of elegance and simplicity. Had he known rubies were her favorite stone? Had he guessed right, or . . .

Uncomfortable with the turn of her thoughts, Mary straightened her backbone and firmed her mouth into a thin, disapproving line. "Did you pick that out yourself? Or steal it from the hand of some unsuspecting ladylove?"

Lee placed a hand over his heart and pretended to fall back on his heels. "Mary, you wound me. You know you're my only ladylove."

"I know no such thing. From what I've seen you propose to women on a regular basis."

"That just goes to show how much you know," he repeated her earlier words. "I chose that ring because I thought it suited you." Lee quirked an eyebrow. "I didn't know you had fondness for pearls in gaudy gold settings."

"I don't," Mary snapped. "And I distinctly remember you shamelessly proposing to my sister-in-law in front of the entire population of Peaceable, Wyoming, not even five full months ago."

Lee nodded. "So I did," he agreed, "but that was different. I was only trying to fulfill my promise to her brother and show your brother what a stubborn fellow he was." Lee smiled. "Are you still holding a grudge over that?"

Mary snorted. "I have better things to do than hold a grudge over something you did months ago."

"I'm glad to hear it," Lee told her, a wry expression on his face. "Nevertheless, I think I should have bought you an emerald instead of a ruby. If I'd known you were so jealous, I would have."

"I'm not jealous!"

"Oh, yes, you are," Lee assured her. "It's probably caused by your unfortunate warrior heritage"—he echoed Pelham's disapproving tone of voice, then winked at Mary—"or, maybe it's because you like me much more than you think you do."

"I do not."

"Oh, don't worry, Mary. I like for my women to be jealous. It makes me feel wanted."

"Women?" Mary repeated. "You said women. Plural."

"And you said you weren't jealous."

He had her there, and Mary knew it. "This isn't a game of flirtation." Mary changed the subject. "I'm serious."

"So am I."

She eyed him thoughtfully. She didn't trust him, at least not completely, but there was definitely something about him that she liked. "Maybe you are serious about this," Mary agreed. "But I'm not some little schoolgirl you can charm out of her clothes. I'm not stupid enough or arrogant enough to believe you're offering marriage because you suddenly realized you're head over heels in love with me." Even as she said the words she knew were true, Mary prayed she was wrong—prayed he had realized he *was* head over heels in love with her.

Lee nodded. Once again, he was tempted to sweeten his answer with romance-laced lies, but he knew his instincts about Mary were right on the money. No matter how unpalatable, she wanted the undiluted truth. "You're right," he told her, "you're not a naïve schoolgirl. You're the teacher, and I'd be stupid if I tried to pull the wool over your eyes because as a teacher, you know all the answers, don't you? You know I didn't come running back because I suddenly discovered I'm in love with you." Lee took a deep breath. "But do you know that I've been thinking recently of leaving the Agency and settling down? And do you know that when I thought of settling down, I naturally thought of you?"

"Naturally," Mary replied dryly. "It stands to reason that a Pinkerton detective would choose to marry a woman who, in the course of their *acquaintance*"—Mary stressed the word—"has twice pulled a gun on him with every intention of plugging him full of holes. And will again," she warned him, "at the first opportunity."

"Not so," Lee said. "I've no doubt in my mind that if you really wanted to shoot me full of holes you would have done so before now."

Mary smiled. "I think I've shown remarkable restraint up 'til now."

"So have I, up 'til now." Lee pocketed the ruby ring, then leaned closer and touched his lips to hers. It began as a light, teasing kiss, something Lee couldn't keep himself from experiencing, but it suddenly grew into something more. A heated rush surged through Lee's body as he kissed her again and felt Mary sway against him. He pulled her closer as he deepened the kiss, then reached up under her wedding veil, tangling his fingers in her thick, silky hair before running them down past her shoulders to feel the weight of her breasts in his hands.

Mary was overwhelmed by her response to Lee's kiss. She leaned toward him, then wrapped her arms around his neck and parted her lips to allow his tongue to slip through and taste the warm recesses of her mouth. Suddenly Lee was on the sofa beside her and Mary was surrounded by his arms. She molded herself against him, enjoying the taste of his mouth under the soft brush of his mustache, and his warm, spicy smell. She breathed in the scent of him and pressed closer to the source. Lee groaned aloud. Mary pushed away from him, gasping for breath. She felt light-headed, giddy, and incapable of rational thought. She opened her eyes and found herself staring up into Lee's gray ones. Mary smiled at him and Lee leaned down to plant a line of kisses from her forehead to her lips. She closed her eyes once again and whispered his name and the sound of it coming from her lips seemed to echo through the room. Mary suddenly realized she was lying on the sofa instead of sitting on it, and that Liam Kincaid had one of his hands on the bare skin of her thigh, under her wedding dress and above the frilly garter holding her silk stocking in place.

"What are you doing?" she gasped, shoving at his chest with all her might as she jack-knifed into a sitting position.

"Kissing you," Lee murmured as he let go of her leg and helped her smooth her satin skirts back into place. "And enjoying the feel of having you kiss me." He sat up and moved a few inches away from her. His breathing was heavy and irregular and his heart seemed to thud against his chest at twice its normal speed. Lee stared at Mary. Her lips were swollen from his kisses, her brown eyes sparkled with emotion, and her cheeks were flushed. She looked the way he imagined every bride should look on her wedding night, but Mary wasn't a bride—at least not yet. He shrugged his shoulders. "Come on, Mary, admit it," he coaxed, "you enjoyed kissing me. Better than old Pelham I bet."

"Much bet—" Mary clapped her hand over her mouth, refusing to say more.

There was a teasing light in Lee's gray eyes when he looked at her and his thick mustache tilted upward in a smile. "Well, Mary Two-shot, what's it to be? Will you marry me? Yes or no?"

Mary wanted to throw her arms around him once again, kiss him senseless, and shout yes loud enough for the whole world to hear, but her instincts warned her not to be foolhardy and reckless. "I don't know."

Lee raked his fingers through his blond hair. "Hell, Mary, what don't you know?"

"I don't know why you're here," she told him, "or what you expect from me. Or why you're in such a hurry to get married."

"I've told you why I'm here and what I want from you." Lee's face was the picture of innocence wronged. "I want us to be a family. I want to marry you. And why not marry you today? You're dressed for it."

Mary didn't hear all of what Lee was saying. She only heard him say, "I want us to be a family." She suddenly had a mental picture of Lee holding the little girl with the dark hair and the bright blue eyes in his arms. Maddy. He'd called her Maddy. Mary shook her head. There were many sides to Lee Kincaid, many faces he kept hidden, so much so that things were never what they appeared to be—not where he was concerned. Suddenly everything seemed so clear. "I should have known," she muttered.

"What?"

"That you have some kind of scheme going and that you want to involve me somehow," Mary replied sarcastically.

"There's no scheme, Mary." Lee reached out to put his hand on Mary's knee.

She batted his hand away. "Then what about the little girl? What part does she play in your marriage plans?"

Lee gritted his teeth, nodded his head a time or two, then stroked one side of his mustache. "Her name is Madeline. Maddy for short. She's the daughter of a Pinkerton detective who passed away nine days ago."

"I'm sorry," Mary murmured softly.

"Yeah," Lee said sadly, "so am I."

"You must have been very close."

"We were partners." He glanced over at Mary.

"And he left his daughter to you?"

Lee winced at her question. "Maddy doesn't have anyone

else. My partner left her in my care and I thought . . ." Lee let his words trail off, not quite sure what to say anymore.

"You thought you could simply waltz onto the ranch and drop her off for someone else to take care of," Mary finished for him.

"No, damn it, I thought I could waltz onto the ranch, sweep you off your feet, and give her a mother to take care of her."

"You don't love me," Mary said.

Lee got up from the sofa and began to pace. "What difference does that make?" he asked. "You don't love me either."

"It makes a great deal of difference," Mary protested, "when two people are thinking about getting married."

"Oh, yeah?" Lee argued. "What about Pelham Everhardt Cosgrove III? I suppose you were madly in love with him."

"Maybe I am."

"And maybe I'm the king of England." Lee quirked an eyebrow at her. "I can tell from your kisses just how broken up you are over his desertion."

"What I shared with Pelham is none of your business! He's a fine upstanding gentleman, which is more than I can say about you."

"Thank God!"

"The simple fact of the matter is that you came to Cheyenne to ask me to marry you because you've gotten yourself into something you don't know how to handle." Mary summarized Lee's situation. "Though why you thought I would do you any favors is beyond me."

Lee looked her right in the eyes. "Maybe I thought I was doing you a favor. Maybe I thought I was doing all of us a favor—Maddy, me, *and* you," he said softly. "Maybe I somehow got the idea into my head that you might be tired of teaching school and having to carry that little silver gun of yours in your pocket all the time for protection against rough cowpokes and amorous Indians. Maybe I thought you might like to have a family all your own. Maybe I thought you'd make a decent wife and a damn good mother." Lee turned away from Mary and walked to the door. "And maybe, just maybe, I'm crazy as hell to think so." He reached for the doorknob.

If he had lied to her or tried to sway her with his Irish charm, she could have turned him down without a second glance, but he had spoken the truth. Her truth. For some inexplicable reason, Lee Kincaid knew how she felt.

"Lee . . ." Mary's voice stopped him.

"Yeah?" he turned back around to face her.

Mary held out her left hand. "Maybe you're not as crazy as you think."

Lee walked over to the sofa and took the ruby and diamond ring out of his pocket. He grasped Mary's hand and slipped the ring onto her finger. "And maybe I'm even crazier."

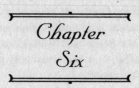

Chapter Six

Lee Kincaid might doubt his sanity, but as Mary watched him slip a thin gold band onto the third finger of her left hand some twenty minutes later, she knew she had definitely gone stark raving mad. She didn't know what had possessed her to agree to this. Lee didn't love her. He probably didn't even like her much—not nearly as much as she liked him. But he needed her. And Mary was more than willing to take advantage of that fact. The man who had filled her dreams in the months since she had met him had finally taken note of her. For once in her life, she wasn't just an aunt, a sister, a daughter, or a granddaughter. And, unlike Pelham, Lee Kincaid wasn't interested in her family connections or how much money she had in the bank. He knew her family's worth. He had worked with David and Reese and been friends with them for over a decade. He might have reasons for marrying her that didn't equal love, but marrying her for her money wasn't one of them. He needed her. No, she ruthlessly reminded herself seconds later, he didn't need *her*—Mary Alexander—he simply needed a wife to mother a motherless child. Any woman would have sufficed.

But, Mary concentrated on the thought, he chose her.

"You may kiss the bride," Father Joseph announced, glancing from Lee to Mary and then back to Lee. "Congratulations."

Mary looked up as Lee lifted her wedding veil from her face, then closed her eyes as he bent down and lightly touched his lips to hers. His mustache softly brushed her cheek, like the flutter of a butterfly's wings. Mary kept her eyes closed, anticipating more. But to her great disappointment, Lee straightened, gently took her by the elbow and turned her around to face the wedding guests.

She froze. Mary hadn't expected to see any guests other than her family, lining the pews of the church. Nor did she remember seeing them when she re-entered the sanctuary, but the pews were packed—even more crowded than before. The people who had come to see her married to Pelham Cosgrove III had stayed to see her become Mrs. Liam Gordon MacIntyre Kincaid. And it appeared that other guests had joined them. Mary spotted the society editor of *The Cheyenne Leader* scribbling away in her little notebook and squeezed her eyes shut, envisioning the write-up her wedding would make.

"Mary?" Lee urged her forward. "They're waiting for us to walk down the aisle as husband and wife. Come on, chin up. You have more than enough courage to handle this." He stepped forward. Mary followed, her head held high. "That's more like it." Lee praised her. "Here, take your bouquet," He reached over, accepted Mary's flowers from Tessa, then handed them to his bride. Their fingers touched beneath the flowers. Mary's were as cold as ice. They were halfway down the aisle when Lee motioned for Judah and Maddy.

"Mary," Lee said when the elderly gentleman and the little girl joined them in the aisle. "This is Mr. Judah Crane. He's an attorney who represents the estate of the friend I told you about, as well as being a close family friend." Lee turned to Judah. "Judah, this is Miss Mary Alexander," he grinned at his slip of the tongue, "I mean the *former* Miss Mary Alexander. She's Mrs. Liam Kincaid now."

Maddy whined and danced from one foot to the other as Judah let go of her hand to shake Mary's. "Pleased to meet you, Mrs. Kincaid."

Lee released his hold on Mary and reached down to pick up Maddy. "You've already met Maddy," he said to his new bride, "but you haven't been officially introduced. Mary, meet Maddy. Madeline Gray." Lee smiled at the child in his arms. "Maddy, this is the pretty lady I told you about. Her name is Mary." Maddy stared at Lee, a solemn expression on her little face, then flung her arms around his neck and held him tight.

Seeing the two of them together—her new husband and his ward—made Mary want to follow Maddy's example and fling her arms around them both and hold them close to her heart. She swallowed the lump in her throat and blinked at the sheen of tears clouding her vision.

"Lovely wedding, ma'am." Judah bowed to Mary. "Thank you most kindly for inviting us." He turned to Lee. "I know I should, but I can't remember who you are." He shrugged his thin shoulders. "I don't think I know any of these people. Lovely bride. Darling little girl. Can we go home now? I'm sure it's time for my nap."

"After breakfast, Judah," Lee said gently.

"Breakfast?" The elderly lawyer sounded as if he'd never heard the word.

Mary stared at Judah. His dark brown eyes were vacant, his face slack, expressionless, and his dark blue waistcoat was turned inside out. Suddenly Mary understood. She held out her hand to him. "Breakfast, Mr. Crane. You know, steak, and eggs and hot biscuits."

"Biscuits?" Judah repeated.

"Never mind," Mary assured him. "When we get home, I'll show you."

"Are we going home?" Judah turned to Lee.

"Eventually," Lee answered. "But right now, we're going to ride out to the ranch for breakfast."

"Good," Judah pronounced. "I'm tired of all these strangers. And I'm sure it must be time for my nap."

Lee turned to Mary, and offered her his arm. "Shall we go to breakfast, Mrs. Kincaid?"

Mary linked her arm through Lee's, then reached out and grabbed Judah by the hand. She smiled shyly at her new husband. She liked this side of Liam Kincaid—the family man side of him. "I'd be delighted, Mr. Kincaid."

He grinned. "Let's go." Lee led his small party down the rest of the aisle and out the front doors of the church. He paused on the top step, turned, managed a slight bow, and smiled at Mary. "Your carriage awaits, milady."

Mary gasped in surprise. Not at the plain hired hack parked on the street, but at the snow-white thoroughbred stallion tied to the back. She recognized him, of course. There was only one horse like him in the country—Pegasus. He belonged to her cousin Reese, but Lee had ridden him into town. She glanced at Lee once again. It seemed Prince Charming had come to her rescue after all. And he had ridden in on a snow-white stallion, just like in the scenes in all the fairy tales—like the scenes from all of her dreams.

The wedding party arrived at the Trail T ranch in time for a late—very late—wedding breakfast. Reese Jordan and his wife, Faith, had sent Daniel ahead to warn the women and the ranch hands, who had remained at home preparing the food and making arrangements for the arrival of guests, that there had been a change in grooms. Reese's instructions asked that anything bearing an association with Pelham Cosgrove III be removed from sight and that no mention of Cosgrove reach Mary's or Lee Kincaid's ears.

Mary and Lee stood side by side in the huge dining room

of the main house and waited for the wedding guests to arrive. The dining table, large enough to seat thirty people, had been moved from the center of the room to one wall, draped in white sheets, and loaded with a buffet of fine foods—from thick juicy beefsteaks to delicate seafood brought in by rail from San Francisco. Smaller tables had been set up in the center of the dining room for the bride and groom, their families, and members of the wedding party. It looked to Mary as if every straight-backed chair on the ranch was lined against the dining room walls. She nervously fidgeted with the skirts of her wedding dress and readjusted her veil before the guests arrived. Although she told herself that everything would be fine, Mary wondered how she would manage to endure the looks and comments of her guests. One look at Lee in his dusty suit and canvas duster standing beside her in her pristine white satin wedding gown would serve to remind everyone on the Trail T that she had left the ranch to become Pelham Cosgrove's bride and had become Mrs. Liam G. M. Kincaid instead. It was only a matter of time before one of the wedding guests forgot their manners long enough to mention it.

Mary shifted her weight from one foot to the other and waited impatiently for the trial by fire to begin. She glanced at Lee, wishing she could appeared as relaxed as he did, wishing she had Judah and Maddy with them. But Maddy was eating breakfast in the kitchen with the other children and Judah. Mary sighed. Nothing about her wedding had gone according to plan. According to her schedule, she and Pelham should have been settling into Reese's luxurious private railroad car for their honeymoon journey to San Francisco by now. But then, no one had planned on having Lee Kincaid ride to the church and make her his bride.

Pelham. His clothes and personal belongings had already been placed in Reese's private Pullman car for the journey west. "Oh no," she gasped loud enough for Lee to hear.

"Wait is it?" Lee turned to her.

"It's nothing," Mary shook her head. She would have to remind someone to unload Pelham's things and send them back to him before she left with Lee.

"Something must be bothering you," Lee said. "You're as stiff as a board." He smiled at her. "I'm afraid to touch you for fear I'll get splinters."

Mary looked down at her hands tightly gripping the fabric of her dress. Her fists were clenched, her knuckles white.

Lee reached out and took one of her hands in his. "I want to help you, Mary. I know we can make whatever it is that's upsetting you better. You can trust me. I'm your husband now." His words surprised, yet pleased him. Until he arrived in Denver two days ago and found himself confronted by Tabby Gray's ultimatum, Lee hadn't expected his way of life to change. Oh, he admitted there were times when he longed for a real home, a wife, and children—maybe even a dog to sleep beside the hearth, but he had never tried to satisfy those longings. The proposal he had made to Tessa Roarke five months ago had been halfhearted at best. Lee hadn't taken it seriously and neither had Tessa. It was, as Lee had tried to explain to Mary, an offer made out of his sense of loyalty and duty to his partner and good friend, Tessa's dead brother. It was a proposal meant to infuriate David Alexander, to spur David into proposing to Tessa himself. And it had worked beautifully. No one had taken it seriously except David, and perhaps Mary. Lee took a deep breath. The scent of Mary's perfume filled his nostrils—a warm, compelling scent of wildflowers and herbs and spice—much like the woman herself. His wife. Lee grinned. He was married, and the knowledge gave him a warm feeling inside. It filled the place in his soul that had been empty for so very long. . . . For the first time in years, Lee believed he might have a future after all.

"Pelham," Mary blurted. "I was thinking about Pelham—

of how we would've been boarding the train for our honeymoon in San Francisco about now."

He stiffened. Her words affected him like a sword thrust through the pit of his stomach. Lee gritted his teeth in an attempt to halt the flow of bitter feelings surging through him. Pelham. While he had been eagerly planning a future with Mary Alexander, she had been thinking of Pelham Cosgrove III and the future they would have shared if he hadn't come along and ruined things for her with his slick scheme to meet the terms of Tabby's will.

"I'm sorry about that, Mary," Lee apologized, "I didn't know you planned to honeymoon in San Francisco."

There was a note of genuine sincerity in his deep baritone voice. Mary looked up at him to see if he really meant his apology.

"I suppose you were going to stay in a fancy hotel and eat in all the fine restaurants," Lee said. "Maybe go to the opera?"

"Yes," Mary agreed. "We had planned to do those things. Pelham had never been to San Francisco. He wanted to take in all the sights."

"What about you, Mary? What did you want to do?" Lee asked softly.

Mary hesitated a moment before answering. "I suppose I wanted to do those things, too. It's been ages since I've been to San Francisco." She studied Lee's face, the way his blond brows framed his mesmerizing gray eyes, his perfect nose—the one she'd asked her brother to break—the thick blond mustache framing his mouth, and the pout of his bottom lip which seemed to issue invitations for her to kiss it. Mary stared at his mouth. Lee Kincaid was her husband now. Less than an hour ago, he had stood beside her in the church after Pelham walked out and solemnly promised to love, honor, and cherish her. Remembering Lee's kiss, Mary smiled shyly, wondering what it would be like to have him love, honor, and cherish her with his body. She blushed at her thoughts. Although she had planned to have a family with Pelham, she had never given any thought to having Pelham cherish her with his body. She had gone out of her way not to think about sharing her bed with Pelham Everhardt Cosgrove III. But the idea of sharing her bed with Lee Kincaid, of creating children with Lee, excited her and made her look forward to her wedding night. Mary nervously licked her lips, took a deep, calming breath, then said, "About San Francisco . . . my honeymoon . . . I mean, I don't suppose you and I . . ." She bit her bottom lip. It wasn't like her to stutter so.

Lee stared down at his bride. Mary's face was so guileless and her thoughts so apparent. While she dreamed of the romantic honeymoon in San Francisco she had planned with Cosgrove, Mary was confronted by the possibility of having to share a marriage bed with him. Lee supposed being married to him would take a little getting used to, especially since she had been in the process of marrying someone else—someone she cared about, and maybe even loved.

He sighed. He wasn't a normally patient man, but he would try for Mary's sake.

"I'm sorry, Mary, but a San Francisco honeymoon is out of the question." Lee focused his gaze on the tips of his dusty boots, trying to figure out how to say what he needed to say. He cleared his throat and ran his index finger under the collar of his white shirt before he spoke in a low, husky whisper. "In fact, I've been thinking that maybe we should wait a while before we, uh"—he swallowed hard—"actually become husband and wife."

Mary gasped. "But we're married!"

"Legally"—he sucked in a breath then slowly released it—"but not actually. I mean, right now, what we have is marriage on paper only. And I'm saying, maybe, we ought to keep it that way for a while."

"Oh." The rejections Mary had endured on this, her wedding day, were enough to send a weaker woman running to her mother for comfort, but she was made of stronger stuff. Mary straightened to her full height, tilted her chin a bit higher, and ignored the sting of disappointment. Pelham hadn't trusted her enough to marry her and although Lee had married her, he didn't care to share her bed. "I see." Her ironic tone concealed the mixture of emotions she felt and the quavering note in her voice.

Lee glanced at Mary's profile. Her lovely face was full of strength, shining with a steadfast determination to endure and to make the best of her situation. He admired her strength, her courage. "It doesn't have to be forever," he told her.

"Only until death us do part," Mary said softly.

"I meant the 'paper only' part," Lee said. "The other can wait until we get to know one another better."

Mary took a deep breath, then met Lee's solemn gray-eyed gaze. "Up until you walked into the church an hour ago, I was planning my life with the man of my choice." Hoping to salvage what she could of her pride, Mary pulled the shreds of her dignity around her and flashed him a look of disdain. "I married you because you offered me a way out of an embarrassing dilemma, but don't think for one second that gives you any rights. As far as I'm concerned, the other can wait forever."

"I'm your husband," Lee reminded her, as the need to assert his masculine claim on her suddenly resurfaced.

Mary gave him a look of wide-eyed innocence. "Not in the way it counts," she countered. "Only on paper and only until death us do part." She saw his eyes narrow as her barb found its mark. She wet her dry lips with a tip of her tongue, then slipped her hand into the crook of Lee's elbow, and pasted a wide, adoring smile on her face. "Smile," Mary hissed at her husband, nudging him in the ribs for good measure. "Our wedding guests are here to congratulate us."

Lee blinked at her quick change.

"Please?" she added when Lee failed to respond. "I don't want my family embarrassed any more than they already have been. As far as everyone else is concerned"—she thought for a moment—"we met and fell in love last year in Peaceable while I was visiting David." She worried her bottom lip with her teeth. "It shouldn't be too hard to convince them. Most of these people were guests at David and Tessa's wedding. They saw us together."

"How do you account for my four-month absence?" Lee asked.

"You left for Chicago on business. I was told you'd been killed in an accident. Later, I met Pelham. Our story is a romantic tale of love lost and found."

"The official story." Lee smiled then, more impressed than he would like to admit. Her expressions and thoughts weren't quite as transparent as he'd thought. He grinned in admiration. She had depths he hadn't even imagined. And if he didn't watch out, William Pinkerton would be trying to recruit her to work for the Agency. Mary Alexander Kincaid gave as good as she got, and she did it with such style and grace. He nodded his head. All in all, he was quite satisfied with his choice.

All in all, it had been quite a wedding day. For both of them.

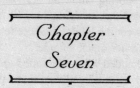

Chapter
Seven

"I'm glad you could make it for the wedding, Liam."
Tessa Alexander bit her lip to keep from smiling as she held
her hand out to him.

Lee stared at Tessa's hand but didn't offer to shake it. He
raised an eyebrow. "As I turned out to be the groom, I'll just
bet you are," he told her. "What would you have done if I
hadn't shown up?"

Tessa looked around and spotted Mary standing across
the room with a couple of the wedding guests. "I might have
had to stand up and object to the ceremony myself."

"You had your opportunity," Lee pointed out.

"I waited for you," Tessa replied. "And although you cut
it close, you finally made it. The real question is what would
you have done if you had gotten here a few minutes later?"

"I would have turned around and gone on my merry way
without a backward glance."

"Ha!" Tessa scoffed. "Why didn't you? You had *your*
opportunity."

"I should have taken it," Lee told her. "Then I wouldn't
have to endure your smug attitude."

Tessa bit her lip even harder. "You couldn't stand by and
let Mary marry Pelham Cosgrove or any other man," she
told him. "You don't have it in you."

Lee shook his head. "How did you know I'd come
running in response to your telegrams?"

"It's your nature," Tessa replied matter-of-factly.

"Ha!" It was Lee's turn to scoff. "I don't risk my neck for anybody."

"You risk your neck for everybody." She gave up the battle and laughed outright. "You, Liam Kincaid, are a born rescuer. I saw it from the beginning. It's one of the things I've always liked about you."

"You obviously have me confused with David." He nodded toward Tessa's husband. David Alexander was an attorney known for championing the weak. "You couldn't have seen anything about me from the beginning, Tessa, because you wouldn't let me get within a foot of you for weeks after we met. You may not remember it now, but you haven't always liked me." Lee frowned at the memory of Tessa Roarke taking a swing at him on the stairway of Myra Brennan's Satin Slipper Saloon in Peaceable, Wyoming.

"That's only because I thought you were after me and Coalie," Tessa explained.

Liam Kincaid had followed Tessa from Chicago to Wyoming Territory, but not for the reason she feared. He hadn't been interested in returning Tessa's traveling companion, nine-year-old Coalie Donegal, to the brutish man to whom Coalie had been apprenticed—the man from whom Tessa had helped Coalie escape. No, Lee had followed Tessa from Chicago because he had promised her brother he would watch out for her. But Tessa hadn't known that, and nothing Lee could say or do had kept her from despising him on sight.

"I didn't know you then." Tessa interrupted Lee's musings. "But I know you now. And I know that you and David are cut from a similar bolt of cloth. You could have left the church quietly once you saw Mary at the altar with someone else. You didn't have to make your presence known. And you certainly didn't have to make such a dramatic entrance."

"What's the matter, Tessa? Aren't you happy with the results of your scheming?" he asked.

"I'm very happy," she said. "And I think you and Marry will be, too. That's why I asked you to come to Cheyenne for the wedding."

"You didn't ask me to come to Cheyenne," Lee corrected her, "you *ordered* me. Dammit all, Tessa, I haven't had a moment's peace since I agreed to try to find Lily Catherine for you. Everytime I return from a trip, I find a telegram from you waiting on my desk." He ran his fingers through his thick blond hair. "I didn't mind it at first because I knew you were anxious for news, but this time there were four telegrams, Tessa. *Four*. And not one of them mentioned a damned thing about a wedding."

Tessa's Irish temper ignited. "I sent more because you didn't answer the first one. Besides, you scared me half to death!"

"I scared you?" Lee repeated. "How did I do that?"

"You took so long getting here, I thought you were going to be too late to save her," Tessa replied. "I expected you two days ago."

"I didn't get into Chicago until two days ago," Lee informed her. "And yours weren't the only urgent messages I had waiting. I do have other cases. I had to make a stop in Denver."

Tessa nodded. "To get the little girl. David told me. And I have to admit when I first saw Madeline, I thought she was Lily Catherine . . . I thought you had found her." Tessa swallowed the lump of disappointment in her throat. "But David told me about Madeline on the way over here from the church."

"How much did he tell you?"

"Everything," Tessa replied.

"Then you know why I married Mary."

Tessa smiled slyly, then slowly nodded her head. "Yes, Liam, I know why you married Mary."

Lee cleared his throat, uncomfortable with the fact that Tessa knew so much about him. "Yes, well, I'd appreciate it if you and David would keep quiet about the reason. I don't want to hurt or embarrass Mary any."

"Neither do we," Tessa reminded him.

Lee glanced over Tessa's shoulder and saw that Mary was heading toward them. "I'll have your promise."

"Our lips are sealed." Tessa heard the sound of soft footsteps, the swish of satin skirts, caught a whiff of Mary's perfume, and turned to embrace her sister-in-law. "You were a lovely bride, Mary, and David and I are very happy for you." She planted a kiss on Mary's cheek.

"Thank you, Tessa," Mary said.

"I was just welcoming Liam into the family," Tessa continued in a rush. "He's so lucky to get you." She smiled at Mary. "I told Liam I think everything has turned out for the best. I was congratulating him on his timing and his success."

"And," Lee said to Mary, as he shot Tessa a knowing look, "I was just congratulating Tessa on hers."

"I don't see why we didn't spend the night at the ranch," Mary grumbled to her husband as she shifted on the hard train seat for what seemed like the hundredth time.

Lee moved closer to the window to give her more room. It was late afternoon and the sun was beginning its descent. They had been married half a day and Mary was already questioning his judgment. He frowned at the thought. Years ago, his first bride had hung onto his arm and onto his every word, but then Mary wasn't anything like Jeannie. And it wouldn't do to compare the two women or the two weddings. Lee sighed. He hadn't told Mary their destination. She thought they were going to Denver. What would she say once they reached Utopia? What would she say when she learned the whole truth? Lee squeezed his eyes shut. He had enough to think about right now. He didn't need to borrow future troubles. "Not a good idea," Lee remarked brusquely.

"Why not?" Mary asked. "I'm exhausted." She glanced at Madeline sprawled across Lee's lap and Judah, who was nodding off in the seat directly in front of Lee. "Madeline and Judah are exhausted, and you look dead on your feet."

"I appreciate your concern," Lee replied, "but I'm doing what I think is best."

"What about what I think? Couldn't you have consulted me about this? Or don't my opinions matter to you?"

Lee sucked in a deep breath, then counted to ten, and slowly let it out. He didn't appreciate her sarcastic attitude or her "schoolteacher" tone of voice—not when he was trying his utmost to hang on to what was left of his patience. He sighed tiredly. "What do you want from me, Mary? A promise to consult you before making any decisions in the future?"

"That would be a nice start," Mary replied sweetly. Too sweetly.

"Fine!" Lee raised his voice, then quickly lowered it as Maddy squirmed restlessly in his lap. "I promise to consult you before I make any major decisions in the future. Anything else?" He shifted his weight on the uncomfortable seat and attempted to straighten his long legs in the limited space between benches.

Mary stared at her husband. He was way beyond exhausted. She noted that his gray eyes were streaked with red and underscored by dark circles. She saw the tired lines bracketing his mouth and the golden stubble marking his cheeks and chin, and was tempted to postpone her questions and doubts, but she couldn't. She had tied her future to this man—this virtual stranger, for better or for worse, and they might as well work out some ground rules before they reached Denver. "You promise to consult with me before *we* make any major decisions," she corrected him in her best schoolteacher tone, "and you promise to explain why we couldn't spend the night at the ranch and get a fresh start in the morning like any sensible family would."

Lee snorted. Damn. He had forgotten how tenacious Mary Alexander could be. She wanted—no, demanded—an explanation. Well, hell, the least he could do was give her one, whether she liked it or not. "If we had stayed at the ranch, where would we have slept?"

"In my house," Mary answered confidently. "I have my own little cabin close to the schoolhouse."

Lee was familiar with the layout of the Trail T ranch. He had been there once before at another wedding breakfast— that one honoring Tessa Roarke's marriage to David Alexander. And although Mary didn't look like any schoolteacher he had ever had, Lee knew her cabin was located next to the schoolhouse because she taught the children on the ranch how to read and write and cipher in three or four different languages.

"How many bedrooms do you have?" Lee asked.

"One," she answered.

"For the four of us?" he nodded toward Judah, then glanced down at Maddy.

Mary looked at him. She hadn't really thought about Judah and Maddy's sleeping arrangements—only hers and Lee's. "No," she admitted. "But Maddy and Judah would have been welcome to stay with Reese and Faith and the girls."

"What about us, Mary?" Lee's voice, deep and sensual, sent a ripple of awareness through her. "Where would we sleep?"

"In my room," she answered softly, hesitantly.

Lee chuckled unexpectedly, then shook his head. "I may be tired, Mary, but I'm not *that* tired." Didn't she realize he was trying to be considerate? Didn't she understand the danger of inviting him to spend the night in her bed? He had willpower, but he wasn't a bloody plaster saint. He would make a mockery of their agreement to keep the marriage chaste before the bedroom door closed, and then her chance for future happiness with the man of her choice would evaporate like morning dew in the sunshine.

"You could have slept on the sofa," Mary suggested.

"If I'm going to be uncomfortable, I prefer to spend the night on a hard bench in a noisy train with a group of strangers. Thank you." That wasn't entirely true, but Lee didn't think he should elaborate on how difficult it would be for him to sleep on the sofa in the living room of her tiny cabin knowing she was tucked into a nice warm bed one door away wearing one of those pretty white lace and cotton nightgowns he liked—or nothing at all.

"We could have borrowed Reese's Pullman car and traveled in comfort," Mary pointed out. "Reese wouldn't have minded. Pelham and I were going to borrow it for the trip to San Francisco anyway."

Lee shifted Maddy's slight weight on his lap, then turned a bit so he could look at Mary. "That's precisely why I refused Reese's offer. I've followed in Pelham's footsteps enough for one day."

Mary sat back against the hard bench, stung by Lee's sullen announcement. "What is that supposed to mean?"

"It means I married his intended bride, ate the wedding breakfast prepared for him, and played host to his wedding guests. But I draw the line at sleeping in his bed or wearing his damned nightshirt or any of the rest of the clothes he left in Reese's railroad car."

"How did you know about the bed or his clothes?" Mary was surprised. No one at the ranch had even so much as breathed a mention of Pelham Everhardt Cosgrove III in her hearing since the ceremony.

"I accidentally overheard Faith tell Reese he needed to send someone down to the depot to pack up the things you had laid out for your honeymoon—including your new white lace peignoir and his striped nightshirt—and have Cosgrove's bed dismantled and sent back to his house. "

"So we're sitting here on our wedding night keeping watch while Maddy and Judah sleep." Mary managed a small wistful smile.

"Yeah," Lee agreed. "It's not much of a wedding night for you."

"Or for you."

"No, I guess not." Lee winced as Maddy sighed in her sleep, flung her arm out, and hit him in the center of his chest. He shifted on the seat again. "But, then, I wasn't expecting one tonight. You were."

Mary blushed and reached for the little girl in an attempt to cover her embarrassment. "Here, let me hold her while you rest your arms."

"You don't mind?"

"Of course not," Mary replied as he settled Maddy into her arms. "I like children."

"I'm very glad to hear it," Lee said, his voice deep and husky and full of meaning.

Mary's cheeks pinkened once again at the look in his gray eyes. She struggled for some way to break the uncomfortable silence. "Speaking of children . . ."

"Yes?" Lee raised his eyebrow and lowered his voice suggestively.

Mary focused her gaze on the child in her lap and cleared her suddenly dry throat before she continued her train of thought, "Tessa told me that when she saw Maddy walk into the church she thought you had found Lily Catherine."

"Yeah, I know," Lee answered.

"Was she very disappointed?" Mary asked, knowing Tessa and David were devastated.

"She hid it very well," Lee said, "but I could tell she was upset."

"Finding Lily for David is very important to Tessa. She and David have adopted Coalie as their son, but they want a big family and although it's still early in the marriage, Tessa hasn't had any luck conceiving a child of her own."

"Not from lack of trying, I understand," Lee commented.

"No, not from lack of trying." Mary couldn't control the wavering note in her voice or the way the blood rushed to her cheeks every time Lee mentioned children. "In fact, my mother thinks that may be the problem. She thinks Tessa and David are trying too hard to have a baby when they should just relax and let nature take its course."

Lee had to fight to keep from leering at his bride. "Is it possible to try too hard?"

"My mother thinks so. She thinks Tessa's is working too hard to make things perfect for David and Coalie. And since it's taking you longer to find Lily than she expected, Tessa is wearing herself and David out trying to have a child of their own. My mother thinks that, deep down, Tessa feels she has to repay David for saving her life."

"I didn't hear David complaining."

"And you never will. He loves Tessa. And she loves him. But she's so stubborn, so independent, and so conscious of the fact that she came to David with nothing but Coalie and the clothes on their backs. It's that Irish pride of hers." Mary turned to look at Lee. "You've got to locate Lily Catherine before Tessa becomes obsessed with producing a daughter for David because my mother says that just makes things worse."

"I see." Lee understood Tessa's obsession. He had spent the better part of the last four months in Washington searching. Why? Because Tessa had asked him to do something no one else could do, just as she had demanded he hurry to Cheyenne and save Mary.

Mary. Lee stole another glance at his wife as she shifted on the hard train seat.

"What happened in Washington?"

"Huh?" He hadn't been paying attention to her words, only the way her lips formed them.

"I confess to being as curious as Tessa is to learn the details of your trip to Washington. What happened? Or are you allowed to discuss it with people other than your clients?"

He debated for a moment on how to respond. Much of his report was classified, but Mary was his wife. And somehow, Lee knew he could trust her. He wanted to trust her. "Senator Warner Millen died unexpectedly."

"What?" Mary breathed the question, clearly surprised. She knew the senator was a vital link in locating Lily Catherine. What would happen to Lee's case now? What would happen to Lily? "How?"

Maddy whimpered in her sleep and Lee watched as Mary automatically redistributed the little girl's weight, so that Maddy lay with her head pillowed on Mary's breast.

"Mrs. Millen's official statement says he died of heart failure," Lee answered calmly.

"But you don't believe her." It wasn't a question, but a statement of fact.

"Well." Lee didn't bother to mask the cynical note in his voice. "His heart definitely stopped beating. But only after he put his gun to his head and pulled the trigger."

Mary gasped. "He killed himself?"

"Unofficially."

"May he burn in hell," Mary fervently prayed.

Lee chuckled. "My sentiments exactly. But I thought you'd be a bit more charitable"—he teased—"you being such a lady and all."

"After what he did to David?" Mary responded indignantly. "Senator Millen ruined David's promising career in Washington with a pack of lies told by his frightened sixteen-year-old daughter! And then, when his daughter needed him most, our noble Senator Millen disowned her and sent her away. And when his only child died in childbirth, did the almighty senator rush to claim his grandchild? No! He abandoned her, his own flesh and blood." Mary turned her fiery gaze on Lee. "Yes, I hope Senator Millen burns in hell for what he did to David, but mostly for what he did to his daughter and granddaughter. A man like that doesn't deserve a family."

Lee couldn't take his gaze off his wife. When riled, Mary displayed all the ferocity of a lioness defending her cubs. He stroked one side of his mustache with the tip of his finger. "Your family means a lot to you, doesn't it?"

"I love them," she said simply. "My family means everything to me."

Lee nodded, becoming more satisfied with his choice and more comfortable with Tabitha's ultimatum with each passing moment.

Mary waited for Lee to say something. But he didn't, so she asked a question of her own. "What about you?"

Lee gifted her with his innocent expression and a lopsided smile. "What about me?"

"Well, I know you met David and Reese during the war, that the three of you became friends and sometimes worked together for Pinkerton. I know you remained with the agency after David and Reese resigned and are still an operative. And I know you've had at least two partners— one was Tessa's brother, Eamon Roarke, and the other was Maddy's father." Mary brushed Madeline's dark curls off the little girl's flushed cheeks as she spoke. "But other than this, I know nothing about you. Where's your family? Where are you from? Do you have any brothers or sisters? Nieces or nephews?" She sighed. "You're my husband and I don't even know your birthday."

"February sixteenth in the year of our lord, eighteen hundred and forty," Lee answered.

"Then you're—"

"I was thirty-three on my last birthday."

"I am a teacher," she reminded him. "I know my arithmetic."

Lee grinned. "It's late, and you've had a rather trying day. I thought I would save you the trouble of calculating my age."

"What about the rest of my questions?" Mary wanted to know.

"I was born and raised in Washington City. My mother died when I was eleven. My father lives in Texas. I have no nieces or nephews because I'm an only child." He shrugged his shoulders as if to indicate that there was nothing more to tell.

Mary shuddered. She had grown up with such a large family that she couldn't imagine not having them around her. "What was your mother's name?"

"Jane MacIntyre," Lee told her. "And my father's name is Patrick Kincaid. My mother was Scots and my father is Irish, and I was named after both my grandfathers. Liam Gordon MacIntyre Kincaid."

"Do you see your father often?"

"No," Lee answered abruptly. "I don't."

"You don't take the time to visit him in Texas when you're working out west?" Mary pressed the issue.

"No."

"Ever?"

"Never." Lee closed the subject of Patrick Kincaid. "What about you?" he asked.

"You know my whole family," Mary answered.

"I don't know your birthday," Lee said softly.

"May tenth."

Lee smiled at her reticence to reveal her age. He studied the soft skin on her face and neck and guessed her to be in her early twenties. She need not worry about aging: She had that timeless quality about her. Mary would be as beautiful at eighty as she had been at eighteen. But he couldn't resist the urge to tease her. "What year?"

"None of your business," she replied sharply.

"So you won't tell me your age." He pretended to ponder the topic. "That can only mean one thing."

"What?"

"You're older than me."

"I am not!"

"Prove it," he challenged.

"May tenth," Mary told him. "In the year of our lord eighteen hundred and forty . . ."

"Yes?" He cocked his right eyebrow.

"Four," Mary ground out.

Lee choked back a laugh. "That makes you twenty-nine."

"Twenty-eight," she corrected. "I won't be twenty-nine until May tenth."

"Which is what? Two weeks away?" He glanced at Mary's rigid posture. "At least that explains it."

"What?" she demanded.

"Pelham Everhardt Cosgrove III." Lee met her dark-eyed gaze. "Now I know why you were in such a rush to marry him."

"I wasn't in a rush to marry him. He was in a rush to marry me. But you're never going to stop reminding me about Pelham, are you?" Mary asked. "You're never going to let me forget that he left me standing at the altar—that he never gave me the opportunity to explain." They wouldn't be able to build much of a marriage if Lee kept reminding her of her public humiliation for the next thirty or forty years.

"I'm not throwing Cosgrove in your face," Lee said.

"Really?"

"Really. I just wondered why you chose a tenderfoot like

him when it was obvious to everyone in town that he could never be the kind of husband you need."

"Such as?" Mary was prepared to do battle.

But Lee Kincaid surprised her with his answer. "A man strong enough to let you be yourself. A man who wouldn't try to mold you into something you're not or force you to deny what you are."

"He couldn't force me to do anything."

"No," Lee agreed, "Maybe you're right. He was too weak to force you. Maybe he simply planned to wear you down over the next few years until you became what he wanted his wife to be."

"And what do you think he wanted me to become?" Mary couldn't contain her curiosity.

"A very pale imitation of the woman you already are. He didn't appreciate you, Mary, and because he didn't appreciate you, Cosgrove could never be the husband you deserve."

His answer took her breath away. "What about you, Liam Gordon MacIntyre Kincaid?" She wiggled closer to him on the hard bench.

Lee recognized the look in her dark eyes and wanted very much to kiss her. Wanted to prove what kind of husband he could be, but he didn't. "Me?" he asked, all innocence once again. "I'm your temporary husband, ma'am. Until you find someone better."

Mary wondered suddenly how he could possibly think someone better would ever come along.

"But I promise you something, Mary," Lee continued.

"What's that?" she asked breathlessly.

"I'll kill the next man who makes you cry," he solemnly swore.

Mary squeezed her eyes shut and rested her chin on the top of Maddy's head, turning her face to hide the tears welling up in her eyes lest Lee see her crying and feel compelled to join the long line of suicides petitioning Saint Peter for the opportunity to pass through the pearly gates.

Chapter
Eight

The train whistle sounded five miles outside the town limits of Utopia, Colorado, just moments after sunrise.

Mary awoke with a start to find herself resting against Lee's upper arm. Remembering that she had been holding Maddy, Mary instinctively tightened her grasp on the little girl. Her arms were empty and Mary cried out in alarm. "Maddy!"

"It's all right, Mary. I've got her." Lee shifted from his uncomfortable position against the window, then rotated his right shoulder to relieve the tingling pins and needles sensation. He turned a bit in the seat and Mary saw that he held the sleeping Madeline cradled in one arm against his wide chest. He stared at Mary for a moment before he smiled at her.

The tender look in his gray eyes unnerved her. "What is it?" she asked.

Lee reached up and gently rubbed at the pink and white indentations on Mary's cheek. "You have wrinkle marks from my coat on your face."

"I'm sorry," she apologized. "I meant to stay awake."

"That's all right. You were tired, you needed to sleep."

Mary stared at her husband and events of the previous day—her wedding day—came rushing back. "What about you?" The sight of him nearly brought tears to her eyes. He sat with his shoulders hunched forward, his large body practically folded to fit into the space between the window and the seat in front of them. "Did you get any sleep at all?"

"An hour or so, here and there."

His gray eyes were bloodshot and two day's growth of blond beard seemed to sparkle on his chin, but he looked as wildly attractive as ever. She hadn't thought it possible for Lee Kincaid to look more handsome than usual, but he did. Dishevelment suited him. Mary suddenly realized that she was entitled to see him this way every morning. She smiled at the intimate thought and a blush brought more color to her cheeks.

Lee was intrigued by the sly smile touching her lips. "Is something wrong?"

"Oh, no," she murmured, "it's just that . . ." Mary lowered her gaze to her lap and quickly began to smoothing out the creases in her skirt.

"What?"

"You look so—so—" Mary couldn't begin to put her feelings into words.

Lee rubbed his hand over his chin, gauging the growth of his whiskers. "Tired?" he suggested. "Rough?"

Mary shook her head. Appealing was the word that came to mind. And attractive, and manly. But she couldn't say those things to him. "Different," she finally answered.

"Yes," Lee said, smiling. "I guess the newness has already worn off the marriage. We haven't been married twenty-four hours and you're already seeing me at my worst."

"No," Mary corrected him. "I've seen you look much worse than this."

"When?" Lee asked.

"In Peaceable after David punched you in the eye. And then later at David and Tessa's wedding when your face was swollen and the bruises had turned that ghastly shade of yellowish-green." Mary reached up and self-consciously smoothed back the locks of hair that had escaped the confines of her chignon. "You don't look nearly as bad now as you did then. But I . . ."

"You look fine," he replied gruffly.

"Are you sure?" Mary glanced around to see if any of the other passengers were paying attention to them, then whispered, "I've never spent the night in the public car before or fallen asleep while traveling alone."

Lee grinned. "Mary, you weren't alone. You were with us." He nodded toward Judah who was dozing in the seat in front of them, then glanced down at the little girl asleep in his arms.

"And it's a good thing you're family," Mary said, "or else my reputation would be ruined." She smiled at him. "Besides, it wouldn't do for anyone to see me looking like this."

"No," Lee agreed, leaning closer to her. "That wouldn't do at all." Her hat had been knocked askew and long straight strands of her shiny black hair had come loose from its neat bun. Her left cheek was puffed from sleep and reddened by the marks of his coat. Her dress was wrinkled, and there was a wet spot the size of a silver dollar on the jacket above her left breast where Maddy had drooled in her sleep, but Lee thought that any man seeing Mary Alexander now, so soft and warm and enticing, in the early morning would be hard-pressed to resist her. Lord knows he was having trouble.

"Other than my husband and family, I mean." Mary stared at Lee's mustache while she nervously tucked another lock of hair back into place. She wondered if he would kiss her good morning. He was her husband, after all, and entitled to a morning kiss.

Husband. The soft spoken word brought a lump to Lee's throat. Family. He couldn't explain the feelings he felt as

Mary matter-of-factly included him and Maddy, and even Judah, into her family circle. Lee stared into her big brown eyes. He recognized the look in them—the softness and warmth she reserved for her family and friends. There was none of the hostility and coldness that ordinarily came his way. He wanted to kiss her, and if she didn't stop staring at him with that soft look in her eyes, he was going to do just that. He leaned down to make good on his promise.

The train whistle sounded again and the conductor hurried down the aisle. "Utopia," he announced, "Utopia station."

Lee moved away from Mary as the conductor passed by. He leaned forward in his seat, and reached out to Judah.

"What is it?" she asked.

"We're getting off the train," he told her before touching the elderly man sleeping in the seat in front of him on the shoulder. "Judah, wake up."

Judah awoke instantly, turning in his seat to face Lee. "Oh, hello, young man. Are we there yet?"

Lee nodded. "The train is just pulling into the station."

Judah straightened his clothing and looked around for any belongings. "That's nice. We'll be home before we know it."

Lee gave a heartfelt sigh of relief. Judah's mental faculties appeared to be intact today.

Mary glanced over Lee's shoulder, out the window at the desolate town's main street, then touched him on the sleeve. "But this is Utopia."

"I know," he answered as he gently awakened Maddy and set her on her feet, then stood up beside her.

Madeline grabbed hold of Lee's coattail, twisting the fabric in her fist as she squirmed in the small space between the rows of seats. "Pretty," she said clearly.

Lee looked from Maddy to Mary, then smiled back at the child. "Yes," he agreed, "Mary's pretty."

Mary flushed with pleasure at the unexpected compliment.

"Pretty," Madeline repeated more forcefully. Her brow wrinkled in frustration as she let go of Lee's coat and grasped the front of her pinafore. She wiggled this way and that, and danced from foot to foot. "Pretty. Go pretty."

As he watched her clutching her dress and bouncing from one leg to the other, Lee suddenly remembered exactly what pretty meant in "Maddy-talk." A look of panic appeared on his face as he studied the passengers crowding into the aisle preparing to disembark from the train to stretch their legs and gauged the amount of time he had. "Just a minute, sweetheart," he said, awkwardly patting Maddy on the shoulder as she squirmed in the space beside him. "I'll get you there."

Mary glanced down at Maddy and understanding dawned. She quickly grabbed her purse from the seat and stepped into the aisle. "Give her to me," she said to Lee. "There's bound to be a facility behind the depot." She sounded completely confident that the town would have public outhouses nearby, but after catching a glimpse of Utopia from the train window, Mary doubted the town had that much to offer.

Lee lifted Maddy and gratefully handed her over to Mary. "Judah and I will wait for you in the depot."

"Go pretty." Maddy was more insistent.

"All right, sweetie." Mary gave Lee a quick wave, then hurried down the aisle and stepped off the train onto the platform. Mary flagged down a porter and asked directions to the nearest necessary.

But the wet warmth seeping through Maddy's undergarments and petticoats onto Mary's arm warned her that it was already too late.

Maddy's lips puckered suddenly and the expression on

her face crumpled as she realized she had disgraced herself. She turned her face away from Mary and began to cry.

"There, there, sweetheart, it's all right," Mary soothed as she continued on the path toward the facility. She reached the outhouse, opened the door, stepped inside, then leaned down to place Maddy on the ground.

"No!" Maddy balked at being set on her feet. She tightened her hold around Mary's neck, buried her face in Mary's shoulder, wrapped her legs around Mary's waist, and cried harder.

"Maddy, sweetie, I must put you on the ground in order to get you out of your wet underthings."

"No!"

"Don't you want me to take off your wet clothes?"

"No!" Maddy shook her head vigorously, setting her dark curls bouncing against Mary's face.

Balancing Maddy on one hip, Mary reached down and tried to pry Maddy's chubby little legs from around her waist. "Please, Maddy," Mary persuaded, "let me put you down so I can remove your drawers and petticoats." Mary tried to remember if little girls Madeline's age wore drawers or if they were still wearing diapers. Although she had been around her cousin Reese's three-year-old daughter since the day Hope was born, most of Mary's practical experience was with school-age children, not toddlers.

Maddy refused to meet Mary's gaze, but continued to cry. It broke Mary's heart to watch the tears run down her cherubic face.

"Maddy, sweetheart, listen to me," Mary instructed in a gentle voice. "This little accident wasn't your fault. We've had a very long train ride and your . . ." Mary faltered for a moment, not knowing how to refer to Lee so that Maddy would understand. "Lee and I should have realized you needed to—" She shrugged her shoulders and tried another tack. "I know you're embarrassed, but there's no need to be. I won't tell anyone."

All at once Maddy seemed to understand that Mary could be trusted with her secret. She stopped crying and scrubbed away the tears with her little fists.

Encouraged by Maddy's response, Mary asked, "Would you like to get down now?"

Maddy nodded.

Mary set Madeline on the ground, then hiked up her own skirts and knelt on the ground beside the little girl. Acting purely on instinct, Mary put her arms around Maddy and held her close. "That's my girl," she praised.

Maddy rewarded her with a smile.

"Okay." Mary reached for the hem of Maddy's royal blue dress and white pinafore. "Let's get you out of these clothes."

Maddy stood quietly cooperating while Mary stripped her of her soiled white muslin petticoat, underdrawers, black leather shoes, and white knitted tights. In a few short minutes she stood barefoot, wearing nothing but her blue dress and white pinafore.

Mary rolled and re-rolled Maddy's wet underclothing into a tight bundle, but no amount of rolling or folding could reduce the size of bundle enough so that she could fit it in with her things. She thought for a moment, wondering how she could conceal Maddy's undergarments, then finally decided there was only one thing she could do. She unbuttoned the jacket of her traveling suit and wrapped the bundle in that. When she finished the chore, Mary turned her attention back to Maddy who waited patiently. "All right, angel, we'll slip your shoes back on," she said, picking up one of Madeline's tiny black leather shoes. "I'll tend to my needs, and then we'll meet Lee and Mr. Crane back at the depot. Okay?"

"No!" Maddy shook her head, vehemently opposed to Mary's suggestion.

Mary sighed, at a loss as to the workings of the two-and-a-half-year-old mind. Being a mother to a toddler was much harder than she ever imagined—and a lot like playing a game of drawing room charades. Mary's admiration for her own mother and her cousin, Faith, grew by leaps and bounds. Still, she had her work cut out for her and Mary wasn't about to give up. "What is it, Maddy? What's wrong? Don't you want to go back to the train?"

"No!" Maddy stared defiantly at Mary, shouted the single word, stuck out her bottom lip, then immediately fastened her gaze on her shoes.

"Maddy?" Mary reached out to touch her but Madeline jerked away.

Stuck in an outhouse with a recalcitrant child, and unable to delay any longer, Mary quickly tended to her own personal needs. And as she began to set her skirts to rights, lowering them to cover her petticoats and silk stockings, Mary found she had gained Maddy's complete attention.

Mary studied the expression on the little girl's face. "So, that's it," she said at last. "You're embarrassed for anyone to see you without your petticoats and tights, aren't you?"

Maddy nodded slowly.

"We've got a problem, don't we?"

Maddy nodded once again.

A solution to the problem suddenly took form in Mary's brain. It was daring and a bit scandalous. And Mary would die of embarrassment if anyone ever discovered the lengths she'd gone to appease a child, but it seemed the only appropriate thing to do. Mary smiled down at Madeline. "Would you feel better about leaving this outhouse if I took off *my* drawers and petticoats, too?"

"Uh huh."

Mary took a deep breath. "All right. Here it goes." She

raised her skirts and hurriedly shed her drawers, quilted underpetticoat, bustle petticoat, and stockings. Maddy looked on in delight as Mary added her neatly rolled-up undergarments to Maddy's bundle of clothing tucked inside her suit jacket, then stood balancing first on one leg and then the other, as she struggled to get her shoes back on.

Maddy giggled suddenly—a deep-throated, husky giggle that sounded disconcerting coming from such a small angelic-looking child.

Mary couldn't help but giggle as well. "I know it looks funny. But remember, young lady, that I'm doing this for you. This will be our little secret, okay?"

"'Kay."

"Mary, are you in there?" The unexpected knock on the outhouse door and the sound of Lee's voice startled her and Mary jumped—tripping over the hem of her skirt, made longer by her lack of undergarments, nearly toppling over in the process.

Maddy laughed out loud.

Hearing the childish laughter, Lee asked, "What's taking so long? What are you two doing in there?"

"Nothing," Mary answered quickly. Too quickly.

"Then hurry it up," Lee ordered. Fatigue made him irritable and more abrupt with Mary than he meant to be.

"Uh . . . we'll be out in just a minute," she replied. "I'm . . . uh . . . putting on my shoes."

"Your shoes?" Lee asked. "What are you doing with your shoes off?"

Mary thought quickly. "I . . . uh . . . meant Maddy's shoes. She had something in them." Mary said a quick prayer, hoping the Lord would understand the need to protect the little girl's sensitive feelings. Mary fastened her remaining shoe, then gathered up the bundle of clothing.

"Hey," Lee called from outside the door. "Can you speed

it up a bit? I left Judah at the depot and I'd rather not leave him alone very long."

"Do you want to walk?" Mary asked Madeline. "Or would you rather have me carry you?"

"Hold me," Maddy answered, lifting her arms up to Mary.

Mary handed the bundle to Maddy. "Can you manage this?"

Maddy nodded, but as she took hold of the clothing, it slipped from her grasp. The ties came loose and an armful of white undergarments fell to the floor. Madeline frowned at the pile of white fabric, then puckered her lips.

Mary hurried to forestall the flood of tears. "Maddy, it's all right. See? Besides, I have an idea." She bent to retrieve the clothes, bundled Maddy's into a tight ball, then quickly stuffed hers inside her jacket. "I'll carry you and Lee can carry these." That said, Mary opened the door to the outhouse. "Here, take this while I get Maddy." Leaving him with no choice, she shoved her jacket-wrapped bundle in Lee's direction, then turned to lift Maddy into her arms.

"What is it?" Lee made a grab for the bundle, caught hold of a jacket sleeve, and watched in astonishment as the hem of a woman's petticoat slipped from beneath the jacket and a pair of women's white muslin and lace-trimmed drawers fluttered to the ground. Curious now, Lee opened Mary's jacket and peeked inside. The unmistakable odor of urine assaulted his nostrils as he untied the white bundle and found Maddy's wet underthings along with an assortment of other feminine undergarments—all dry and, except for the quilted underpetticoat, practically sheer, and much too large to be Maddy's.

Lee sucked in a breath at the thought of Mary wearing nothing beneath her prim skirt. Smiling at the image, he took Maddy's doll out of his coat pocket, then whisked

Mary's lacy drawers off the ground, and hurriedly stuffed them into the coat pocket before she exited the privy.

He barely managed to tuck the other bundle of clothes back into place when Mary stepped through the outhouse doorway. She carried Maddy on her hip and Lee noticed that the chubby little legs locked around Mary's waist were bare. Mary followed his gaze and the expression on her face warned Lee not to comment. Lee didn't say a word. He simply let his gaze roam downward over Mary's skirt which, he noted with a great deal of satisfaction, now hung past her shoes—several inches longer than it had been when she left the train wearing her bustle and petticoats. He grinned as a gust of wind flattened the green serge against her body. Nice legs, he thought. Nice long legs.

Lee would have continued his contemplation of Mary's legs, but Maddy took one look at him and the doll he still held in his hand, reached out her arms, and yelled, "Mama!"

"No," Mary corrected gently. "Papa. Not Mama." She looked up at Lee. "Is it all right if she calls you Papa? She's so young, she won't remember her real papa. As far as she's concerned, you'll be her father."

"Papa is fine with me," Lee replied. His chest swelled with pride and his heart seemed to skip a beat at the thought of Maddy calling him papa.

"It won't be a completely accurate term," Mary continued.

"It will be accurate all right," Lee explained. "I plan to adopt her and raise her as my own."

Mary's eyes lit up and the smile she gave him could have warmed the coldest winter night. "Oh, Lee, that's wonderful!" She stepped closer to him.

"Hey, don't look at me like that," Lee warned.

"Like what?"

"Like I'm some kind of knight in shining armor." He didn't know why he suddenly felt the need to warn her away from him. Maybe it was lack of sleep, or his uncharacteristic lapse in willpower. Or maybe he just felt too damned deceitful to take advantage of her moment of weakness. "I'm only adopting her to fulfill the terms of the will."

"Oh." A deep disappointment settled in the pit of Mary's stomach. The warm rosy glow disappeared and all at once, she began to feel the cold seeping into her bones. She shivered involuntarily as the cool wind cut through her thin blouse and the fabric of her skirt.

"Mama!" Maddy shouted again.

"Papa," Mary corrected automatically.

"No," Lee interrupted, intent on further disillusioning Mary. "It's Mama."

"I don't understand." Mary's expression of puzzlement echoed her words.

"She means her doll," Lee explained, handing the doll over to the little girl. "Mama equals doll in 'Maddy-talk.'"

Remembering Maddy's dramatic entrance into the church, Mary narrowed her gaze at Lee, only half-watching as Maddy hugged the porcelain-faced toy to her chest. "Her doll?"

"That's right." He shrugged noncommittally.

"And how long have you known that?" Mary demanded.

Lee met her gaze. "Oh, I figured it out on the train from Denver to Cheyenne." He turned to head up the path.

But Mary stopped him by grabbing hold of his coat sleeve. "So you knew! At my wedding, you knew what she meant all the time!"

"Yeah, Mary," Lee admitted. "I knew."

"And you didn't say anything. You let Pelham think . . ." She let her words trail off when she realized she was too angry to form coherent sentences.

"Yeah, well, I'd be willing to bet over half the people in the church knew. But they didn't say anything either."

Everything he said was true. Mary couldn't dispute it, but

she couldn't let him have the last word. Something in her refused to let the matter rest. She knew the truth, but she wanted him to say it—dared him to say it. "You didn't save me from humiliation. You set me up!" She flung the words at him like a gauntlet. "Admit it! I was set up!"

Lee looked down at her. "Yeah, well, welcome to the club."

"What's that cryptic little remark supposed to mean?" She tugged on his sleeve once again like a belligerent little bulldog holding on to its catch.

Lee sighed. "It doesn't mean anything, Mary, except that I'm not going to argue with you anymore. What's done is done, and if you can't accept that now, well then, you'll just have to live with it. Now, I'm tired and sleepy, and sick of carrying on what should be a civilized discussion beside a damned outhouse! Come on. There's no need to stand here freezing. We can argue when we get home."

He was right. There was no sense standing out in the cold when they could argue within the warm confines of a Denver hotel. "Fine." She bit off the word in a manner that eloquently warned him that their discussion was far from over.

"Fine," Lee repeated as he took hold of Mary's elbow and helped her negotiate the narrow path from the outhouse to the depot. The train engineer blew the warning whistle to inform passengers it was time to begin boarding. Shivering with cold, Mary hurried up the path. Lee tightened his grip on her elbow, steadying her as she tripped over the hem of her skirt.

"What's wrong with your skirt?" he asked, knowing full well what was wrong.

"Nothing is wrong with my skirt." She glared at him.

"Then slow down," he warned, "before you fall and break your neck. I didn't go to all this trouble to get married just to become a widower the first day."

"You couldn't be so lucky," Mary shot back. "And if we miss the train, don't blame me."

"It doesn't matter if we miss the train."

"Of course it matters," Mary told him. "If we miss the train to Denver, we'll have to wait for the next one."

"We aren't going to Denver. This is the end of the line for us."

"What?" Mary stopped in her tracks and turned to face Lee. "You're abandoning me, too? You married me just to leave me here in the middle of nowhere?"

Lee recognized the note of indignation in her voice but he also heard the fear. "No, I'm not abandoning you, Mary. I'm staying here in Utopia," Lee told her as they reached the depot and climbed the two steps leading to the platform.

Judah struggled from the rocking chair beside the ticket window, grabbed hold of his cane and rose to greet them. He tipped his hat to Mary. "Morning, ma'am."

Mary forgot her anger at Lee in her pleasure at finding Judah Crane lucid. "Good morning, Mr. Crane."

Judah glanced at Lee.

"Judah, you remember my wife, Mary Kincaid," Lee prompted.

"Yes, of course," Judah responded. "A pleasure to see you again, Mrs. Kincaid."

"Please, call me Mary," she said.

"Mary is it," Judah agreed. "And you must call me Judah. Mr. Crane is much too formal a way to address a friend."

Mary smiled. "Thank you, Judah."

"You're welcome, Mary." The elderly attorney matched her smile with a smile of his own. "And welcome to Utopia. I hope you'll be very happy living here."

Mary turned to Lee for confirmation. Live in Utopia?

Lee nodded. "That's right. Welcome to Utopia, Mrs. Kincaid." He smiled his most charming smile. "Welcome home."

Chapter Nine

"I don't believe it," Mary said, staring at Utopia's nearly deserted main street as the gusting wind sent spirals of red dust and bits of trash whirling about.

"Believe it," Lee told her. "Because according to the directions I got from the stationmaster, our house is at the end of Main Street."

"House?" Mary was genuinely confused.

"Yep. You and I are the proud owners of a house and silver mine in Utopia, Colorado."

"You bought a house and a silver mine here? In this town?" Mary looked around. As far as she could tell, there wasn't much to Utopia—certainly nothing to recommend it. The town had obviously already peaked in popularity and was currently on the downswing. Utopia was dying. Anyone with an eye and a modest amount of intelligence could see that.

"I've never been to Utopia before," he told her. "And I didn't buy the house or the silver mine. I inherited them. Or, rather, Madeline did. Ettinger House and the Ettinger Silver Mine."

"Maddy's father left her a house and a silver mine?"

To keep from lying outright, Lee nodded.

Mary sucked in a breath as another gust of wind caught the hem of her skirt, lifting it a few inches. "So we came here to look at the property?"

Lee didn't hear her. He focused his attention on the wooden floor around Mary's feet, hoping to catch a glimpse of her bare ankles. He was vastly disappointed and vastly amused when she grabbed a handful of fabric and pulled her skirt tight to keep the wind from lifting it higher. By doing so, she inadvertently managed to give Lee a wonderful view of the outline of her lower body and her long, luscious legs.

"Lee?"

"What?" He jerked his gaze away from her skirt.

"I said we came here to have a look at the property, right?"

"Wrong."

"But . . ." Mary protested.

"Hey," Lee smiled at her. "We haven't seen the house yet and the stationmaster says it's the biggest one in town."

Mary glanced around. "That's not saying much."

"Come on, Mary, where's your spirit of adventure?" Lee teased.

"I left it on the train," Mary replied glumly as she watched the train chug down the track toward Denver. "Along with my luggage."

Lee laughed out loud. "I took care of our luggage. It's being delivered to the house."

"By whom?" Except for their little group and the man behind the cage in the ticket window, the depot appeared to be as empty as the town.

"I paid the porter to deliver it," he answered. "And he left with our luggage right before I left to get you and Maddy." Lee stared at her meaningfully. "He should have reached the house by now."

Mary shivered at the thought.

Lee, thinking it was the cold, placed Mary's bundle of clothing on the rocking chair Judah had vacated, and removed his canvas duster. "Take this." He draped the coat over Mary and Maddy, buttoned the top button, and tucked the ends around Maddy's bare legs.

"Thank you."

"Yeah, well," he shrugged. "It's a shame to cover up your pretty skirt with my old canvas duster." And an even bigger shame to hide those wonderful legs, he thought. "But . . ."

She glanced at him sharply. The look in his gray eyes contrasted with the all too innocent expression on his face. "But what?"

"But I imagine you need it more than I do."

"Why . . ." Mary stopped to clear her throat and start over when her voice came out several octaves higher than normal. "Why would you imagine that?"

Lee struggled to keep a straight face. "Our new abode is at the end of this street. And you seem to be having some trouble with the wind catching your skirt." He watched as Mary straightened her back and raised her chin a notch higher. "Are you ready?"

"As much as I'll ever be," she muttered beneath her breath.

"Okay." Lee picked up Mary's bundle and led the way down the platform steps. "Let's go home."

During the walk through town, Judah pointed out the meager sights. "There's Kinter's Livery Stable on the right. And the Ajax Saloon and Assayer's Office. Used to be soiled doves in the Ajax," Judah confided to Lee. "But not anymore. Now it's just a place for drinking, gambling, and mining business. The Silver Bear, across the street," Judah continued, "that's the place to go for women—" Suddenly remembering Mary's presence, Judah tipped his hat. "Beg pardon, ma'am. I was just saying the Silver Bear is the place for young men to go if they're unmarried. Of course, Mr. Kincaid won't be frequenting the place."

"No offense taken, Judah," Mary replied. She couldn't object to Judah's commentary on the town watering holes because she was so very relieved to know he remembered them—for today, at least. "Please, continue," she encouraged him.

"Over there's Sherman's General Store." Judah pointed to a building with the windows boarded over.

"Is it open?" Mary asked.

"Yes, ma'am. Mr. Buford, the owner, keeps it open six days a week. Every day but Sunday."

"The owner's name is Buford?" Lee asked.

"Yes."

"Then why is it called Sherman's General Store? Was that the name of a previous owner?"

"No." Judah smiled and shook his head. "It's just Jed Buford's sense of humor. You see, Jed's originally from Georgia. General Sherman's troops burned his first home and business during their march to the sea—after they had looted it, of course. So Jed came west, settled in Utopia during the silver boom, and made a comfortable living supplying the mine owner and the miners. He says he's better off now than he ever was back in Georgia. Naming his store after General Sherman is his idea of a jest."

"But why does he keep the windows boarded?" Mary wanted to know.

"Has to," Judah admitted. "The southerners around here and the Southern sympathizers keep breaking them."

"But Buford is a Southerner," Lee remarked, impressed by Jed Buford's stubborn resistance.

"I guess the other Southerners don't appreciate Jed's sense of humor."

"Or his property," Mary added. "Why doesn't the sheriff do anything about it?" She nodded toward the sheriff's office.

"Well, we have a sheriff's office," Judah replied. "But we don't have a sheriff anymore."

Mary gasped. She didn't want to ask the question, but her knowledge of the danger inherent in Lee's occupation frightened her. "Was he killed in the line of duty?"

"No, ma'am," Judah replied. "He ran off last summer with one of the women from the Silver Bear. I heard he took up gambling down in Dodge City, but I can't say for sure. Utopia's become rather boring, I'm afraid." Judah shook his head. "There isn't much for a sheriff to do. Not like the old days."

Judah sounded so sad, Mary hurried to change the subject. "What was that, Mr. Crane?" she asked, indicating the pile of burned and blackened debris situated on the lot between the sheriff's office and Sherman's General Store.

"That was my office," Judah replied matter-of-factly. "That's where I set up my practice. Judah Crane, Attorney-at-Law."

"Oh, Judah, I'm so sorry," Mary apologized. "I didn't know."

"That's quite all right," the elderly gentleman assured her. "I didn't expect you to. You're new to Utopia. You couldn't have known the crazy old lawyer forgot to bank the coals in his stove and burned his office down." He stared at Mary and the look in his brown eyes was perfectly lucid for a moment longer, but it started to fade with his next words. "I lived there, too, you know. I had a nice, cozy little apartment in back. A real nice place." Then the intelligent, articulate gentleman lawyer vanished before Mary's eyes. "It's around here somewhere." He glanced around at the ashes, then became childlike once again. "I'll find it."

Devastated by the change she felt she had caused in Judah, Mary turned to Lee. "I'm so sorry. I never meant . . ." Her voice broke, "I mean I never would have mentioned it if I had known or even suspected . . ."

"Mary." Lee touched her elbow.

"Why didn't you tell me? Why did you let me go on?"

"I didn't think anything about it," Lee told her. "I knew he had accidentally set fire to his office, but I didn't think about it until . . ." He let his words trail off.

"Until I mentioned it." Mary hugged Maddy tightly. "I feel so horrible. He was so intelligent, so witty and entertaining. Now he's like a child again, and it's all my fault."

"It isn't anybody's fault. Not yours, not mine, not Judah's. It's part of aging, Mary. Just a part of living a long life. We'll take him home with us until he remembers where he's supposed to be." He stared at Mary, and the earnest expression on her lovely face tugged at Lee's heartstrings. She cared so much—maybe too much, and she could be hurt so easily. He reached out and touched her cheek with the tip of his finger. "Don't agonize over it," he said. "You didn't mean any harm. Judah won't remember an innocent blunder for long."

"How can you be sure?"

"Because he is like a child." Lee touched the tip of her reddened nose. "He dismisses the bad and remembers the good."

"Thank you." Mary smiled at him.

Lee shrugged his massive shoulders. "We can't have you worrying about little things when there are bigger things to agonize over." He pointed to the wrought-iron fence surrounding the building at the end of Main Street. Lee whistled in awe. "The stationmaster was right when he said we couldn't miss it. Look."

The house standing before them was an amalgam of nearly every architectural style known to man. Made of wood, stucco, and stone, it combined Moorish and Gothic styles on a Queen Anne frame. It resembled a castle, and boasted turrets, gargoyles, stained glass windows, and a collection of statuary depicting various Greek gods. There was even a faded red pennant flying from a staff on the roof of one of the turrets. Ettinger House wasn't just a house; it was a bonafide mansion situated on a lot the size of a city block, and was quite impressive despite its peeling paint and neglected state.

"Oh my goodness," Mary breathed, overwhelmed at the

massive task ahead of her. "Would you look at the size of this house?"

"House," Maddy echoed. "My house."

Lee reached over and ruffled Maddy's dark curls. "Yeah, sweetheart, it's your house."

"It must have cost a fortune to build," Mary said.

Lee nodded. "It's too bad Maddy didn't get the fortune along with the house."

Mary wasn't too surprised that there was no money to go along with the house. A house this size would cost a small fortune to maintain. And it was obvious that Maddy's father hadn't been able to afford the upkeep. How could he have afforded it on a Pinkerton agent's salary? And for that matter, how would Lee? She glanced over at her husband. "We're not actually going to live here, are we?"

"I'm afraid so," Lee said. "It's one of the conditions listed in the will."

Mary chewed on her bottom lip. She had money of her own left to her by her uncle, and the interest from investments Reese and David had made for her. It might be enough to support them for a while, but not indefinitely.

"Cheer up, Mary." Lee tried to reassure her. "It won't be forever."

She had an idea that there was a lot more about the house, the silver mine, and the terms of Maddy's father's will that Lee wasn't telling her. Mary didn't like the jovial note in his voice. She didn't trust it. Her instincts warned her that she wasn't going to like the answer to her question, but she asked it anyway—and dreaded his reply. "How long?"

"Until Maddy reaches her majority."

"Eighteen years." The number horrified her. She didn't have enough money to support them and this huge monstrosity of a house for eighteen years!

Lee winced. "The actual number in the will is twenty."

"I guess he added two extra years for good measure,"

Mary muttered in the exact same way a judge would pronounce sentencing on a condemned man. "Are you sure Maddy's father was your friend?"

"Positive."

"Hmmf," she sniffed.

Lee couldn't help but laugh. "Mary, Mary, what am I going to do with you? I never dreamed you were such a pessimist. We haven't seen the inside of the house yet."

"I've seen all I want to see."

"Yeah, well, cover your eyes because we're going inside." Lee unlatched the iron gate and pushed it open.

Mary didn't budge.

"Come on." Lee reached out, gripped Mary's arm and gently urged her forward. "You'll see, it won't be all bad."

"I'll bet the inside is every bit as bad as the outside."

"If it is, we'll have it put to rights in no time." Lee held the gate open and waited for Mary to enter.

"That's easy for you to say," she accused. "You won't have to clean this place."

"Mary." He spoke her name in a firm voice that brooked no further argument.

"All right." She grabbed a handful of skirt, lifted it a few inches as she stepped through the gate, then preceded Lee up the brick walkway to the house. She paused as she reached the porch. A pile of luggage was neatly stacked beside the front door. Mary stood tapping her foot impatiently as Lee inserted the key into the lock and opened the front door. "Let's get this over with." Mary took another step forward but Lee stopped her.

"What is it?" she demanded, her brown-eyed gaze shooting sparks at him.

"Princess, your castle awaits."

"I don't understand."

"I believe it's customary to carry the bride over the threshold, and you're the only bride around." Lee gave her his most devastating smile, then bent and lifted her and Maddy into his arms and carried them into the house.

His romantic gesture surprised her as much as it charmed her. Mary melted into his embrace and let herself enjoy the unique pleasure of being cradled in Lee's arms. She sighed and released a measure of her pent-up anxiety. Perhaps he was right. Perhaps it wouldn't be so bad after all.

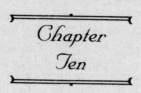

Chapter
Ten

The inside of the house was cleaner and in better shape than Mary expected, but it was cold and as much a mix of styles and furnishings as the exterior. The interior designer had shared the architect's appalling lack of taste and had apparent delusions of grandeur. She studied her surroundings as Lee set her down on the marble floor of the entrance hall, before he returned to the front porch for Judah and the luggage. The intricate stained glass window above the door depicted a jousting tourney of a much earlier time where a knight on a black horse tilted against a knight riding a white charger. The stained glass window panels on either side of the massive front door continued the theme—a king, possibly Arthur, stood on the right side of the door and a queen, possibly Guinevere, occupied the left. Curious to see whether the rest of the decor continued the castle theme, Mary ventured farther down the hall and peeked into the front parlor.

"Oh my goodness!"

It was red. And gold. Ruby-red flocked wallpaper covered the walls, while the woodwork and moldings—even the mantel above the fireplace—were coated in gold. A gilt chandelier, decorated with dozens of crystal droplets, hung from the plaster ceiling. Even the ceiling, some sixteen feet above the hardwood floor, was painted red.

As if that weren't bad enough, a huge billiard table dominated the room. Two smaller game tables, several leather chairs, and a built-in mahogany bar occupied a good deal of the remaining floor space, along with a marble statue of Merlin that overlooked the gaming tables. Silver ash stands stood beside the leather easy chairs and brass spittoons occupied each corner of the room. The red Turkish carpets were dotted with tiny burns and brown tobacco stains.

A gilt-framed portrait of a female reclining nude hung above the fireplace, and a replica of Excalibur hung over the bar. A roulette wheel took up most of the area along one wall, and two floor-to-ceiling windows—covered in heavy Chinese-red velvet drapes fringed in gold that reeked of cigar smoke—overlooked the unkempt front lawn.

"What's wrong?" Lee asked, coming up to stand behind her.

"This room," Mary told him. "It's every bit as bad as I feared. It looks like . . ." Mary shifted Maddy to her hip.

Lee leaned over her shoulder to get a view of the parlor and began to laugh. "At least this castle has some creature comforts. This room reminds me of nearly every private gentlemen's club I've ever visited." That was his polite way of telling Mary the front parlor of her new home could have doubled as a gaming room in some of the most exclusive brothels this side of the Mississippi.

"And I'll bet you've seen quite a few," Mary snapped back.

"I've seen my share," he replied good-naturedly. "After all, I am a grown man." Lee let his gaze wander over the attractive blush spreading across Mary's cheeks. "And I do travel a lot."

He was right. She was acting snappish. But the house was such a shock. And this room . . . Mary didn't know what to make of it. She turned to Lee. "You don't suppose Maddy's father ran a gambling house, do you?"

"Nah," Lee said. "Not with a two-and-a-half-year-old daughter around." He turned Mary to face him, then unbuttoned his duster so that she could put Maddy down. Mary leaned over and set the child on her feet. "Then why do you suppose he had a parlor like this?" Mary couldn't imagine anything reputable taking place in a red room furnished with a bar, a billiard table, and roulette wheel.

"A lot of big houses have rooms like this. Places where a man can entertain his friends and business acquaintances. It comes in handy. A man can play cards and gamble, shoot billiards," Lee walked into the room and over to the bar where he picked up a bottle of Scots whisky. "And consume vast quantities of expensive liquor and tobacco without leaving the privacy of his home." He turned to Mary and grinned, waiting to see her reaction.

"Something you know a great deal about," Mary replied acidly, remembering Lee's days masquerading as a barman at the Satin Slipper Saloon in Peaceable. "You'll probably feel right at home in no time."

"So will you, if you give it half a chance," Lee told her.

"I'll never feel at home with that," Mary pointed to the painting of the nude woman hanging over the mantel, "hanging in my parlor."

Lee studied the painting. "It's not so bad," he said. "In fact, I'd say the artist was rather good. Think of it as having a Rubens on display in your very own home."

"It's not a Rubens," Mary reminded him. "It doesn't look anything like a Rubens."

Lee looked at the painting again, then raised his right eyebrow at Mary. "It doesn't?"

"I was referring to Rubens' style of painting, not his choice of models."

Lee smiled at her. "You're being a little prudish, don't

you think? Even for a schoolteacher? After all"—he teased—"we're talking about art."

"That painting isn't art," Mary informed him. "It's a cheap, tawdry advertisement, just like all the other nude pictures you find hanging in saloons. It's designed to entice men into the bar so they can spend their hard-earned money on liquor."

"I kinda like it."

"Don't tell me you plan to leave this room as it is." Mary wasn't trying to pick a fight with Lee, but the house, the town, the situation with Judah and Maddy, and marriage to Lee was so daunting. So overwhelming. She felt like a failure before she had even begun. She didn't know the first thing about really young children. She didn't understand "Maddy-talk," as Lee called it, or know how to be a good mother. And although she understood the basic nature of Judah's illness, Mary didn't know enough about the elderly gentleman to avoid inadvertently touching on unpleasant memories that triggered Judah's retreat into childhood.

But worst of all, she didn't know what to expect from her new husband. He had kissed her before the wedding with tenderness and passion and hunger, then rejected her after the ceremony. He wanted a marriage on paper and a mother for Maddy, not a wife and lover for himself. But Mary didn't know if she could settle for the kind of marriage Lee wanted—not when she wanted more. The very thought of another rejection at his hands frightened her more than she liked to admit. He *had* carried her over the threshold, but the *least* he could do was take her in his arms once again, kiss her senseless, and promise her that everything was going to work out.

"Okay," he agreed. "I'll tell you I plan to take the luggage upstairs and fall into the first bed I see."

"You don't know what we'll find upstairs," Mary reminded him. "Or if the beds have clean linen."

"I don't care."

"You must care. The beds could be filled with fleas, or bedbugs, or worse . . ."

Lee stared at his wife, and recognized the look of apprehension in her beautiful brown eyes. Unfortunately, he had reached the end of his physical reserves. He wanted to allay her fears, but he was too damn tired to be diplomatic. He couldn't think straight anymore—he needed sleep. Still, he made an effort to humor her. "What could be worse than fleas and bedbugs?"

"Well, you know."

"What?" He was too tired to play guessing games or dance coyly around the subject.

"You heard what Judah said about the Silver Bear Saloon." When Lee looked at her blankly, Mary decided she needed to prod his memory. "You know what he said about the women there." She lowered her voice to a whisper so Maddy wouldn't hear. "What if this house is a place like that? What if the beds upstairs are all occupied?"

Lee couldn't help but grin. "Fortunately, I easily adapt to almost any situation."

"Lee!" Mary's face turned a bright shade of pink.

"Just look how well I've adapted to being a family man. After spending nearly a week on a train and practically crossing the continent, I inherited a little girl and the company of an old man who can't remember his name or where he lives most of the time, and a beautiful bride—not to mention a house, a silver mine, and a load of unexpected responsibilities. I'm dead on my feet and nearly delirious from lack of sleep.

"I had to persuade my wife to enter her new home when all I want is a bed and a few hours of uninterrupted sleep. And now that I've got her inside the house, I find myself standing in the entrance hall calmly discussing the possibility of whor—soiled doves—residing upstairs with my bride who's upset because the town I've brought her to is too small and the mansion I've given her isn't quite up to standard and has a billiard table, a roulette wheel, and a Rubenesque nude in the front parlor."

"I'm sorry you feel I'm being ill-tempered or petty, but this isn't a joke, Lee Kincaid. This is serious. We don't know what we've stumbled into," Mary reminded him in her prim schoolteacher voice.

"I know I've stumbled into a house with beds upstairs and that's all that matters to me right now."

"But, Lee . . ."

"Good God, woman, where did you get your tenacity?" Lee removed his hat and raked his fingers through his hair, then mumbled, "It must be the result of your 'unfortunate heritage.'" He had hoped to provoke a smile from her or a heated comment at his mention of her pedigree, but Mary didn't respond. She simply stood there and looked at him. He stared down at her. Her brown eyes appeared bigger and darker in her face than he remembered. Her lips were red, chapped from the cold, and marred by abrasions from her teeth. Mary was so capable, so intelligent, so strong and decisive, that he forgot she probably had as many anxieties about their partnership as he did, maybe more. She was, after all, a bride miles away from her family and friends, saddled with a host of new and unfamiliar responsibilities—himself among them. Lee reached out and touched her bottom lip, tracing the tiny marks with the pad of his thumb. "Mary, I'm fairly certain there aren't any other women upstairs, but if there are, I promise not to take advantage of them. Or let them take advantage of me."

"I wasn't . . ."

"I know," he replied gently. "I was just trying to allay your fears." He grinned suddenly, and his thick blond mustache tilted at the corners. "I am, after all, a married man now. I have no interest in any woman who isn't my wife."

He traced the contours of her lip one more time, then reached down for his leather satchel. "Don't worry so much." He raised up and met her solemn gaze once again. "All I need is a few hours' sleep. When I wake up, we can sit down and try to work out a plan. Okay?"

Lee looked so exhausted that Mary had no choice but to relent. "Okay."

He turned toward the stairs at the end of the hall and slowly began to climb them.

"Lee!" Mary called out when he reached the top of the stairs.

"Yes?" Lee leaned over the rail so he could see her. He needed to assure himself that Mary would be all right in this mausoleum, with only Judah and Maddy for company, during the few hours it would take for him to get his long-delayed and much-needed sleep.

"What do I do while you're sleeping?"

He wanted to suggest that she tuck Maddy and Judah into beds of their own, then come up and join him, but he didn't. He smiled down at her instead and tried to make useful suggestions that would provide a couple of hours of busywork to keep Mary from dwelling on her anxieties. "You can find Maddy's bag and get her some more clothes to wear. And you might see to whatever it is you have bundled in your jacket. Then, you might want to do a little unpacking yourself. Oh, and check out the kitchen and see if there's any food. I'm sure Maddy and Judah must be hungry. Make a list of the supplies we need and explore the house. Just make yourself at home. I'll be down in a couple of hours."

Chapter Eleven

"Make yourself at home, check out the kitchen, find something for Maddy to wear. I'll be down in a couple of hours," Mary grumbled as she poured a measure of rolled oats into the farina boiler. "And I might fly to the moon tomorrow. Who does he think he is, leaving me to cope with everything while he takes a nap?" She wiped a stray lock of hair off her forehead with the back of her hand. Her husband, that's who. Mary's heart seemed to skip a beat as she answered. The bridegroom who had sat up on the train all night watching over her and Maddy and Judah while they slept. He was her legal spouse, and as such, Lee had every right to expect her to take care of Maddy and Judah while he slept. He was her husband. She was his wife and lady of the house. There was nothing wrong with his suggesting she perform a few necessary household chores, as long as he didn't make a habit of it. As long as he didn't expect her to behave like a well-trained servant rather than his wife. They were, after all, marriage partners. Equals. And Mary expected Lee to contribute as much to the upkeep of this monstrosity of a house as she did.

She held her tongue and had waited until Lee disappeared from view before she had began rummaging through the carpetbags he had left in the entrance hall. She found Maddy's bag, pulled out a petticoat, drawers, and a pair of thick black stockings, and dressed the little girl in those. Once she had Madeline warmly dressed, Mary took a bottle of bath salts and a pair of soft deerskin moccasins from one of her trunks, then picked up the jacket-wrapped bundle and began a search for the kitchen.

She finally located it and an adjoining food pantry in the servant's wing. The food pantry contained the usual bulk staples of flour, lard, sugar, coffee, tea, rice, rolled oats, and molasses, as well as an assortment of spices, dried foods, canned goods, and a barrel of salted pork. Wasting no time, Mary took off her black lace-up shoes, slipped on her comfortable moccasins, rolled up her sleeves, and built a fire in the stove.

After carefully priming the pump, she pumped water into a kettle for tea, filled a farina cooker to make boiled oat porridge with molasses, then filled a large pot with water, poured a bit of the bath salts into it, and hefted it onto the stove to boil. She didn't attempt to locate the springhouse to see if there was any butter or eggs, nor did she try to find a smokehouse that might contain meat other than salted pork because she would have had to leave the house to do so, and she couldn't leave Maddy and Judah unsupervised.

Once the porridge was done, she fried a few slices of pork, dished up bowls for the three of them, and opened a can of peaches, which she served along with the rolled oats. Rather than eat in the dining room, they sat at the worktable in the warm kitchen. It wasn't much of a breakfast, eaten as it was, without milk, butter, or fresh meat, but it was hot and nourishing and Maddy and Judah seemed to enjoy it.

When she finished eating, Mary unwrapped the bundle of clothes. She counted the garments twice—Maddy's muslin petticoat, drawers, and knitted tights—her silk stockings, quilted underpetticoat, bustle petticoat, and. . . . Mary frowned. There was no doubt about it. Her drawers were missing. Left behind in the necessary, no doubt, although

Mary distinctly remembered bundling them inside her jacket. She shrugged her shoulders and swallowed an embarrassed giggle at the thought of another passenger on the Cheyenne to Denver train, or one of Utopia's residents, stumbling across her frilly underwear. But there was nothing she could do about that now. Mary shrugged her shoulders once again and scooped up Maddy's pile of laundry. At least Lee hadn't noticed anything unusual about her appearance, except that her skirt seemed longer.

She put Maddy's soiled linen and stockings in the pot with the bath salts, and covered it with a lid. She let the linen boil for a few minutes, then drew up a pan of cold rinse water. She lifted the pot off the stove and set it into the sink before she fished Maddy's undergarments out of the hot water with a long wooden spoon and dumped them into the pan of cold water. Mary added her own silk stockings to the cold rinse water and, once the laundry had cooled sufficiently, she wrung it out by hand, then carried the linen into the scullery and cranked it through the wringer. Mary hung Maddy's tights and petticoats on the wooden clothes racks in the scullery to dry along with her own pair of stockings. She didn't attempt to launder her massive petticoats or her green jacket, but simply hung them up to air out. And throughout the process, Madeline and Judah finished their breakfast and watched quietly as Mary made several trips from the kitchen to the scullery and back.

After breakfast, Mary put a pot of pork and beans on to simmer for the next meal, washed the breakfast dishes, and tidied up the rest of the kitchen. Taking a mug of tea with her, Mary ushered Judah and Maddy back to the main wing of the house. She found paper and pencils in a desk in the library and, using a book as a writing desk, made a list of the kitchen and food supplies they would need, then set out to explore the rest of the rooms of the main wing.

She found that the servant's wing housed the kitchen in

the turret room at the back of the house, a water closet, and a large dining hall furnished with an oak trestle and matching benches, a china closet, butler's pantry, several storage closets, and food pantry. In addition to the front parlor and the entrance hall, there were four other rooms in the main wing of the first floor: a Baroque dining room complete with carved niches displaying china and overflowing with furnishings decorated with the curves, bumps, lumps, and knobs indicative of the rococo period; a Gothic revival style study with arched doorways, a frescoed ceiling, a massive walnut desk and matching chair, as well as a pair of huge book cabinets with stained glass fronts; a Renaissance-style sitting room which opened onto the study and the library, which was located in the front turret. The library had a high ceiling and large floor-to-ceiling clear glass windows for light, built-in bookshelves, a marble fireplace, windowseat, and Jacobean furnishings.

Mary studied the rooms with a critical eye. The furniture, paintings, wallpaper, and rugs, even the assorted bric-a-brac were of the highest quality, but the mix of styles, colors, and fabrics jarred the senses. She made copious notes, numbering, describing, and, in some cases, even sketching the pieces of furniture in each room, ending her journey in the study where she sat down on one side of the massive two-person desk to make the list she hoped would help her devise a decor of her own—something she could live with—by keeping the furnishings she liked and relegating the rest to the third floor for storage. Strangely enough, she decided she liked the Arthurian touches in each of the rooms. The woven tapestries hanging in the library, the paintings of Arthur and Guinevere in the dining room, and the other items appealed to her whimsical side, and Mary decided to keep them.

She finished making her notes, then took Judah and Maddy with her back into the warmth of the kitchen and set them down at the table where she could keep an eye on them while she prepared lunch.

She gave Judah some paper and a pencil to write or draw on while she worked. Maddy sat down on the opposite side of the table and played quietly with her doll as Mary mixed up a batch of biscuits and a cobbler, made from dried apples, to go with the pork and beans.

Lunchtime came and went with no sign of Lee. Mary left the pot of beans warming on the stove as she cleaned up the kitchen once again, then sat down at the table beside Maddy to savor another cup of tea. A little while later, Mary realized Judah was growing tired and restless. She looked at the watch she'd taken off her jacket and pinned to her blouse. Lee's two hours of sleep had stretched to five and a half hours. It was afternoon and probably time for Maddy's nap . . . and Judah's as well. Mary remembered that her grandfather, who was around Judah's age, always took a nap after lunch.

Almost as if he'd read her thoughts, Judah announced, "I want to go to bed."

"Judah, I'll be happy to make up a bed for you upstairs," Mary told him. "Or if you'd rather, I can try to locate your house, so you can sleep in your own bed in your own home."

The elderly attorney looked up at Mary from his place at the table and yawned widely. "I'm sleepy."

Mary sighed. She'd managed to avoid the upstairs all morning, but it didn't look as if she was going to be able to delay any longer even if she wanted to. Judah was a guest in her home, and Mary couldn't ask him to sleep on one of the downstairs sofas.

Maddy laughed suddenly, then covered her face with her hands. She peeked through her fingers, teasing Mary.

Mary stood up and took Maddy by the hand.

Judah got to his feet as well, then grabbed his hat and cane off a chair and limped out of the kitchen and into the entrance hall.

"Judah, where are you going?" Mary asked, following him.

"I'm going home," he answered. "I've got work to do. Papers to review. And court on Monday. I need to get some sleep."

"But, Judah, I didn't mean for you to leave. You can't go home," Mary tried to explain. "Not until you tell me where you live." She let go of Maddy's hand and rushed over to take Judah by the arm.

Maddy giggled again.

Mary looked down at her. "Do you know where Judah lives?"

"Uh huh." Maddy nodded.

"Can you take me there?" Mary asked.

"Uh huh." Maddy nodded again. She picked up her doll, then walked over and tugged on Mary's hand, leading her toward the stairs, away from the front door.

Mary understood. "Sweetheart, we'll go upstairs later. But right now, we need go to Judah's house."

Maddy giggled again and Mary realized she hadn't understood at all. Until now. "Maddy," she asked, "where does Judah live?"

"Up'tairs," Maddy answered.

Upstairs. The word took the wind out of Mary's sails. She plopped down on the bottom stair. Judah lived upstairs. She was responsible for him, right along with Maddy and Lee. Mary bit her bottom lip. Somehow she hadn't expected that added responsibility. Somehow she had thought that when they reached Denver someone else would be responsible for Judah. But they hadn't gone to Denver. They'd stopped in Utopia.

Utopia had come as a surprise to Mary. But Lee had

known where they were heading all along. She wondered if Lee knew Judah was a permanent resident of Ettinger House and not a temporary guest. Mary wondered if that was another one of Lee's secrets—something else he hadn't told her.

Madeline cuddled closer to Mary on the stairs and touched her sleeve. "Zhudah wants go to sleep," she reminded.

Mary sighed as she got to her feet. She couldn't avoid the upstairs any longer. She had to explore the rooms on the upper floor. She had to venture into intimate territory, a place full of bedrooms and beds where people slept—and her husband lay sleeping. "Okay," Mary said. "Let's go upstairs."

"One, two, three, four." Mary let go of Maddy's hand at the top of the landing, then followed behind as the little girl led the way to Judah's room. Mary paused in front of each door she passed, quietly opened them, and peeked inside. All of the rooms were bedrooms and, Mary noticed, so far all of the bedrooms were unoccupied and none of them seemed appropriate for a little girl or suitable for an elderly gentleman until they reached the fifth door on the left side of the hall.

"Zhudah's room," Maddy announced as she reached up and patted the wooden door with the palm of her hand.

Mary turned to Judah and pasted a bright smile on her face. "Here we are, Judah." She turned the cut-glass doorknob and pushed open the door into a warm, welcoming room, full of dark wood furniture and packed with shelves of leather-bound volumes. Law books. "Home at last."

Judah didn't budge. He simply stared at the room as if he'd never seen it.

Mary didn't quite know how to handle the situation, but Maddy apparently did.

"Come on, Zhudah." Madeline took the elderly man by the hand and walked him to the large half-tester bed across the room. She tossed her doll, Mama, on the bed and issued another instruction to the older man. "Turn 'round, Zhudah."

Judah turned.

"Sit down." Maddy nudged him on the leg just above the knee and Judah obediently sat down on the edge of the bed.

Maddy turned to look at Mary who hovered in the doorway. "Me help Zhudah," she said, before she reached down to tug at Judah's shoelaces. She pulled the lace through the loop and the laces knotted.

Mary realized suddenly that Maddy knew a great deal more about Judah's illness than she did. Maddy recognized Judah's lapses in memory and understood that his loss of memory resulted in the loss of his basic skills. When that happened, he wasn't like other adults. He couldn't remember how to tie or untie his shoes, or how to button or unbutton a shirt. At two-and-a-half, Madeline had mastered some of the skills Judah lacked and had taken it upon herself to help him. Mary watched as Maddy patiently worked at undoing the knot she had made in his shoelace.

"Here," Mary said, as she crossed the room and knelt beside Judah's bed. "Let me undo that while you untie the other one."

Maddy let go of the knot and turned her attention to Judah's other shoe.

"Now what?" Mary asked, when Judah's shoes were neatly lined up beside the bed.

"Zhudah's coat." Maddy took hold of Judah's arm and lifted it.

Judah sat with his arms extended as Maddy tugged at his coat sleeve, undressing him as if he were a doll. After his coat, came his waistcoat and tie. And while Mary removed Judah's collar and unbuttoned his dress shirt, Maddy walked over to the armoire and took a blue-striped cotton nightshirt out of the bottom drawer.

The sight of Judah's bare chest, sprinkled here and there with gray hair, took Mary by surprise. It wasn't as if she'd never seen a man's naked chest before. She had seen her brothers, Reese, and her father strip off their shirts in summer. She had caught glimpses of shirtless cowhands as they washed up for meals, and even helped nurse her brother, David, through a bout of measles after he returned from the war, but helping Judah was different. His illness wasn't like the measles. Judah's illness was worse than the fever and pain of measles, much worse, because his illness took away his ability to take care of himself. It robbed him of his memories and threatened his dignity. He was a grown man, not a child, and no matter how hard Mary tried to think of him as a child like Madeline, she remembered the articulate, intelligent, sensitive gentleman she had seen earlier. Judah would be embarrassed to know Mary and Maddy had undressed him and put him to bed—tucked him in—the way Maddy tucked in her doll. He would be ashamed to know Mary had witnessed his weakness. And even though she doubted Judah would remember, Mary didn't want to take the chance. Judah deserved to keep his dignity. "Maddy, it's still daylight. I don't think Judah should wear his nightshirt before dark."

Relishing her role as the boss, Maddy refused to give in. She shook her head. "Zhudah go sleep. Zhudah nightshirt," she insisted.

"I don't think so."

"Nightshirt!" Maddy shoved the garment at Judah.

Mary snatched it away. "No, Maddy. Judah can nap as he is." Mary moved Madeline's doll off the bed and placed it on the nightstand. She turned to Judah, motioned for him to scoot down to the foot of the bed, waiting as he did so, then flipped back the covers. "In you go," she said as Judah lay back against the pillows and raised his legs so Mary could tuck the covers around him. "Sleep well." Mary reached out and patted Judah's gnarled hand. "Maddy, say goodnight to Judah," Mary instructed.

But Maddy had other ideas. "No!" She grabbed hold of Judah's nightshirt and tried to pull it out of Mary's grasp. "Zhudah, nightshirt!"

"No, Madeline," Mary said firmly. "It's too early in the day for Judah to be wearing his nightshirt." She tried to reason with an unreasonable two-and-a-half-year-old.

"No!" Madeline argued, still tugging on the garment.

It appeared Maddy was one of those children who demanded explanations for every decision contrary to her own. "Lee . . . Papa . . . is sleeping now, too, and I'll bet he isn't wearing a nightshirt."

Maddy looked up at Mary and Mary could almost visualize the little wheels turning in Maddy's brain.

"Go see," Maddy said, as she suddenly let go of her end of Judah's nightshirt, grabbed her doll, and ran out of the room.

Realizing what Maddy intended, Mary tried to stop her. "Maddy, wait!"

But Maddy was already opening and closing doors down the hall.

Mary hurried after her. "Maddy!" Mary didn't know if Lee slept in a nightshirt or not, but she was willing to bet money that, as tired as he had been, Lee was sprawled, fully clothed, on top of the covers, across the nearest bed.

She came to an abrupt halt in the doorway of what had to be the master bedroom suite. It was a good thing she hadn't bet money because she would have lost it. Lee had been exhausted when he stumbled upstairs to sleep, but he had taken the time to see to his comfort. He wasn't sprawled atop the covers, but laying face-down between the sheets of an enormous polished brass bed. The bedspread and quilts had been pushed to the foot of the bed and bunched against the footboard. Lee had his right arm curled around a feather pillow and a white sheet draped over his hips.

Chapter
Twelve

She was right about the nightshirt.

He wasn't wearing one, or anything else. His broad back, baked a golden color by the sun, was bare. And Mary wanted to reach out and touch him—to place her palm against his shoulder to see if his skin was as smooth and as warm as it looked.

She glanced around the room. Lee's shirt and pants hung over the brass footboard and his gunbelt was looped over the brass bedpost, while his hat crowned the top of it. His tall black leather boots lay in a heap on the floor beside the footboard as if he had sat on the side of the bed to tug them off, then tossed his boots aside.

Lee lay in the center of the bed. The thin cotton sheet draped across his lean hips and over his firm buttocks was the only thing covering him and the white fabric drew her gaze the way a magnet drew iron filings. Lying there, he seemed younger than his thirty-three years. His hair was tousled in sleep, his jaw shimmering with a two-day growth of beard, and his thick eyelashes fanned against his face. But there was nothing boyish about him. The tiny wrinkles marking the corners of his eyes, the powerful muscles of his shoulders and back, and the puckers and ridges of long-healed scars proclaimed him fully grown. Lee Kincaid was a gloriously healthy man in the prime of his life, and although it seemed to Mary that sleep should have given him a harmless appearance, the opposite was true. He looked dangerous instead. More dangerous and irresistible than she'd ever imagined.

Mary bit her bottom lip and clenched her fists to keep from giving in to her almost overwhelming desires. Heat rushed to her face. Her lips ached to be kissed and her body begged to be touched. Mary wanted to throw off her clothes and climb into bed beside Lee—to watch him open his eyes, to see those gray eyes darken with desire to an even deeper shade. She wanted to feel him run his hands over her. All at once, she understood how Faith and Tessa felt when they looked at their husbands. Now she recognized the urgency—the desire—the need to be with a man. And not just any man, but her husband, the man she desired. The man she loved.

Loved? Mary shook her head, trying to push the unbidden, unwanted thought aside. Not love. She couldn't be in love with Lee Kincaid. She was an intelligent, practical, levelheaded schoolteacher. And he was a carefree rogue. She couldn't be foolish enough to fall in love with him. It was desire, she told herself. Desire, pure and simple. Lust, healthy animal lust. That's what she felt for Lee Kincaid. But if that were true, she asked herself, why hadn't she desired other men, handsomer men, nicer, more suitable men? Why hadn't she wanted Pelham Cosgrove? Mary actually began to quake. When had she taken the tumble? When had she fallen in love with her husband?

"Come on," she whispered urgently to Maddy, intercepting the little girl as Maddy approached the bed. "Let's go before we wake Papa."

"No!"

"Maddy, you can see Papa's not wearing a nightshirt. Now, come along." Mary looked down at the watch pinned to her blouse. "It's time for your nap."

"Nap with Poppy." Maddy decided. She tossed her doll

onto the bed beside Lee and pulled against Mary's restraining hand.

"No," Mary whispered. "Papa's not dressed for company," she explained. "He needs to be alone. And little girls like you . . ."

"Big girl," Maddy corrected. "Mine big girl."

Mary smiled. "All right," she said, careful to keep her voice low. "You're a big girl. And big girls like you sleep in their own beds. They don't sleep in the bed with their mamas and their papas. Right?" Mary waited for Maddy to agree or disagree with her explanation.

Maddy was quiet.

"Okay," Mary said, finally, when it appeared Maddy wasn't going to answer one way or another. "Show me your room."

"Mama," Maddy said reaching toward the bed, puckering up to cry.

"Ssh, angel, I'll get your doll," Mary promised. Although a part of her wanted Lee to wake up, open his eyes, and invite her to join him in the big cozy brass bed, Mary didn't want Lee to wake up to the sound of Madeline's crying. Taking a deep breath to steady herself, Mary tiptoed to the bed and bent to retrieve Maddy's doll.

At that moment, Lee sighed in his sleep and rolled from his stomach to his side. The mattress dipped and shifted with his movement, and Mama rolled with him. The sheet, which had been modestly draped over his hip, slipped a bit lower as the doll rolled into the curve of his body. Mary stopped abruptly and stared at the thick blond hair that covered Lee's chest then tapered into a golden line that snaked down to where it disappeared from view beneath the sheet. She didn't move for a moment for fear of waking him—and barely dared to breathe, fearing he would hear the heavy pounding of her heart against her rib cage. Mama was within her reach, if only she dared to reach for her. Quickly, she made a grab for the doll. Reaching blindly,

Mary closed her fingers around the doll's satin wedding dress, intending to jerk Mama toward her, but froze when the back of her hand grazed the sheet above Lee's loins. Mary sucked in a breath. She wanted to snatch her hand away, but found she couldn't.

Lee had reached out and gripped her wrist.

"You're exploring dangerous territory, Mary Two-shot," he said, slowly opening his gray eyes.

"I was trying to g-get M-Maddy's d-doll," Mary stammered nervously. "Sh-she threw it on the bed beside you."

Lee smiled, and his mustache tilted at an angle guaranteed to send Mary's heart racing. "You nearly got more than the doll, didn't you? You almost got more than you bargained for, huh?" He lowered his gaze.

She felt the hot blush creep from her neck to her face. "I-I d-didn't mean . . ."

His smile broadened. "My mistake." Lee slowly let go of Mary's wrist.

But Mary didn't move her hand. She didn't move at all. She simply stood there staring at him.

"When I woke up and found you groping . . ."

"I wasn't groping," she replied indignantly.

"Exploring then . . ."

"I wasn't exploring either," she said. "I was trying to reach Maddy's doll."

"Whatever," Lee yawned widely and waved away Mary's explanation. "As I was saying, when I awoke and found you reaching for certain parts of my anatomy, I thought you might be interested in . . ."

Mary's blush deepened. "I'm not."

"You didn't let me finish, Two-shot." He sounded hurt.

"I'm not sure I'm ready to hear the rest of what you have to say."

"Hmmm." Lee yawned again and settled himself more comfortably against the soft mattress to give Mary's answer more thought. He had been about to ask Mary if she was ready to forget about her aborted marriage to Pelham Cosgrove III and the honeymoon that should have followed and concentrate on making a real marriage with him.

Lee thought about his relationship with Mary. It was a different sort of relationship than the one he had had with his first wife, Jeannie, and worlds apart from the brief affair he'd had with Tabby Gray, but there was something—a foundation—to build on. He was sure of it. There was a spark of desire between them that might flame into a fire big enough to burn their entire lifetime. Lee smiled at the idea. He wasn't stupid, nor was he blind. He knew how it felt to kiss her, and how it felt when she responded. He understood the significance of Mary's stuttering. Lee had heard her sting her brother with her sharp tongue. And he had been on the receiving end himself a few times. But now, he also realized he made her nervous—knew that he, alone, had the power to make her forget how to form coherent sentences. He recognized the look in her eyes, the challenge coupled with something more. . . . She was ready for a honeymoon all right. But who would she be sleeping with—him or the memory of Pelham Cosgrove?

Lee braced himself on his elbow so he could look at Mary. "Maybe you're right. Maybe you're not ready. But I'll be here when you are, Mary Two-shot. I'll be right here waiting."

"For how long?" His confidence shook her a bit. He'd be waiting for her, he said. But for how long? Until the next case came along? Until Pinkerton wired him telling him to report to Chicago or Washington or London or wherever the Agency needed him? Lee had told her he had decided to quit the Agency, but would he go through with his decision? And if he did, when would he resign? A week from now? Six months? A year? Would he fulfill his obligations before he resigned? Would he find Lily Catherine for David and Tessa as he promised? And what about him? What about his fidelity? His commitment to their marriage. Was he planning to stay with her for a lifetime, or just until the next pretty woman came along?

Lee had proposed to her on impulse and married her on the spur of the moment. And Mary had heard him propose to Tessa once as well. Did he make a habit of it? Was she his only wife? Or did he have a string of them in other little railroad towns like Utopia? Did he love her at all, or even like her? Mary sighed. She wanted to share his bed. She couldn't deny it. But should she trust him with her body when she wasn't sure she could trust him with her heart?

"As long as you want me," he said.

"What happened to 'till death us do part'?" Mary asked.

"I don't know, Mary," Lee said quietly. "You tell me."

"Mama," Maddy whined, reaching for the doll Mary still held in her hand.

"She wants her doll," Lee prompted.

"I know what she wants," Mary snapped at him.

"Do you?"

"Yes." Mary had to blink back the sudden sting of tears as she jerked the toy off the bed and handed it to Madeline. Maddy called her doll Mama. She wanted it to comfort her. She wanted it to serve as substitute for the mother she didn't have. But she didn't want a new mother any more than Lee wanted a wife. "She's tired and sleepy. It's time I put her to bed for her nap."

Lee yawned again. "Well, I guess there's nothing more for me to say. I might as well go back to sleep."

Maddy considered Lee's statement for a moment, then rushed to the bed and started to climb on. "Maddy sleep with Poppy," she announced.

"Maddy, no, you shouldn't . . ."

But it was too late.

Madeline had already crawled onto the bed and settled herself comfortably against Lee's wide chest and curled her little rump against Lee's flat, hard stomach. Mary watched as Maddy grinned at her—a tiny blue-eyed, dark-haired imp who had gotten her way—extended her arm, and motioned for Mary to lean forward. She obeyed and Madeline wrapped her arms around her neck and gave Mary a hug. When Maddy let go of her hold on Mary's neck, she patted the side of the bed with one pudgy little hand and said, "Marwy sleep Maddy, Mama, and Poppy."

Out of the mouths of babes. Madeline must have read her mind. Mary straightened, then smiled down at the pretty little girl and the porcelain-faced doll lying pressed against Lee Kincaid. Maddy's oatmeal-splotched pinafore and the doll's grubby white wedding gown appeared pristine white beside Lee's sun-bronzed flesh. And as she watched, Lee pushed himself higher against the pillows and lifted Maddy away from him. "Mary's right, sweetheart," he told her. "I'm not accustomed to having little girls share my bed."

"Big girl," Maddy interrupted. "Maddy big girl."

Lee frowned.

A tiny smile began at the corners of Mary's mouth. Let him wiggle out of this one, she thought as she waited to see how he would handle the situation.

"Maddy big girl," Madeline insisted again.

"Yes, yes you are," Lee told her. "You're much too big to want to sleep with me."

"Hmmf," Mary snorted, unable to hold her tongue any longer. "I doubt girls come that big."

Lee shot her a sharp look. "You'd be surprised," he answered cryptically.

"Maddy pease sleep Poppy?" Maddy put her arms around Lee's neck and hugged him tight as she planted wet, sloppy kisses on his face.

"No." Lee took a deep breath, then replied firmly, "Papa sleeps in his bed, Mary sleeps in her bed." He thought for a moment. "For the time being, and Maddy sleeps in her bed."

"No!"

"Yes," Lee said as he held Maddy close and kissed her cheek. "Run along with Mary and take your nap. I'll be here when you wake up." He motioned for Mary to take the little girl.

Mary lifted Madeline into her arms. "Don't make promises you may not be able to keep." Mary warned him.

"Mary Two-shot, I never make promises I can't keep," Lee told her.

"You made one yesterday," Mary said.

"So did you," Lee reminded her.

"I know that." She lowered her voice until it was a mere whisper.

"But I intend to keep mine," Lee challenged.

"So do I!" Mary shot back.

"I'm delighted to hear it." Lee grinned.

"I fully intend to keep m-my p-promise," Mary said. "When I'm ready."

"I'll be here." He glanced out the window and gauged the time by the position of the sun in the sky, then rolled onto his back and stretched lazily. "For the rest of the afternoon and on into the night. You're welcome to join me after you tuck Maddy in."

"I'm not sure I'm big enough," she admitted.

"You look big enough to me." Lee sat up in bed.

Mary recognized the look in his eyes. He reminded her of a lion sniffing the air for a scent. "Lee . . ." she began.

He sat up against the pillows, then reached for Mary. Lee tangled his hand in her hair, pulling her closer to him. "Maddy remembered her manners. She had a welcoming kiss waiting for me when I opened my eyes. You didn't."

Then he was kissing her and Mary couldn't bring herself to think of any protest. She felt her knees give way. She sat down on the edge of the bed, allowing Lee to pull her even closer.

Chapter Thirteen

Mary lost herself in Lee's kiss.

She hadn't thought it was possible for a man's kiss to steal her heart and her soul, but she learned it was more than possible . . . it had just happened. She felt like the princess in the fairy tale, sleeping for years, waiting for her handsome prince to come along and awaken her. Lee Kincaid kissed her as if she were the most desirable woman in the world. He reawakened all the dreams and desires Mary had put aside when she realized Pelham Cosgrove III would never be able to fulfill them. Lee teased, he coaxed, he promised. He held her as if she belonged in his arms. And that was exactly where Mary wanted to be.

Within the protective circle of Lee's arms, Mary suddenly realized that the dreams she thought would never come true had. She could have the same things Faith and Tessa had. She could have a home of her own with a husband and children and family to love. She already had the house, and in Madeline, she had her first child—a daughter—to teach and to love. She had Judah to learn from, to protect, and care for, and, for the moment, she had Lee as her husband. His desire was an emotion she could build on, and with time, Mary knew she could persuade Lee to build a real marriage with her. And maybe, one day, he would learn to love her.

Mary tasted him, feeling the roughness of his tongue

against hers as Lee deepened the kiss. She pressed closer, willing the kiss to go on forever.

But Madeline had suffered enough neglect. "Let go me!" she ordered, pushing against the two of them, twisting and squirming in Mary's arms. "No!" She put her hand on Lee's chin and tried to push him away from Mary and when that maneuver failed to separate her papa from Mary, Madeline reached out and pulled at the short blond hairs on one corner of Lee's mustache.

Lee ended the kiss abruptly and yelped in pain. "Yeow!"

Maddy giggled at his reaction.

And Mary opened her eyes to find Lee rubbing the corner of his mouth, and Madeline smiling triumphantly. "What happened?" she asked. "What did we do?"

"We forgot about Maddy," Lee explained, "We had her sandwiched between us and when she tired of us squashing her, she got my attention by grabbing my mustache."

Mary moved back, away from Lee, and turned her attention to Maddy. "Did you pull Papa's mustache?"

Maddy nodded enthusiastically, pleased with herself for accomplishing her goal.

"That wasn't very nice," Mary scolded. "You should apologize."

Maddy frowned, then stuck out her lower lip, threatening tears.

"Oh, no, you don't," Mary warned. "You were wrong to pull Papa's mustache. Now, tell him you're sorry for hurting him."

But Madeline ignored her. She looked at Lee instead, squeezing a couple of tears from her big blue eyes for his benefit.

"Don't worry about it." Lee rushed to console her. He pointed to the corner of his mustache, made a funny face, and said, "See, Maddy, it doesn't hurt anymore."

Maddy's smile was bright enough to light up a room.

"You're going to spoil her," Mary warned.

"So?" Lee grinned. "Little girls are meant to be spoiled."

"That's what you say now," Mary told him. "But what are you going to say when Madeline learns to cry in order to get her way?"

"She wouldn't do that."

"Are you sure?" Mary asked, convinced that Lee couldn't be unaware of Maddy's manipulations.

"She's a little girl," Lee said. "She doesn't know about ulterior motives or using tears to get her way." He winked at Maddy. "Do you, sweetheart?"

Maddy shook her head, winked both her eyes in reply, then giggled again.

"See?"

Madeline put on her prettiest smile, then reached for Lee.

He leaned closer so she could hug him, and then Maddy moved in for the kill. "Maddy sleep Poppy. 'Kay?"

Mary looked at Lee knowingly as she raised one elegantly curved eyebrow. "You were saying?"

"I was saying that I defer to your superior knowledge of children," Lee improvised. "And that you were right about it being time for our little girl to take a nap. In her own room," he added hastily when Maddy's blue eyes brightened. "In her own bed. Alone."

Mary nodded in agreement. "Maddy's on her way to bed right now." She turned toward the door, then stopped. She hadn't seen anything that even resembled a little girl's room across the hall. Mary looked back at Lee. "Any ideas where her bed is?"

"There." He pointed to a door on the opposite side of the bedroom. "Through the dressing room. It connects Maddy's bedroom to this one."

"Thanks." Mary headed toward the dressing room door with Maddy in her arms.

"Mary?"

"Yes?"

"Are you coming back to join me?"

"I don't know," she teased. "What did you have in mind?"

"A few more kisses," Lee replied.

"Is that all?" Mary asked.

"We'll start with kisses."

"And then?" she prompted.

"And then, I'm open for suggestions," Lee replied as he stretched his arms over his head, then yawned, and lay back against the pillows. "Hurry back," he urged. "And we'll discuss our options."

Mary tried to follow Lee's suggestion and hurry back to his bedroom, but Madeline wasn't cooperating. She fought sleep and balked at Mary's authority. Maddy whined when Mary removed her dress and pinafore, cried when Mary took her to the pretty pink-and-white–papered water closet adjoining her bedroom, and refused to close her eyes and go to sleep until after Mary tucked her into bed and read two stories.

By the time Maddy fell asleep, Mary was tired, cranky, and close to tears herself. Although she wasn't normally given to tantrums and tears, Mary knew she was in danger of succumbing. A half hour battle of wills with a determined two-and-a-half-year-old girl left her feeling more like the evil witch in the fairy tales than the beautiful princess. But Mary knew the remedy for what ailed her. A few private hours with Lee and a few more of his magical kisses would restore her good humor before she knew it and make her feel like a princess once again.

Mary pulled the covers up to Madeline's chin and tucked the ends beneath the mattress. She bent and pressed her lips against Maddy's flushed cheek, then smoothed the tangle of curls off the child's brow.

"Mama," Madeline murmured.

Mary leaned over and retrieved the doll from the foot of the bed, where Maddy had thrown her in a fit of temper, then lifted the layers of sheets and blankets to place the doll beside Madeline. "Mama's here," Mary said softly as she nestled the doll in the curve of Maddy's arm.

Maddy sighed in her sleep, turned onto her side, pressed her face against the feather pillow, and felt her way across the cool sheets until she touched Mary's hand. "Mama?" Maddy tightened her grip on Mary's fingers.

"Mama's here, little one," Mary whispered again. "Right beside you for as long as you want me." She didn't move from the bed, but sat quietly until Madeline let go of her hand.

"I'm sorry," Mary announced from the doorway of Lee's room some thirty minutes later. "I didn't mean to be so long, but Maddy took longer to fall asleep than I thought." She crossed the room and sat down on the side of the big brass bed. "Lee?"

He answered her with a snore.

"Lee?" Mary touched his shoulder.

But he didn't wake up.

She felt like crying once again—this time from disappointment. Lee Kincaid had fallen asleep on her. Mary considered her options. She thought about removing her dress, stripping down to her chemise, slipping into bed beside him, and pressing herself against him. But she rejected the idea as an act of a desperate woman, and she wasn't desperate. At least, not yet. Besides, she wanted her first time to be special. She wanted Lee Kincaid to make love to her because he wanted to—because he desired her—not just because he awoke to find a warm, willing body in his bed. Mary stood up. She grabbed hold of the covers and pulled them up around Lee, tucking him in bed the same way, she'd tucked in Judah and Maddy, then quietly left the room. She still had her unpacking to do, supper to fix, and other chores to see about. And she might as well take advantage of the solitude while everyone else slept.

*   *   *

Unpacking proved to be more of a job than Mary thought. Her trunks were too heavy for her to carry. She had to make numerous trips up and down the stairs from the entrance hall, where Lee had left the bulk of their luggage, to the bedroom she selected for her use in the back turret above the kitchen and down the hall from Judah's room.

Mary loved the turret room, with its many windows, window seat, and bookshelves built into the niches. It was decorated in the Queen Anne style, the furniture made of a light cherry wood. The half-tester bed had white crocheted net hangings, and the matching armoire, desk, and highboy dresser were similar to the furnishings in the bedroom of her cabin on the Trail T.

Unfortunately, the room reminded her of her bedroom back home in other ways, too. As she unpacked her trunks, Mary discovered the room didn't have anywhere near the amount of storage space she would need for her clothes or her personal items. She had already filled the hanging space of the armoire with dresses and all the dresser drawers with feminine undergarments and accessories and three trunks still remained to be unpacked—including the one that contained most of her trousseau. Mary dropped an armload of dresses on the bed. Where was she going to put them all? She stood in the center of the bedroom, debating for a moment before she decided to inspect the other bedrooms more closely. Maybe one of them would have a larger closet. Mary bit her bottom lip. She hated to give up the turret bedroom, but what else could she do? She had to have a place to put her clothes.

There was no point in moving into another bedroom, she decided after inspecting the storage area in the other rooms. None of the other rooms had any more space than hers. But she could use the armoires and closets in the remaining bedrooms if she separated her clothes by seasons and uses—leaving her winter and spring dresses and everyday dresses in her bedroom, putting her evening gowns and summer and fall clothes in the other rooms. Mary frowned. If only she had a dressing room like the one that connected Maddy's bedroom to Lee's.

A dressing room! Mary smiled. If she had to farm her clothes out to the other bedrooms for storage, why not simply use the dressing room? She hadn't really looked at it when she put Maddy down for her nap, except to notice, in an abstract sort of way, that it was very large and packed with clothes. Why not store those clothes in trunks and use the space for herself? Mary decided to give the dressing room a closer inspection.

She walked down the hall and quietly entered Maddy's room. The little girl was fast asleep, her breathing deep and even. Mary tiptoed across the room, opened the door that connected Maddy's room to Lee's, and stepped into the magnificent dressing room. Maddy's parents had probably shared the dressing room since it connected the two bedrooms of the master suite, but the man of the house hadn't used it as much as his wife.

The room was utterly feminine. A skirted glass-topped vanity table, covered with crystal perfume bottles, decorative hairpin boxes, silver-framed photographs, and an assortment of cosmetics occupied the space to the left of the pass-through hall, and an enormous dressing area took up every available inch on the right side.

Indulging her curiosity, Mary stopped to investigate. Although Mary's family, the Jordan-Alexander clan, was wealthy, they were also conservative. The main house of the Trail T ranch was large and comfortable, but it was a ranch house, not a modern-day replica of an English castle. Mary was astounded by the extravagance displayed throughout Ettinger House and intrigued by the luxury of having a separate dressing room of this size with cedar-lined walls and one whole wall of floor-to-ceiling shelves for hats, shoes, and accessories. Not to mention the amount and variety of fine ladies' clothing hanging on the rods below the shelves. There were morning gowns, day dresses, walking dresses, afternoon dresses, evening gowns, delicate nightwear, and wraps of every description. Mary moved closer and began to rifle through the hanging clothes. Odd. There wasn't a single article of men's clothing in the entire room.

Apparently Maddy's father hadn't used the room at all. Mary frowned. Where had he slept? In the big brass bed Lee currently occupied? If so, where had he kept his clothes? Lee's room didn't contain a closet or even an armoire. It didn't need them. Not with a complete dressing room next door. And Mary had already checked all the other bedrooms for closets. The rooms with closets had *empty* closets and the rooms with armoires and dressers were just as empty. Mary thought back to her tour of the house. The red parlor—with its roulette wheel, lewd painting, billiard table, drinks bar, and stale cigar smoke—and Judah's bedroom were the only two rooms in the house that showed any sign of ever having had a male occupant. And Maddy's bedroom was so thoroughly little girlish—with its pink and white wallpaper, child-sized furniture, pink canopied bed, and toys—that it was impossible to tell if it had once been a man's bedroom.

Mary bit her bottom lip as she fingered the silk fabric of a gray day dress. The pungent aroma of some exotic perfume drifted up to tease her nostrils. She walked over to the skirted vanity and began studying the objects crammed atop the glass surface. She lifted a large silver-framed photograph from behind an etched perfume bottle. Mary couldn't think of any reason why she hadn't come across any of Lee's former partner's belongings. Unless . . .

Mary stared down at the photograph of a man and a woman, and found her husband's sepia-colored face staring back at her.

Chapter Fourteen

Lee awoke with a start as something cold and heavy landed in the center of his chest. He opened his eyes to find Mary standing over him, her brown-eyed stare shooting sparks at him. A silver picture frame rested against his breastbone. "What the . . . ?"

"You lied to me," she accused. "I thought you said you had never been to Utopia before," she challenged.

"I haven't." Lee sat up in bed. The covers fell to his waist and the silver picture frame slid off his chest onto the mattress.

"Then how do you explain that?"

"What?" He yawned and wiped the sleep from his eyes, then absently rubbed his chest where the picture frame had landed.

"That!" Mary pointed to the photograph.

Lee picked up the frame and looked at the picture. He and Tabitha embracing in a photographer's studio in Denver. He thought back. What was it now? Three, three and a half years ago? He couldn't remember the exact date, but he remembered the day—a crisp, cold January day in Denver. Tabitha had insisted they stop at the photographer's studio on the way to the depot. She had wanted a picture of them together. A memento of the time they had spent as partners, as friends, and as lovers. Lee smiled at the memory. Their brief romance had been a month out of time. Four special weeks they'd shared before they went their separate ways. He had boarded the train for Chicago shortly after that photograph was taken and Tabitha—lovely, young, vibrant Tabby Gray—had remained behind in Denver to continue her work for Pinkerton. Now Tabitha Gray was dead at the age of twenty-seven. "I didn't lie to you, Mary. I've never been here before. This photograph was taken in Denver," he answered quietly. "In January eighteen seventy."

"What about your partner?" Mary already knew how Lee would answer, but she asked the question anyway.

Lee met Mary's clear brown-eyed gaze. "I never told you my partner was a man."

"But you let me continue to think it."

Lee shrugged his shoulders. "It seemed less complicated at the time. At least I thought it would be." He smiled. "I guess I was wrong."

"Then she was your partner?"

"For a while," he answered evasively.

"I see," Mary replied in a tight voice.

Lee hadn't planned to explain the circumstances of his partnership with Tabitha. It had begun and ended long before he met Mary, long after Jeannie died. He had been unattached, and lonely. He didn't owe Mary any explanation. His affair with Tabby had happened years before he met her. Years before he even learned David Alexander had a sister. His relationship with Tabitha had nothing to do with Mary. Or did it?

Lee took a deep breath and laid the picture aside. He wasn't being honest with himself or completely honest with Mary. His relationship with Tabitha Gray had everything to do with where he and Mary were now. He was living in Tabby's house, sleeping in Tabby's bed, and taking care of her daughter. And Mary Alexander was right there beside him because Tabitha had been forced to tie up the loose ends of her life before her time. Maybe he didn't owe Mary an explanation for his involvement with Tabby, but he suddenly realized he wanted to give her one. He wanted to talk about it. He wanted to tell Mary everything—to share that part of his life with someone else. And he knew he could trust Mary. Despite their first meetings, or perhaps because of them, Lee had realized from the beginning that Mary Alexander was trustworthy and loyal. "For two months," he burst out. "She was my partner from December of eighteen sixty-nine until the end of January eighteen seventy."

Mary nodded. "I see," she said again.

"No, you don't," Lee contradicted her. "But you're going to after I explain what happened."

"You don't have to explain," Mary said, suddenly sure she didn't want to learn the depth of Lee's involvement with Tabitha Gray.

"Please stay," Lee said. "I want to explain." He scooted over in the bed, shoved a feather pillow behind his back as he leaned against the brass headboard, then patted the empty place beside him. "You might as well sit down. It's a long story."

Mary eyed the empty space on the bed. The thought of sitting in bed beside Lee seemed so inviting, so warm and cozy—so married.

Lee saw the look in her eyes and discerned the reason for her hesitation. "It's all right," he assured her. "I promise not to bite."

She smiled. "I wasn't worried about your biting me."

Lee grinned as he pulled the sheets and the wool blankets to his chest, then tucked them tightly around him before propping one of the feather pillows, beside him, up against the brass poles of the headboard. "You can sit on top of the blankets and pull the top quilt over your lap for warmth."

Mary continued to waver.

"Even if I promise to keep my hands where you can see

them?" He held the top quilt open, inviting her to enter the warmth of the bed. "Come on, Mary, be adventurous. Take your shoes off and climb in. It's warmer."

She sat on edge of the bed, then stretched her long legs, and toed off her deerskin moccasins. They fell to the floor with a soft plop.

"No wonder I didn't hear you come in," Lee said. "You were wearing moccasins." He flipped the heavy quilt back over so it covered Mary's legs up to her waist.

"You didn't hear me come in because you were snoring too loudly," she replied.

Lee shrugged. "I guess there's a first time for everything."

"Sleeping that soundly and snoring that loudly can get a man in your line of work killed," Mary reminded him.

"I'm at home."

"Yes," Mary retorted dryly, "I can tell that from the family pictures."

Lee reached over and gently tucked a stray lock of her straight black hair back into place, then let his fingers graze the line of her jaw. Mary shivered in reaction. "Ah, yes," he said. "The family pictures." He lifted the silver-framed picture and looked at it once again. "Her name was Tabitha. Tabitha Gray. But I always called her Tabby for short. Allan Pinkerton assigned me to work with her in Denver that December." Lee paused for a moment, remembering. "Counterfeiting was a lucrative operation. There were only two chartered banks and way too much paper money floating around. Paddy Carnahan, the owner of Paddy's Saloon in Denver asked Pinkerton to investigate. You see, Paddy's Saloon also provided banking services for its boarders and tavern customers, and the counterfeiting was interfering with Paddy's banking business. The Agency tried several times to infiltrate the ring but failed each time. At first, Pinkerton thought the counterfeiters were tavern

owners themselves, one or two of Paddy's rivals, but the
operatives sent to investigate the taverns couldn't find any
evidence of that. And the paper money flooded the saloons,
threatening their very existence. So Pinkerton looked else-
where. He began to suspect that the counterfeiters were
from a higher level of society than the tavern owners.
Someone working in one of the town's two banks; someone
who mixed with investors, bankers, and businessmen from
different areas of the country. Tabitha posed as a wealthy
widow from St. Louis and I became her escort, a rich
investor from back east."

"What happened?" Mary couldn't help but be caught up
in the story.

"The territorial governor invited us to his home and in a
matter of days, Tabitha and I were receiving invitations to
all the Denverites' social gatherings. The doors of the inner
circle opened. All at once, The Pinkerton National Detective
Agency gained access to all kinds of information it hadn't
been privy to before."

"But you were outsiders."

"Yes, we were," Lee agreed, stroking one side of his
mustache. "But we were rich outsiders. And Denver, like all
frontier towns, was desperate for cash. The city government
needed investors, very wealthy investors, and the city
fathers welcomed potential financial backers with open
arms. Tabitha attended all the society ladies' functions,
contributed to numerous charities, and became, in a very
short time, an intricate part of Denver society."

"Were you accepted as well?"

Lee smiled. "Of course. I drank and gambled with the
cream of society, and gained memberships to the most
exclusive gentlemen's clubs. I was accepted completely.
And while Tabitha garnered bits of information from the
wives and daughters, I picked up all sorts of investment and
financing ideas—some legal—some not so legal from the

men. Eventually, we were able to send evidence to Pinkerton, who contacted Treasury officials. They arrested everyone involved in the forging, except the pen man."

"Pen man?"

"The pen man is the actual forger—the artist or engraver who alters bills, bonds, or drafts, or copies real currency. The pen man in the Denver forgery ring slipped out of town before the federal marshals arrived to arrest him."

"And the Denver businessmen never suspected you?"

Lee shook his head. "Not at all. In fact, I still maintain my membership in several of the clubs."

"I knew you were good at your job, but I must admit, I'm as impressed as I am concerned."

"Concerned about what?" Lee asked. He shifted his weight on the bed so he could see Mary's expression.

She smiled at him, a teasing light in her dark brown eyes. "I'm concerned for myself," she told him. "How will I ever know when you're telling the truth and when you're simply acting a part?"

"I try to always tell the truth," Lee replied solemnly.

Mary turned to face him. "As you did about our partner?"

"Exactly," Lee agreed. "I never said my partner was a man, I just didn't correct your inaccurate assumption."

"Failing to correct an erroneous assumption is almost the same as telling the inaccuracy."

"That's true to a point," Lee admitted. "But the fact is that I did not lie to you. I told the truth. And always telling the truth, or as much of the truth as possible, is one of the first things Allan Pinkerton taught me. If you make it a point to tell the truth, then if it ever becomes necessary for you to lie, there is a greater chance that you'll be believed."

"Interesting theory," Mary mused. "You tell the truth to keep from being caught when you're compelled to lie. I don't remember reading that theory in the ten commandments."

Lee chuckled. "Moses wasn't a Pinkerton operative."

"What about the aliases you use? And the roles you assume?"

"I always use a part of my name in my aliases—even my traveling names."

"Traveling names?"

"I always travel under the name Smith or Jones. It makes me harder to trace," Lee said. "But I'm always L. K. Jones or G. M. Smith."

"Liam Gordon MacIntyre Kincaid," Mary said softly, repeating his full name. "Very clever."

"Very safe," he corrected. "And anonymous."

Mary stared at her husband's handsome face—his beautiful gray eyes, classical masculine features, and tantalizing mouth, and wondered how he could ever consider himself anonymous. "What about the roles you play?"

"I don't think of it as playing a role exactly," Lee told her. "It's more like changing jobs. You thought I was a bartender in Peaceable when you met me and I was, but at the same time I was working on a case and trying to help David prove Tessa was innocent. It's always like that. At various times, while working on cases, I've been a gambler, a cowpuncher, a guard, a bank clerk, a newspaper reporter . . ."

"And a handsome escort for a wealthy Denver society matron," Mary added, deliberately turning the conversation back to Tabitha Gray and Lee's relationship with her.

"It was part of the job."

"Only part of the job?" Mary couldn't keep herself from asking the question. She leaned closer to Lee and studied the picture once again. "What happened to Tabitha after you solved the case?"

"I returned to Chicago and Tabby remained in Denver where she continued to work for the Agency."

"But your personal relationship ended when you left Denver?" Mary probed.

He shook his head, amazed at her persistence. "I never said we had a personal relationship."

"You must have seen her from time to time when you traveled to Denver."

"I never returned to Denver until a few days ago when I went to claim Maddy."

"Not once in over three years?"

"No."

"Never?"

Lee sighed. "I knew I should have bought you emeralds to go with your jealous nature."

"I don't have a jealous nature." At least she hadn't had one until she met Lee Kincaid.

"Oh, yes, you do," Lee told her. "You're jealous of Tabby Gray."

"All right," Mary admitted. "Maybe I am jealous. But what do you expect? You've brought me here to live in her house."

"So?" Lee didn't understand.

"What was she to you? Why would a bachelor like you agree to take on the responsibility of a two-and-a-half-year-old child?"

"Tabby was my partner," Lee answered. "She made me the executor of her will and guardian of her child."

"Why?" Mary persisted.

"Why? Why what?" Lee was beginning to lose his temper.

"Why did she make you Madeline's guardian? Why not someone else? Why not a relative? Where's Maddy's father?"

"Tabby Gray didn't have anyone else. She was married once, before the war, then widowed. She wasn't married to Maddy's father. And according to her letter, if I refused to take her, Maddy would've grown up in a St. Louis foundling home—just like her mother."

"And you couldn't let that happen."

"No, I couldn't let that happen," he replied. "Could you?"

"Of course, I could," Mary replied. "Unless I knew I that by fulfilling the terms of a will and agreeing to adopt a little girl, I could get my hands on a mansion and a silver mine."

Lee couldn't believe what he was hearing. "That's not why I agreed to adopt her and you know it! Or you *should* know it! I don't give a damn about owning a mansion or a silver mine!" Unable to sit still any longer, he flipped back the covers, got up from the bed, and began to pace the confines of the room—in all his naked male glory. "And if that's the kind of man you think I am, then why the hell did you marry me?" He stopped pacing and turned to face her.

Mary swallowed the lump in her throat. Her imagination hadn't done him justice. Goodness, but he was handsome. "I could ask you the same question." She swung her legs off the bed, stood up beside it, and slipped her feet into her moccasins. The sight of Lee Kincaid standing in front of her, as naked as the day he was born, practically took her breath away. It was all she could do to keep from flinging herself at him. "If all you wanted was someone to cook and clean and care for Judah and Maddy, you could have hired a maid. You didn't need a wife. You didn't need me. Unless . . ." She grabbed hold of the top quilt and took a step toward him, dragging the quilt along on the floor behind her. "Unless I was part of the deal, too. Was I, Lee? Was I one of the terms of Tabby's will?" Mary stopped just inches away from her husband and boldly placed her palm flat against his broad chest before she trailed her index finger down over his stomach.

Lee shivered in response, then reached out and caught hold of Mary's wrist, preventing further exploration. "Why do you want to know?"

Mary shrugged. "Maybe I'm wondering just how far you went to meet the terms of your partner's will. And how much farther you're prepared to go. Or maybe I just want to know if you'll feel compelled to lie to me again like you did when you told me why you planned to adopt Madeline and if I'll believe you this time, too. But most of all, I'm wondering if I'll ever know whether you wanted to become my husband or simply do a job."

Lee stared at her. Her doe-brown eyes softened as she met his gaze. He leaned forward slightly, then reached out and lifted her chin with the tip of his finger. "Trust me," he said, bending down to kiss her. "When the time is right, you'll know." He gently touched his lips to hers.

Mary tried to push her doubts aside. She had put her trust in Lee Kincaid when she agreed to marry him and she wasn't going to back away now that she had him.

She had known from the beginning that Lee didn't love her, and suspected that he was using her for his conveniences, but still it hurt to have her suspicions confirmed. It hurt to know Lee had deliberately misled her by allowing her to believe his former partner was a man when all the time he was planning to bring her to Tabitha's house to live. Mary understood that Lee had had a life before he married her. And secrets. But somehow, she had expected him to confide those secrets and to pretend to love her even though he didn't.

Somewhere along the line, she had confused the real Lee Kincaid with her idea of Prince Charming and expected the two to be the same. Just as she expected her one-sided marriage to be filled with love and warmth and sharing like the marriages of her parents, and grandparents, Reese and Faith's, and Tessa and David's.

She had thought herself mature and sophisticated. She thought she was old enough to resign herself to a loveless marriage to Pelham Cosgrove or to Lee Kincaid. But she was wrong. She'd made a mistake when she married Lee. Pelham had been safe—she didn't love him and knew she never would. But she'd fallen for Lee Kincaid. And once she realized she loved Lee, Mary knew she hadn't really grown up at all. She couldn't settle for a loveless marriage to him, not when she still believed in fairy tales—especially in happy endings.

She wanted to live happily ever after. Desperately so. She needed to believe it was possible. So she pushed her nagging fears aside and told herself over and over again that Lee's reasons for marrying her didn't matter as much as the fact that he had. And then Mary prayed she could make it be true. She was his wife, bound to him for better or for worse and it was up to her to prove that having her as his wife was better than letting her go.

Lee had ended the kiss quickly. Too quickly for Mary's satisfaction. It was over almost as soon as it began. He released her and stepped away.

Not knowing what else to say or do, Mary handed Lee the quilt. "Supper will be ready in half an hour."

Realizing he was standing before her without a stitch on, Lee gratefully accepted the covering.

Mary turned and headed toward the bedroom door. She opened it as Lee called out.

"Hey, Two-shot."

"Yes?"

"Thanks for listening."

Mary smiled. "You're welcome," she whispered.

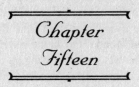

Chapter
Fifteen

"You must be Miz Gray's sister-in-law."

The sound of a woman's voice startled Mary, who stood at the worktable with her back to the door, daydreaming about Lee—the naked Lee—the one she'd just seen striding across the bedroom floor. Mary whirled around, nearly upending the pan of biscuits she had just made to go with the beans, to find a middle-aged woman wearing a black dress, black bonnet, and a black crocheted shawl standing in the doorway. "I beg your pardon?"

The woman stood just inside the kitchen door and Mary saw that she had a wicker hamper over one arm. "I said, you must be Tabitha's sister-in-law."

"I . . ."

She didn't give Mary a chance to reply, but walked farther into the room and set the hamper on the kitchen table beside the stove. The woman held out her hand. "I'm Louisa Shockley, but my friends call me Lou."

Mary shook hands. "Mary Alexan . . . Mary Kincaid. I'm pleased to meet you."

Lou took off her bonnet and shawl and draped them over the back of a chair. "I'll bet you're wondering what I'm doing here."

"Yes, I am," Mary admitted.

"I help out around this place," Lou told her. "It's way too

big for one woman to manage alone, so Tabitha hired some of us women to help cook and clean and wash. I do most of the cooking for everybody. Nan and Birdie clean, and Katrina comes on Mondays to do the washing and ironing." She glanced at the wet garments hanging in the scullery. "I see you've been doing a little laundry yourself."

Mary managed a smile of relief. "Madeline had an accident when we arrived."

Lou walked into the scullery and examined the laundry. "Looks like you did a pretty good job of it." She turned to Mary. "It's a good thing, too, because Katrina is real touchy about the wash. She takes real pride in having the whitest linens this side of the Mississippi."

"I noticed that the house was dusted and that the beds had fresh clean sheets and the water closet had fresh towels. I thought everything looked as if someone was expecting us," Mary said.

"We've been expecting you," Louisa told her. "Tabitha said she'd made arrangements for her brother, Lee, and his wife to come take care of little Maddy and poor old Mr. Crane within the month. We've been keeping the house ready and keeping a lookout for you and your husband, but since we weren't exactly sure when you'd get here, I didn't stock any perishables. When I heard you all had come in on the morning train, I decided to give you a while to rest up from your trip before I came by. I bought some eggs, milk, and butter from Sherman's General Store and I stopped by the smokehouse and cut down a ham before I came in." She nodded toward the hamper.

"That was very kind of you," Mary told her. "Let me get my purse and I'll be happy to reimburse you for expenses."

"Oh no, ma'am." Lou stopped her. "Ain't no need for that. I put the groceries on Tabitha's bill just like I always do. You can settle up with Mr. Buford later."

"Thank you," Mary said. "I can't tell you how relieved I

am to know I won't have to tackle this huge house all by myself. When I saw it, I wasn't sure how I was going to manage."

"Yeah," Lou agreed. "It does kinda take your breath away, don't it?"

"Yes, it does," Mary admitted. "It's so big and empty." She shivered involuntarily. "I'm used to a smaller house and having lots of people around me most of the time. Do you or any of the other women live in?"

It took Lou a moment to understand what Mary meant. "You mean here in the castle?"

Mary nodded.

"No, ma'am. We live just outside Utopia closer to the mine. We have children and houses of our own to look after."

"Oh."

Louisa unbuttoned her cuffs, rolled her sleeves up to her elbows, and began to unpack the hamper. "Now, don't you worry about being lonely. Come morning, you'll have plenty of people around you."

"What happens tomorrow morning?" Mary asked.

Lou chuckled. "Breakfast."

"But there's only four of us. Five, counting you."

"Honey, come breakfast time, that big trestle table in the room next door will be slam full of people."

"Who?"

"Just about everybody left in Utopia. Hand me an apron from that drawer over there," Lou directed. "And that butcher knife," she pointed.

Mary did as Lou asked, handing her first the apron and then the knife. "Are we running a boardinghouse?" Mary asked.

Lou laughed. "If we were, we'd go broke." She stopped slicing ham long enough to look at Mary. "We don't have any paying customers."

"I don't understand."

"Well, Tabitha probably didn't put everything in the letter she wrote to her brother. Or if she did, maybe he forgot to tell you."

"Tell me what?"

"Tabitha Gray's been practically feeding the whole population of Utopia ever since the mine shut down."

"The mine is shut down?" Mary felt like a parrot and an ignorant parrot at that. It seems Tabitha Gray had left a great deal out of her letter to her "brother." Or, as Lou suggested, "Brother" Lee had conveniently forgotten to tell his wife.

"The mine's been shut down for close to a year now," Lou told her. "And most of the miners—nearly all our menfolk—have been gone almost as long."

"You're all living by yourselves?"

"Yes, ma'am." Lou laughed again. "With the exception of a handful of men—three crippled miners, Carl Baker and Ned Sampson, who work in the Depot, Mike Kinter at the livery, Hugh Morton at the Ajax Saloon, Jed Buford at Sherman's General Store, old Mr. Crane, and your husband—what we have here is a town chock-full of women and children."

Mary bit her bottom lip in concentration. How was she going to afford the upkeep of Ettinger House and food for an entire town on her monthly allowance and Lee's Pinkerton salary?

Lou wiped her hands on her apron, then reached over and patted Mary on the hand. "Now, don't fret about things. We're not going to descend on you like locusts at supper tonight. We decided it was best to give you and your husband a little time to get used to the idea of having us around at mealtimes in case you didn't know anything about it."

"I . . . we . . . didn't."

Lou nodded. "I figured as much." She patted Mary's hand

once again. "Well, don't worry, we'll work something out if you . . . that is . . . if you and your husband decide to continue to exchange our services for meals."

Mary heard the question in Louisa's voice and recognized the tension behind the older woman's casually spoken words. "Of course, we plan to continue to exchange services." She smiled at Louisa. "Like you said, this house is much too big for one woman to handle alone, especially a woman trying to look after a two-and-a-half-year-old little girl and an elderly gentleman."

Louisa immediately relaxed and continued her supper preparations. "Tabitha didn't mention whether or not you had children of your own," Lou said as she bent to pull a cast-iron frying pan from the bottom cabinet beside the stove.

"We don't have any," Mary said.

"Hmmm. Something smells good." Lee entered the kitchen wearing a charcoal-colored shirt and a pair of buckskin britches. His hair was damp and neatly combed into place and his face, except for his mustache, was freshly shaven. He looked wonderful as he walked over to the worktable and peeked over Mary's shoulder, watching as she carefully rolled out a pie crust. "Who are you talking to? And what don't we have?"

Mary moved away from the worktable as Lou pulled herself up from her bent-over position so Lee could see they that they had a visitor. "Lee, this is Louisa Shockley." Mary made the introductions. "Lou, this is my husband, Lee Kincaid. Tabitha's *brother*." Mary stressed the last word as she raised an eyebrow at Lee. "Lou was asking if we had children of our own."

"Mrs. Shockley." He extended his hand in greeting.

Louisa automatically reached out to shake hands with Lee, then stopped when she realized she was still holding the cast-iron frying pan in her right hand. "Call me Lou," she told him. "All my friends do."

"Pleased to make your acquaintance, Lou," Lee said.

"Same here," Louisa answered, studying Lee closely. She set the frying pan down on the stove and began to pile the ham slices in it. "There ain't much of a family resemblance between brother and sister, is there?" Lou asked, turning to Mary.

"I'm sorry to say I never met Tabitha," Mary told her. "I've only seen a photograph of her."

Louisa turned to Lee. "Then shame on you for never bringing your wife to meet your sister while she was alive."

"Tabitha and I were never really close," Lee answered. "We had different fathers. I grew to favor my father and I believe Tabitha resembled hers."

Louisa nodded. "That explains it then, and probably explains why Tabitha never mentioned having a brother or a sister-in-law at all until she got sick." She sighed. "Well, we all have our family secrets and our family squabbles." Lou turned her attention back to Mary. "Anyway, like I was saying, Tabitha had a different look about her. She wasn't a blond-haired blue-eyed beauty, but she had the most beautiful skin, masses of dark hair, and big brown eyes—like you." Lou smiled at Mary. "You could have been related."

"I doubt it," Mary answered honestly. "I'm Cherokee Indian with a dash of Scots blood thrown in." Mary saw the look in Louisa's eyes at the mention of her Indian blood and waited for the moment when the older woman would turn her back on her and walk away in disgust. She didn't even realize she had gone into a rigid defensive posture until she felt Lee give her shoulder a gentle squeeze.

Louisa took a deep breath, then smiled at Mary. "I'm originally from the Carolinas, myself," she said. "And I daresay there's probably more than a dash of Cherokee blood in my family tree. I certainly won't be holding your bloodlines against you."

Mary relaxed. "Thank you."

Louisa wiped her hands on apron. "If I'm gonna be working here with you, we might as well come to an understanding. I won't hold your Indian blood against you as long as you don't hold my backwoods upbringing against me."

"It's a deal," Mary agreed. "By the way," she said to Lee, "Louisa is going to be working here."

Lee turned his roguish smile on Mary. "Then I guess she ought to know why we don't have any children of our own." He put his arm around Mary's shoulders and squeezed affectionately. "Yet," he added.

Mary gasped.

"My wife and I are newlyweds," Lee said. "In fact, Mary and I are still on our honeymoon."

Louisa glanced from Mary to Lee and back again. "In that case," she said to Mary, "you shouldn't be slaving in the kitchen. Not on your honeymoon. Get out of that apron. I'll finish up here."

"But my pie . . ."

"Go on now. Don't worry about your pie. I'll make it. You go spend some time with your husband," Louisa shooed them out of the kitchen. "Check out that bedroom upstairs with the big brass bed. Get a start on those children you're wanting."

Mary blushed.

But Louisa replied matter-of-factly, "It's what I'd be doing if my man were at home. Run along. I'll call you when supper's ready."

"Now what do we do?" Mary asked as soon as she and Lee left the kitchen.

Lee glanced over his shoulder to see if Louisa Shockley was watching them. She waved at him, then walked to the doorway and motioned him toward the stairs. "Since she's standing in the doorway watching, I guess we go upstairs." He rested his hand at the small of Mary's back and guided her through the hall way to the central staircase. "Where in the hel . . . devil . . . did you find such a nosy, talkative woman?" he asked, once they were out of Louisa's hearing.

"I didn't find her," Mary told him, whispering furiously as they climbed the stairs side by side. "She found me. She worked for Tabitha and she dropped by this afternoon to make sure she still had a job. It seems she's been expecting us—expecting me. Your partner"—Mary stressed the word—"told Louisa that her brother and his *wife*"—she emphasized that word as well—"would be arriving in Utopia within thirty days to take over the house and to take care of Maddy."

"What?"

"You heard me," Mary said. "Louisa is our new cook."

"Damn it all to hell," Lee muttered beneath his breath. He didn't think there would be any way to keep anything secret from Louisa Shockley—especially his and Mary's sleeping arrangement. "Does she live in?"

"No."

"Thank God!"

"But that's not all," Mary continued. "Nan and Birdie help clean the house and Katrina comes every Monday to do the washing and ironing."

Lee breathed a heartfelt sigh of relief as they reached the landing at the top of the stairs. "This morning you said you needed help with the house," he reminded Mary. "Now you've got it."

"We've got more than help with the house, Lee. We've got major problems." Mary hurried down the hall and opened the door to Lee's bedroom.

He followed her inside, closed the door behind him, and leaned against it. "I'm sure it's nothing we can't handle." He was already trying to figure out a way to appear to be a loving couple without really being a loving couple. Lee sighed. The idea hadn't worked the last time he'd tried it—with Tabitha—and Lee was afraid it didn't have a snowball's chance in hell with Mary, either. Especially since he and Mary were, in fact, a legally married couple. Lee raked his fingers through his hair, then stroked the corner of his mustache. Hell, he'd think of something. He had to.

"Are you listening to me?" Mary asked.

"Huh?" Lee made an effort to follow Mary's conversation.

"Lee, how are we going to afford this house and all these people?" Mary asked.

"We'll manage, Mary." Lee tried to set her mind at rest.

"How?" She demanded. "I know what Pinkerton operatives earn."

"Two-shot, I assure you I make enough money to support a family, a cook, two housecleaners, and a weekly laundress."

"If that's all we had to worry about," Mary said. "I could pay Louisa and the others a salary from my monthly allowance."

"No!"

"Lee, be reasonable . . ." Mary began.

"I'll support you, Mary. I don't want you to use your money on Maddy or Judah, the house, or to pay the help. Your money was meant for you to spend on yourself." Lee didn't understand why it was so important for him to support their household, but it was. He didn't want Mary using her share of the Jordan-Alexander fortune on the upkeep of Ettinger House. Besides, she might need it later. . . .

"Lee, the money I inherited from Reese's father belongs to both of us now," Mary insisted.

"No, it doesn't. It belongs to you. Mary Alexander."

"I'm not Mary Alexander any longer," Mary reminded him. "I'm Mary Kincaid. We took vows, remember? For better, for worse, for richer, for poorer."

"Nevertheless," Lee insisted stubbornly, "I'll support the household."

Mary threw her arms out in exasperation. "With what?"

"With the income from the silver mine," Lee answered. "The mine doesn't bring in a whole lot of money, but I'm sure it will provide enough to support us."

"No, it won't," Mary stalked over to the bed and sat down on the edge of it. "The mine is closed."

"What?"

"According to Louisa, the mine's been shut down for over a year and all the miners have gone to other mining towns looking for work. Utopia is practically deserted. There's only a handful of men left in town—including Judah and yourself. The rest of the population is women and children."

"But Tabby's letter . . ." Lee thought back, trying to remember everything Tabitha had written.

"That's another thing we have to talk about," Mary got to her feet and began to pace the room. "Tabitha's letter."

"What about it?" Lee was immediately defensive.

"I don't know what it says, but it's apparent that she didn't see fit to mention that the mine was closed."

"Christ, Mary, Tabby was on her deathbed!" Lee burst out. "Her concern was for Madeline. She wanted to make sure that Maddy was provided for. The rest of her responsibilities, the mine and the house, Tabby left to me."

"Tabitha left you more responsibility than you thought. Did she mention that Judah was one of those responsibilities? Did she tell you in her letter that Judah Crane lives in Ettinger House?" Mary studied Lee's stunned expression. "No? Well, she didn't tell you about the mine closing either, or make mention of Louisa, Nan, Birdie, or Katrina. So you can't possibly know that the reason we now have a cook, two maids, and a laundress is because Tabitha made a deal with them. She agreed to provide meals in exchange for services."

"What's wrong with that?" Lee demanded.

"There's nothing wrong with exchanging meals for services," Mary said. "I think it's a wonderful idea. I'm impressed by Tabitha's ingenuity."

"It won't break us to feed Judah or Louisa, Nan, Birdie, or Katrina and their families, Mary. If they're going without, it's the very least we can do, especially when they're going to be working with us." Lee answered.

"I agree."

"Then where's the problem? Why are you so upset?" Lee moved away from the door, crossed the room and halted Mary in mid-stride by placing his hands on her shoulders.

"I'm upset because Tabitha didn't give you a choice. This arrangement involves more than just Maddy or Judah or even Louisa, Nan, Birdie, and Katrina. It involves the entire mining town population. Come morning we'll be sitting down to breakfast with nearly every man, woman, and child in Utopia. We provide the food, and not just for breakfast, but for dinner and supper, too."

"What?" Lee was beginning to get the picture and he didn't like what he saw. Oh, it wasn't that he minded feeding the town of Utopia. He didn't. And he was certain Mary felt the same way. What he objected to, and what he realized Mary objected to, was Tabitha's manipulation of him. Of them.

"But don't worry, Lee," Mary was saying, "because Tabitha thought of you," she said quietly. "Tabitha provided you with a helpmate. In fact, I'll bet she demanded you have one, and worded her will in such a way that you couldn't possibly refuse. It was either take Madeline or have her grow up in a foundling home. I'm upset because Tabitha manipulated you, Lee. It was for a good reason—the best of reasons. I know she did it out of love for her daughter, but still, she arranged your life *and* mine. Because Tabitha didn't leave all these responsibilities to you alone. She left them to you *and your wife,* didn't she, Lee?"

Lee didn't answer. He simply stood there looking at Mary. He didn't want to reveal the terms of Tabitha's will. But above all, he didn't want to hurt Mary. And Lee knew the truth was going to hurt.

"But you didn't have a wife, did you, Liam Gordon MacIntyre Kincaid? So you had to get one. Within what . . . thirty days or so?" Mary paused. "I'm just guessing, but I'm willing to bet that getting married within a certain amount of time was one of the terms of Tabitha's will, wasn't it?"

Lee remained silent.

"Answer me!" she ordered. "And don't give me any more of Pinkerton's theories concerning the truth. I want the real version. Do the terms stated in Tabitha Gray's will say anything about you getting married within a certain amount of time? Yes or no?" Tears sparkled in Mary's brown eyes.

"Yes," Lee answered quietly.

Mary stepped back away from him. Suddenly, she couldn't bear the thought of Lee Kincaid touching her, comforting her. The truth shouldn't hurt so much. She had known all along that Lee had a specific reason for marrying her, and had suspected that his partner's will had played a part in his decision. But she hadn't known for sure. And she had learned the hard way that ignorance was sometimes bliss. Until this afternoon, Mary hadn't known that Lee's former partner was a beautiful woman. No, the fact that Lee had married her to fulfill a personal agenda hadn't come as a big surprise, but that his reason had been mandated by his former partner—by a woman he had obviously loved— came as a terrible shock. Mary took a deep breath before she asked the next question. "Did she name anyone in particular? Or did she leave the choice up to you? Was I first choice, or the only one foolish enough to agree?" Her voice broke.

"Mary, don't do this," he begged.

"Answer me!"

"She didn't name anyone in particular," Lee said. "I chose you."

"And how much time did she give you to select your bride?"

"Thirty days from the date of her death."

"Ah," Mary said. "The standard amount. And how much time had elasped between the date of her death and the moment you barged in on my wedding?"

"Nine days." Lee watched as silent tears rolled down Mary's face.

"I suppose I should be flattered," she told him. "You still had twenty-one days to find the girl of your dreams before the deadline expired and you settled for me."

"I didn't settle."

"Hmmf," Mary snorted derisively. "Excuse me if I don't believe you. It seems I've heard one too many of Pinkerton's theories."

Lee shrugged his shoulders.

"Tell me the other terms." Mary's normally calm voice sounded brittle, as if she was on the verge of hysteria.

"You know most of them already."

"I want to know *all* of them," she insisted. "As your chosen helpmate, I think I have that right."

Lee gritted his teeth at Mary's stubborn insistence and a muscle in his jaw ticked under the strain. "There were five unalterable terms. I had to agree to keep the mine and the house for a period of no less than twenty years. I must resign from The Pinkerton National Detective Agency within ninety days from the date of Tabitha's death, and I must agree not to work in any area of law enforcement. The fourth condition of the will was that I marry and settle in Utopia within thirty days of her death, and that I allow Judah Crane to witness the marriage."

"And the final condition?" Mary prompted when Lee grew silent.

"My wife and I have to agree to adopt Madeline and raise her as our own child."

"Tabitha Gray has my utmost admiration," Mary said softly. "She was very thorough." And very sure of Lee. Tabitha had been so sure of Lee that she made unreasonable demands on him and expected to have those demands realized. She had manipulated him, demanded that he rearrange his life to suit her needs, and Lee had agreed to her terms. Just as he had asked Tessa to marry him to fulfill Eamon Roarke's deathbed wish. Mary envied Tabitha for that feeling of confidence. But most of all Mary envied her for knowing how much Lee would do for her and how much he loved her. Because Lee Kincaid had to have loved Tabitha very much to make these sacrifices for her.

"Supper is ready!" Louisa's voice carried up the stairs and down the hall.

"I'll wake Judah," Lee volunteered.

"I'll get Maddy. You can take both of them down to supper."

"What about you?" He was concerned.

"I'm not hungry."

"Mary, you have to eat."

"No, I don't," Mary told him. "I only have to see that the rest of Utopia does."

Lee stroked the edge of his mustache and his voice, when he spoke, was husky and deeper than normal. "Mary, I never meant to hurt you."

But whether he meant to or not, the fact was that Lee Kincaid had hurt her. And a small part of Mary wanted to hurt him back. He didn't care about her at all. He was still in love with Tabitha Gray. "You say a lot of things you don't mean," she told him. "Just this morning you promised to kill the next man to make me cry." Mary put her hand in her skirt pocket, pulled out her pearl-handled, silver two-shot derringer and handed it to him. "It's not very accurate at a distance, but at close range, it will do the job nicely." With that parting comment, Mary turned her back on him and exited through the dressing room door.

Lee watched her leave, then focused his attention on the tiny silver gun she had placed in his hand. She was right. He had promised to kill the next man who made her cry. And if he had any sense of decency—of chivalry—he'd put the gun to head and pull the trigger right away. Before he hurt her again.

Chapter Sixteen

Mary awoke the following morning to find herself burrowed into the thick goose down mattresses and the mound of quilts on the big brass bed in Lee's bedroom. The room was dark and Mary fought her rising panic as she quickly reached out and found the lamp and the matches. Her hands shook as she lit the lamp and turned to identify the warmth pressed against her.

Mary breathed a sigh of relief when she realized it was Maddy who lay cuddled beside her. Her head ached from the hours she'd cried before she finally fell into an exhausted sleep and her eyes were puffy and swollen, but her memory was intact. Mary knew she hadn't wandered into Lee's dark room by accident or fallen asleep in his bed. But the trouble was that she had no recollection of how she came to be there—until Lee entered the bedroom. His blond hair was damp, and his face was freshly shaven. A thick, white towel was draped over one bare shoulder and a pair of well-fitted black trousers, only partially buttoned, rode low on his slim hips.

"Good morning." He greeted Mary politely, not the least bit surprised to find her in his bed.

"I see you're still living and breathing," she answered icily.

"Disappointed?" he asked.

"Very."

"Well, I guess there's no point in asking if you're still angry. But you're talking to me and that's always a good sign." He smiled at her as he casually buttoned his pants.

"Signs can be deceiving," she reminded him.

Lee chuckled. "I see the morning isn't your best time of day."

Mary turned toward the window. "How do you know it's morning? The sun's not even up yet."

Lee lifted a gold pocket watch off the bedside table. "I carry a watch," he replied. "And I know how to tell time. It's"—he turned the wick up on the lamp, then opened the watch and looked down at the face—"seven minutes after five." He snapped the lid closed, then placed the watch in his trouser pocket.

Mary groaned.

"And even if I couldn't tell time, *I* could hear the racket going on downstairs and smell the coffee brewing. We've been invaded. Louisa's downstairs cooking."

Galvanized by the fear of being discovered lying abed while everyone else was downstairs helping with breakfast, Mary flipped back the covers and scrambled to get to her feet. "How did I get in here? I distinctly remember going to bed in the room across the hall."

"Would you believe you sleepwalked? That you followed your desires and came straight to me?" Lee deadpanned.

"No, I would not!"

"Well, then, the truth is that I brought you in here and put you to bed as soon as I heard Louisa moving around in the kitchen. You were dead to the world."

"Then I didn't . . . we didn't . . ." Mary stopped abruptly.

Lee winked at her. "I was tempted." He stared down at her shapely legs exposed to his view as her white nightgown rode up her thighs while Mary struggled out of the bed. "I admit to being partial to your long, lovely legs."

Mary grabbed the hem of her gown and tugged it down as she stood up. "How did you get into my bedroom?" she demanded. "I know I locked the door." Mary stomped around the bedroom searching for the fine linen wrapper that matched her nightgown.

Lee shrugged his shoulders, then grinned. "I unlocked it."

She stopped searching and spun around to face him. "How?"

He lifted her robe from the back of a chair and handed it to her. "By picking the lock."

Mary grabbed the wrap, shoved her arms into the sleeves, and tied the ribbon at the waist in three quick jerky motions. "Why?" Her voice rose.

"Keep it down," he cautioned, glancing at Madeline asleep on the bed. "Please. You'll wake Maddy."

Mary took a deep breath, then nodded slowly.

"I woke up early," Lee explained. "I couldn't go back to sleep, so I decided to go downstairs and put on a pot of coffee." He didn't tell her that he hadn't slept at all after their argument; that he had left Ettinger House after supper and walked to the depot to telegraph William Pinkerton, or that he'd received a reply around midnight and spent the remainder of the night packing and pacing the bedroom floor until he had decided what he should do next. "I was halfway down the stairs when I heard Louisa and a couple of other women come in the back door. I heard Louisa tell them we were newlyweds and that she wanted to surprise us with breakfast in bed."

"How sweet!"

"Yeah, well, it wouldn't be so sweet if they had to serve the honeymooners breakfast in bed in two different rooms. It would tend to spoil the romance. Besides, it doesn't take a genius to figure out that we would look more like a happily married couple—a honeymooning couple—if we were sleeping in the same bed. So I crept back up the stairs, went into your room and got you, then carried you back in here." He pulled out his watch and checked the time once again. "That was about fifteen or twenty minutes ago. They should be knocking on the door any minute now."

"What about Maddy?" Mary asked.

"I don't know," he said. "She must have come in while I was washing up. I saw her curled up beside you when I came back into the room to get a clean pair of pants."

The image of Lee striding naked back and forth across the room popped into Mary's brain. She felt the rush of warmth color her cheeks. She didn't have to imagine how he looked. She had seen him yesterday and couldn't get the image out of her mind.

She cleared her throat. "You explained what happened," Mary told him. "And how I came to be here. But you didn't explain why I'm here."

Lee took a deep breath. "Mary, I know you're hurt. I know I hurt you—I heard you crying last night. And you had every right to be angry, to feel betrayed, and to say what you said to me. But we've made a promise to each other. And despite what you may think of me, I don't take that promise lightly. I married you. You married me." He held up his hand when Mary would have interrupted. "Hear me out. The fact is that *we* married each other, and right now the reasons we made the choices we made don't really matter. I tried to tell myself this whole idea was a mistake, but I don't believe it. Regardless of how it came about, this marriage between us feels right to me. And I want my second chance. I want this union to work."

Mary's heart seemed to skip a beat at his words. The last thing she had expected Lee to say, after last night's fiasco, was that he wanted to make the marriage work. But he had.

Lee Kincaid had offered her an apology and said he wanted to stay married to her.

Lee continued, "So I carried you in here this morning because I think it's important that we try to play the part of the happy couple for the people of Utopia. If we work at it some, we might even become a happy couple, and if not, then I intend to play at being happily married until I'm able to adopt Maddy."

"Until *we're* able," Mary corrected. "And if not . . . what about after the adoption? What happens then?"

He froze at the sound of china and silver clattering against a tray coming up the stairs. "I don't know," Lee answered honestly. "I only know that I don't want to do anything to jeopardize my . . . our . . . chances of becoming Maddy's parents." He looked at Mary. "This is as important to me as looking happy on our wedding day was for you. After that, well, then, I guess it's up to you. If you're still unhappy, if you want to call it quits and go back to Cheyenne, well, then . . ." He let his words trail off.

Mary recognized the expression of uncertainty that crossed his handsome face, even though she was quite sure he hadn't worn one often. For whatever reason, this pretense of wedded bliss meant a great deal to him. It was every bit as important to him as he said it was. But Mary didn't believe Lee's wanting to keep Maddy was his sole reason for pretending. There was something more, some other reason that he left unsaid. And her instincts told her that the feelings Lee couldn't put into words were just as important to him as the reason he gave her. Perhaps even more important. Mary remembered how Lee had allowed her to coerce him into pretending to be her long lost love, her hero, at their wedding reception. He hadn't asked why she wanted him to pretend. He had simply asked how she wanted him to play the part. She had been grateful for his understanding that she needed to save face—to pretend she was a blissfully happy bride. Lee Kincaid had played along for her two days ago, and now she would return the favor. She would show him she could forget the hurt she'd felt last night, forget her anger, and meet him halfway. No man wanted a whole town to know his bride had cried herself to sleep on her honeymoon. No man wanted a whole town to know he had slept alone. No man wanted to admit that he had failed. This was a matter of pride, and after living in the company of a ranch full of strong men, Mary understood Lee's need to protect his masculine pride.

During the long wakeful hours of last night, she had come to terms with the reality of her marriage. She loved Lee Kincaid. But he didn't, couldn't, return her feelings. He loved someone else. He still loved Tabitha Gray.

Mary had come to her moment of truth. She had to make a decision—to accept her present situation and work toward building a future with Lee, even if that future didn't include his loving her, or to give up and go home to Cheyenne.

She marveled at the change in her thinking. Two days ago, she'd been willing to marry Pelham with no hope of ever loving him or having him love her. But it was different with Lee. With Lee she wanted—no, demanded—the fairy tale happy ending. He had ridden up like Prince Charming on a white stallion and rescued her from the terrible mistake she'd been about to make. She had known the risks when she willingly accepted Lee's marriage offer . . . had known there was more to his offer than he let on, and yet she had jumped headlong from the frying pan into the fire. Could she blame him for the burns she'd suffered? And if she gave up on her marriage and Lee Kincaid now, could she live with her regrets? She had made a huge leap of faith when she agreed to marry him, trusting in her belief that love would conquer all and make things right. If she went home to the Trail T, could she live the rest of her life with the thoughts of what might have been and what she might have had if she had stayed?

Mary shook her head. She wasn't a quitter, she was a fighter. And if she couldn't have Lee Kincaid's love, then she would work to get the next best thing. She could build upon the physical attraction between them. She would use the desire she saw in his eyes each time he looked at her to her advantage. She loved Lee Kincaid, and she was about to embark on a course of no return. Even if she never had his love, she *could* have his children. She could give him the family she sensed he needed so desperately. She could provide a place for him to come home to—a house filled with warmth and love—with Maddy and Judah and the people of Utopia. Eventually, if she was lucky, she would earn his friendship and his respect, if not his undying devotion. And fifty years from now, if she worked at making him happy long enough and hard enough, Lee would forget that he didn't love her and remember that he couldn't live without her. Mary smiled. Friendship and respect and sexual attraction were good foundations for a lasting marriage. Lots of marriages had started out with less and had grown into more. She could do it, and she could start right away. Now. Before she had time to think things through—before she lost her courage. Thinking quickly, Mary ordered, "Take Maddy back to her room."

"What are you going to do?" he asked.

"Don't worry about me. Take Maddy and hurry. They're coming."

Lee didn't waste any more time. He bent and whisked the sleeping child off the bed and hurried through the dressing room door to her room.

Mary threw off her wrapper and climbed back into bed. She propped herself up against the pillows and hastily unplaited her long black hair. She bit her bottom lip, debating for a moment, before she daringly untied the top ribbon on her white ruffled nightdress and unbuttoned three of the tiny pearl buttons.

She barely had the buttons undone when Louisa tapped on the bedroom door and called cheerily, "Good morning! I've brought your breakfast. Are you decent?"

Mary opened her mouth to answer, but Lee stopped her. He put his finger to his mouth, gesturing for her to be quiet as he slipped between the covers. "Lovers never answer the first knock," he whispered as he rolled into bed beside her. "Let her wait a minute or two."

"But . . ."

"Ssh," he whispered again, his face a fraction of an inch from hers, "this has to look real." Then Lee closed the distance between them, kissing Mary thoroughly before she had a chance to say anything more.

"How are you feeling this morning, dear?" Louisa asked as Mary opened the bedroom door to admit her, moments later. "Mr. Kincaid said you were too tired to come down to supper last night. Are you feeling better now?"

"Uh . . . yes . . . thank you," Mary stuttered, glancing over her shoulder at Lee, who raked his fingers through his thick blond hair and put on a big show of yawning and stretching for Lou's benefit. "A good night's sleep works wonders."

"You look a little flushed," Louisa commented as she placed the breakfast tray on the night table. "Are you sure you're feeling all right?"

Mary pressed her palms to her cheeks, then gently touched her puffed and reddened lips. "I'm fine," she assured Lou. "More than fine. Really." Mary turned her attention to the breakfast tray. "Breakfast smells wonderful, Lou. Thank you so much. But you shouldn't have gone to all this trouble for us."

"It's no trouble," Lou said. "Besides, you missed supper last night. I figured you must be starving."

"I am," Mary assured her. "It's just that . . ."

"What my wife is trying to say," Lee interrupted, "is that it's a bit early in the morning for her breakfast. She wakes up early, but she likes to linger in bed awhile, sleep in a bit longer, and breakfast later. Especially when I'm home," he added in a huskier tone of voice.

"So you see," Mary broke in breathlessly before Lee could embarrass her further, "while we truly appreciate your thoughtfulness in bringing us breakfast in bed this morning, it won't be necessary for you to continue to do so. We'll go downstairs for our morning meal, just like everyone else."

"And if we're a little late," Lee added, "we'll settle for whatever is left over or wait until later."

"You will not," Louisa responded indignantly. "Nobody in this house goes without food unless they choose to do so, especially the owners. Not while there's a breath left in my body. Do you think I would let you"—she shot a glance at Lee—"or your sweet wife go without a meal when she agreed just yesterday that the two of you would continue feeding my family? Continue Tabitha's practice of feeding just about everybody in the whole town? Why, I'll fix meals for you no matter what time of day or night it is. Or how long you two honeymooners linger in bed."

Lee was genuinely touched by Louisa's dedication and loyalty. "Thank you, Louisa, for breakfast and for your understanding."

"Oh, I understand, all right," Lou told him. "I'm not so old that I don't remember whiling away the hours in bed with my man." She turned to Mary. "Now, you just hop into that bed and let me put this tray over your lap."

"But . . ." Mary protested.

"No buts," Lou told her. "I intend to see that you get this breakfast in bed. We'll worry about future breakfasts later."

She turned to Lee as Mary climbed into the bed as bidden. Louisa placed the tray in Mary's lap, poured two cups of tea, one for each of them, then gave them a friendly smile and a wave. "Just put the tray outside the door when you've finished," she said. "Birdie or Nan can pick it up later. Oh, and since you're not coming down, I'll have Rolf come up to see if Mr. Crane needs any help. Don't worry about a thing, and enjoy your breakfast."

"We need to talk," Mary said as soon as Louisa left the room.

Lee popped a piece of bacon into her mouth. "After we eat," he said.

Maddy woke up and toddled into the bedroom as Mary and Lee were eating. "Go pretty," she announced, flinging Mama up onto the bed beside Lee. "Maddy go pretty."

Mary handed the tray to Lee, slipped out of bed, then took Madeline by the hand and led her to the pink and white wall-papered water closet.

When they returned a few minutes later, Lee was pouring a second cup of tea into Mary's cup.

Mary lifted Maddy onto the bed and the little girl quickly scrambled over the mound of covers to sit beside Lee. She curled her little body close to his, then reached for Lee's plate. "Bidcut," she said, as she pointed to emphasize her request.

Lee grinned. "Would you like butter with your biscuit or strawberry jam?"

Maddy nodded.

"Butter?"

Maddy nodded again.

Lee sliced through the fluffy center of the biscuit, coated the bread with butter, then wrapped it in a napkin and handed the biscuit to Maddy.

Madeline handed it back. "'Berry zham," she instructed.

Lee chuckled as he added a teaspoonful of strawberry jam

to the buttery biscuit. "It appears Maddy has very definite ideas about her likes and dislikes." He handed the bread back to the child and watched as she took a big bite.

Mary pulled the chair up next to the bed, sat down on it, took the breakfast tray from Lee and set it on the night table, then picked up her plate to finish eating. "Madeline is very smart and very strong-minded. She's definitely her own person."

"You sound as if you like that."

"I do," Mary admitted. "I'm pleased to see she's an outgoing child. I know from personal experience that shyness and timidity can be a burden." She set her plate aside.

"Personal experience?" Lee reached around Maddy and handed Mary her cup of tea. "There isn't a shy or timid bone in your body."

Mary sipped her tea, remembering. "I was a tomboy growing up. I followed Reese and David around and tried to do everything they did until I was ten or so," Mary told him. "Then I changed—" She blushed, then continued on matter-of-factly. "I guess you could say I matured early."

"I'd say you matured nicely," Lee replied in his deep husky tone of voice. "Very nicely."

Mary blushed more furiously. "Anyway, after that, I became very shy and withdrawn. I began to keep to myself. I didn't know myself anymore. So, I began to read and study more, to help with the women's work, and stayed as far away from men as possible."

"When did you start carrying the derringer?" Lee asked.

"I got it as a present for my fifteenth birthday. A year or so before we left the Indian Territory for Wyoming."

A gun as a birthday present for a fifteen-year-old girl? Unusual to say the least. Unless, Lee thought, the fifteen-year-old girl was part Cherokee Indian and living in a territory where all too many men considered Indian women, and most especially half-breed Indian women, as theirs for the taking. And white men weren't the only men who posed a threat. The territory was full of outlaws, mixed bloods, and Indians who felt the same way. "Who gave you the gun as a gift?"

"Uncle Benjamin," Mary smiled at the memory. "Reese's father. He gave me the gun, then asked my mother to make sure that, in the future, all my skirts had pockets on the right side. He taught me how to shoot and made me promise to keep it loaded and carry it with me at all times."

"What prompted your uncle to give you a gun?"

"I don't know," Mary answered quickly. Too quickly.

"Yes, you do," Lee insisted.

Mary took a deep breath. "I decided I wanted to continue my education so I could become a teacher. The family talked it over and decided that I should attend a very expensive, very exclusive girl's school back east in Boston. I didn't want to go to school that far away from home, even though I knew Reese and David were attending Harvard University nearby, so Uncle Benjamin suggested I attend a school in St. Louis. He had a friend there who operated an exclusive school of higher education for girls.

"I agreed, and Uncle Benjamin traveled with me to St. Louis. He was going to Washington on business and promised to stop by and see how I was getting along on his way home. Everything was difficult at first." She took a deeper drink of tea, then cradled the cup in her hands. "Oh, there were the usual adjustments, I suppose. It took a while for the other girls to become accustomed to sharing space with me. I knew I was different.

"I understood that most of the girls had never seen an Indian and had heard all the horrible stories about Indians— how we massacre and mutilate innocent men, women, and children in their beds. But after the third month, I thought everyone was adjusting. Unfortunately, I didn't realize the other girls hadn't adjusted to my presence at all. They had simply schemed to get rid of me at the end of the term. I never realized girls could be so vicious."

"What did they do?" Lee asked, almost afraid to hear the answer.

"The school held an end-of-term social the last week of April—a dance. And young men from one of the area military academies were invited to be our escorts. After the dance," Mary recited the story in a flat unemotional voice that told Lee more about the trauma she had suffered than an avalanche of tears. "I went upstairs to bed, full of high spirits, because the social was my first real dance. After I fell asleep, someone sneaked two of the young men from the academy into my room."

Lee's breath caught in his throat, and he could barely get the words out of his mouth. "What happened?"

"I don't think they meant to hurt me," Mary answered. "The plan was for me to be caught with a man in my room so I'd be sent home in disgrace. But the young men had other ideas. I woke up to find one of the boys standing over me. He held me down while the other one tried to . . ." She took a breath.

"Did he?"

Mary shook her head. "No. One of the girls, one I had helped tutor, got scared. She knew about the plan to teach the 'Injun girl' a lesson. She ran to the headmistress who arrived in time to prevent it. The next morning, the headmistress wrote a letter to Uncle Benjamin requesting that he come to take me home. I was being expelled from school for lewd behavior."

"What about the other girls or the boys?" Lee demanded. "What happened to them?"

"I don't know. Nothing more was said about the incident to me. I was expelled for having men in my room." Mary swallowed hard. "After all, rules were rules, and I had broken them. My uncle came to St. Louis and rescued me. I think Uncle Benjamin could have bought my way back into the school, but I didn't want to return. I just wanted to go home. The following year, I did attend a school in Philadelphia, but I never forgot what happened. Since the day of my fifteenth birthday, I've always carried my derringer in my pocket and kept a lamp burning in my room so I never have to wake up in the dark and worry that someone might be there."

Lee thought it was a measure of just how exhausted Mary had been, that he had been able to enter her room and carry her from her bed to his without waking her, or having her shoot him, in the process.

"Bidcut," Maddy interrupted, pointing to the biscuit left on Mary's plate.

Mary handed her biscuit to Lee, who spread it with butter and jam and gave it to Maddy, whose nightgown was covered with crumbs and whose face was smeared with butter and jam as well.

"She's getting crumbs in your bed," Mary commented.

"That's okay," Lee said. "I don't think I'll be needing it for a while."

"What?"

"I did a lot of thinking last night, Mary, and I don't see how either one of us can plan for the future until I get some of Tabitha's demands out of the way."

"You're leaving me," Mary said flatly.

"I'm leaving town later this afternoon," Lee explained. "But I'm not leaving you. I'm coming back to Utopia, but for now, I have to return to Chicago."

"I don't understand."

"I telegraphed William Pinkerton last night after supper, and I received a reply from him around midnight. He said that if I planned to resign, I had to do so in person. He wouldn't accept anything else." Unable to sit still any longer, Lee rolled out of bed and, barefooted and shirtless, began to pace the width of the room. "So I'm returning to Chicago."

"You can't resign from the Agency."

"I can't do anything else," Lee reminded her. "It's not as if Tabitha left me with a lot of choices. If I want to keep Maddy, I must resign from the Agency."

"Within ninety days of Tabitha's death," Mary reminded him. "She's only been dead eleven days. You still have almost three months before you have to make a decision."

"I've already made the decision. And I would like to be able to give the Agency as much time as possible to find a replacement for me. They'll need every moment to brief a new operative on the status of my cases."

"What about the status of your cases? What about Tessa and David? What about the promise you made to them? What will happen to their case if you resign now? Who will replace you on that case? Who will continue the search for Lily Catherine if you don't?"

"I'll find someone," Lee said. "I promise you that. I'll find a good man to continue the search."

"But you won't be there to make sure he's good enough, or works hard enough—that he leaves no stone unturned."

Lee raked his fingers through his hair in exasperation. "Dammit, Mary, do you think I want to leave the Agency this way? It's been my life. I'm thirty-three years old. Do you think I look forward to starting over in a new career?"

"No, I don't," she said softly. "I think you're trying very hard to do the right thing by Tabitha and by Maddy. But if you resign from the Agency before you locate Lily Catherine, you'll be trading one child for another."

"The search for Lily Catherine will go on," he promised again. "I'll find someone to continue it and I'll get William Pinkerton's word on it. Besides, I told Tessa when she asked me to search that finding Lily would be like looking for a needle in a haystack. I've been looking for the past four months and I've come up with more questions than answers."

"Then you're prepared to jeopardize your long-standing friendship with my brother and with Tessa?"

Lee leveled his gray-eyed stare at Mary. "They'll understand."

Mary nodded. "David might, but not Tessa. She'll never understand why you chose to honor some other woman's promise and not the one you made to her."

"Hell, Mary! Who are we talking about here? You or Tessa? How many times do I have to explain that Tabitha Gray was my partner?"

"Tessa's brother was your partner as well. You made a promise to him, too. You promised to look after his sister."

Lee stopped. "Actually, I promised to marry her," he reminded Mary with an ironic little laugh. "Fortunately, Tessa had the good sense to turn me down and marry someone who loved her."

"Unlike me." Mary's voice was a barely audible whisper, but Lee heard her.

"I didn't mean it that way."

"But you don't deny it."

Lee couldn't take his eyes off his wife. Suddenly, he understood just how much Tabitha had asked of him. If he abandoned the search for Lily Catherine, Tessa would never forgive him, but more importantly, Mary would never forgive him. He could live with Tessa's disappointment if it meant keeping Madeline, but Lee realized he would never be able to live with the knowledge of having failed Mary. "Suppose I use the time I have left to look for Lily Catherine. Suppose I hold my resignation until the last possible moment and still am unable to find Lily; are you willing to risk losing Madeline"—he glanced down at the dark-haired, blue-eyed moppet busily wiping her sticky hands on the sheets—"if it comes to that? Are you willing to lose Maddy *and* Lily Catherine?"

Mary shook her head.

Lee barely managed to contain his explosion as his frustration mounted. There was simply no pleasing the woman. He was damned if he did and damned if he didn't. "Dammit, Mary, what do you expect me to do?"

Mary smiled serenely at her husband. "I expect you to find Lily for David and Tessa *and* resign from the Pinkerton Agency before the time limit expires so we don't run the risk of losing Madeline."

"You expect a miracle," Lee told her.

Mary got up from her chair, then bent and lifted Madeline from the center of Lee's bed and headed toward the water closet. "Yes," she said, "I guess I do." She turned back to fix her gaze on Lee. "But then, I believe in miracles."

"Believing that miracles exist doesn't guarantee you'll get one when you need it," Lee warned.

"Then I'll just believe in you." Mary smiled sweetly. "And trust that you'll be able to create the miracle I need."

Chapter Seventeen

Mary put on a good front later that afternoon as she, Judah, and Maddy all lined up at the front door to see Lee off. Judah wore a black suit, brocade waistcoat, and silver watch, while Madeline wore a dress of robin's-egg blue and a sparkling white pinafore, white ribbed tights, and shiny black patent leather shoes. Maddy held her doll in the crook of her elbow as she sucked her thumb. And Lee noticed that someone, probably Mary, had tied a matching blue ribbon around Mama's curls while Madeline's dark baby-fine curls remained ribbonless.

In his traveling suit and canvas duster, Lee felt positively underdressed. He smiled at the picture Judah and Madeline made in their best Sunday clothes. But Mary . . . Mary simply took his breath away. She wore a red day dress. The neckline was heart-shaped, which emphasized the elegant lines of her slender neck. And the front of the dress molded against her, accentuating her willowy figure and the length of her legs. In the back, the fabric covered a small bustle, then cascaded, like a waterfall, into layers of ruby red down to the floor.

"You look lovely, Mary," Lee breathed at last. "What's the occasion? My leaving?"

"No." She shook her head. "We're dressed in our best clothes, and lined up on parade, to cheer our hero in one last adventure." She nodded toward the stained-glass panels above and beside the front door depicting a jousting tournament. "As we live in a castle," she said, trying very hard to show Lee that she really didn't mind his leaving her alone on their honeymoon, "and are surrounded by images of Excalibur, Merlin, Arthur, Lancelot, and Guinevere, it somehow seemed appropriate."

Lee followed her gaze to the stained glass, then turned his attention back to his wife and raised his right eyebrow in question, "Are we surrounded by reminders of Camelot?"

"In every room," she told him.

"Then I guess it only fitting that I ask for favors from my two ladies."

Mary leaned over and whispered into Maddy's ear. "Give Papa his favor."

Maddy held out her hand to Lee, then opened her palm to show him a blue hair ribbon.

Lee took the ribbon and handed it to Mary. "Would you tie it on for me?" He turned so that Mary could tie the blue ribbon around his upper arm over the canvas duster.

Maddy clapped her hands together and giggled in delight.

"I have something for you, too," Mary said.

Lee watched as she reached into the pocket of her skirt. "That reminds me." He searched the inside breast pocket of his suit coat until he located Mary's little silver derringer. He pulled it out and offer it to her. "Don't forget about this. I won't be needing it just yet." He grinned at her. "I think it would be better if you kept it while I'm gone. In your skirt pocket where it belongs."

Mary looked up at him. "Thank you." She took the gun from him and slipped it into her pocket.

Lee turned to Judah and gently gripped his gnarled hand. "Good-bye, Judah. Take care of our ladies until I return."

Judah nodded gravely. "You can count on me, young man."

"I know." Lee knelt on one knee to hug Maddy. "You be a good little girl while I'm gone. Mind Mary and help Judah and Louisa. Okay?"

"'Kay." Maddy nodded.

Lee kissed her on the cheek.

Maddy hugged him tightly, then planted several wet kisses on his face. "Mama!" she demanded shoving the doll at Lee's mouth.

He kissed the doll as instructed by Maddy, then rose to his full height and grabbed his hat from its resting place on the newel post.

"I shouldn't be gone more than three weeks," Lee said to Mary. "I'm going to Chicago first, then on to Washington. I left a man there working on the case, so with any luck . . ." He let his words trail off.

"I understand," Mary told him.

"I hate leaving you alone," Lee admitted, fiddling with the brim of his hat. "Are you sure you want me to do this?"

"Yes." She bit her lip to hide its trembling. Lee had a job to do—a job she wanted him to do—and Mary couldn't let herself interfere with its completion, no matter how much she wanted him to stay.

"Well," Lee said, "the train leaves in fifteen minutes. I'd better be going." He picked up his leather satchel. "You know if you need me, you can telegraph the Agency. William Pinkerton knows how to contact me."

"I know."

"Or you can telegraph Reese or David."

"I know."

"I'll be traveling under the name G. M. Smith," Lee reminded her.

Mary nodded.

"Are you sure you don't want to return to Cheyenne to stay with your family at the ranch while I'm gone?"

The train whistle sounded in the distance.

"I'm sure," Mary said. "And you had better hurry or you'll miss the train."

"But . . ."

"I'll be fine," Mary assured him, moving to stand between Judah and Maddy. "We'll be fine. Go slay the dragons. Go rescue the fair little maiden."

Lee jammed his hat on his head, opened the front door and headed toward Utopia's dusty Main Street. He had passed through the wrought iron gate to Ettinger House and was halfway down the street when he heard Mary behind him.

"Wait, Lee!"

He stopped and waited as Mary, skirts in hand, shapely legs visible, caught up to him. "What is it? Did I forget something?"

She let go of her skirts. "You didn't let me give you my favor." Mary held out a red ribbon.

Lee stared at her. Her face was flushed from the exertion of running in skirts and corset, her lips were reddened, and several strands of inky black hair had come loose from her elegant chignon. Lee shook his head in wonderment. She had gathered her skirts in hand and run out of the house, and exposed her long lovely silk clad legs to anyone who cared to look, just to give him a red ribbon. "Have I your favor now, Mary?" he asked in a husky baritone voice.

"Yes," she answered breathlessly, staring up into his pewter gray eyes.

"And when I return from Washington?"

"Yes."

"Then tie it on." He dropped his leather satchel in the dust and extended his arm so Mary could fasten her favor beneath Madeline's.

"Are you certain?" He had to ask because afterward, there could be no turning back.

"I'm certain." Mary smiled up at him. "You see, I had

another reason for getting everyone all dressed up to see you off."

"And what was that?"

"To remind you of what you have to come home to."

Lee stepped closer to her and traced the heart-shaped neckline of her dress with his finger. "Some reminder."

"Do you like it?"

"The dress is okay," he teased.

"Only okay?" she questioned.

"Yeah, but the woman inside it is pretty special." He leaned toward her. "One favor from you isn't enough. I need another."

"Then, take it," she said as she closed her eyes and waited for his kiss.

Lee thought about Mary all the way to Chicago. He thought about her as he gave his report to William Pinkerton and dreamed of her as he dozed on the east-bound train and after he reached his destination and had settled into a comfortable room at the Madison Hotel. He dreamed of her good-bye kiss, the way she looked in her ruby red dress running down the walkway to catch him and tie her favor around his arm. But most of all, Lee dreamed of the other favors she had promised when he returned. He told himself to turn around and head back to Utopia. He told himself that the best thing he could do for Mary was to send her away from him before it was too late—before he ruined her for Pelham Cosgrove. Lee told himself that he should send her back to Cheyenne so she could have the kind of life she deserved with a better man than he was, but deep down, Lee knew he couldn't . . . *wouldn't* do it.

He wasn't that noble or self-sacrificing. Mary had reached a decision. She was ready to explore the attraction between them, and Lee intended to take full advantage of her curiosity and her temporary weakness. He had been fighting his attraction to her from the first day they met and he'd be damned if it wasn't time to do something about it. She'd married him in a church before God and witnesses, and while he might not have been her first choice, he was the man she ended up with. And Lee meant to end up in her bed, just as soon as he finished his business in Washington.

Washington. The topic of conversation in the city had changed in the few days Lee had been gone. The shocking news of Senator Warner Millen's tragic death had been replaced by other news. Lee sat the bar of the Madison Hotel sipping a cup of Irish coffee and listening to the talk around him while he waited for his contact, Dan Willis, to join him.

Five minutes later, a smartly dressed gentleman slipped onto the barstool beside him. "Hello, Kincaid."

"Hello, Willis," Lee replied as he motioned the bartender over. "What will you have?"

"Beer."

"Beer for the gentleman," Lee said to the barman, "and another Irish coffee for me." He waited until the bartender moved to the other end of the bar, out of earshot, before he spoke again. "Good to see you again, Willis. What have you learned?"

"Pretty much what you expected," Willis said. "It appears to be harder for a rich prominent man to hide an illegitimate granddaughter than the late Senator Millen bargained for, especially after the senator became involved in some questionable business dealings with some less than honorable men."

Lee smiled. "Someone as well known as Senator Warner Millen would need help concealing his daughter's fall from grace. And that help would have to come from someone he trusted. If the person who helped Millen keep his little secret demanded payment for keeping it, then the distinguished senator would have no choice except pay or be exposed."

"Right," Willis confirmed. "I've been following various members of the late senator's staff, and one of the senator's most trusted staff members has made some very interesting trips since the senator's death."

"Let me guess," Lee said. "James Sarrazin."

"Exactly. The late senator's personal clerk has been a very busy man. He's made two trips to Pennsylvania since you left, and at least one trip to the Millen residence in Georgetown."

"As Millen's personal secretary, Sarrazin was privy to almost everything that went on around the senator— personal as well as professional," Lee told him. "It's inconceivable to me that Sarrazin didn't know about Lily Catherine's birth. Someone had to arrange a place for Caroline to stay until the baby was born. When Caroline left Washington, Senator Millen mentioned to several of his cronies that his daughter was going to visit relatives in Pennsylvania for the season. Later, Millen announced that Caroline had died suddenly while visiting those same relatives. Did you have any luck questioning them?"

Willis shook his head. "I wasn't able to locate anyone in Philadelphia who saw Caroline Millen during the last year of her life. As far as I can tell, there isn't any branch of the Millen family or of Mrs. Millen's family, the Gaynors. *The Inquirer* ran her obituary when she died, but there isn't a single newspaper article to corroborate the Senator's story that his daughter was visiting in Philadelphia—not even on the society pages. And I didn't talk to a single soul who remembered meeting or seeing Caroline Millen at any of the society functions that season. And you would think that someone would remember meeting the daughter of a powerful and influential senator; someone would remember dancing with her or escorting her." Willis finished his beer and motioned for another one.

"Which means the senator lied about his daughter's whereabouts," Lee concluded. "And it doesn't make sense for him to have lied when the facts could easily be checked."

"But," Willis pointed out, "the senator circulated the first story when he sent Caroline away—after he learned of her disgrace. Now, all of Washington knows Millen had a falling out with his attorney, your friend David Alexander, which resulted in David's leaving Washington. But only a handful of people know why the senator took it upon himself to ruin Alexander's promising Washington career." Willis took a breath. "Millen sent his daughter away to avoid a scandal during an election year. In the natural course of things, Caroline Millen would have given birth to her child, the senator would have arranged for someone to take the child and raise it as their own, and Caroline would probably have spent a season in Philadelphia, then returned to Washington as if nothing had happened."

"But Caroline didn't return to Washington," Lee said. "She simply disappeared. And eventually the disappearance of the daughter of a popular United States senator was sure to be noticed by someone." He took a sip of his coffee. "Her disappearance from Washington society had to be explained, and the senator couldn't risk telling the truth. He couldn't announce that his daughter had died delivering his illegitimate grandchild."

"How did David Alexander find out?" Willis asked.

"David returned quietly to Washington several months after the senator and Mrs. Millen sent Caroline away. David demanded to see the senator because he was concerned about Caroline's well-being. That's when the senator informed him that Caroline had died, but that the bastard half-breed child had survived. When David asked about the baby, Senator Millen told him that on her deathbed, Caroline had insisted on naming her daughter Lily Catherine Alexander. The senator and Mrs. Millen granted their daughter's last wish, then promptly sent the child to an orphanage."

The bartender set another mug of beer down on the bar in

front of Willis. Willis cleared his throat and shifted his weight on the barstool. "I've confirmed what you said about David Alexander. He isn't Lily Catherine's father. Now that the senator's dead, people have begun talking, mentioning things here and there. And I've learned that there was never any relationship between Alexander and the senator's daughter."

"How did you manage to breach Washington's close-knit society?" Lee asked.

"I've been temporarily assigned to Secretary Fish's staff," Willis told him.

"I'm impressed by your connections," Lee raised an eyebrow at Daniel Willis. Hamilton Fish was President Grant's very capable Secretary of State.

"Not my connections," Willis said. "Pinkerton's. But the job has been an asset. I've been introduced to all the Washington hostesses and I managed to meet Caroline Millen's closest friend. Her name is Anne Greenberry, and I've been escorting her for two weeks now. Anne told me that Caroline Millen told her that she had only met David Alexander twice—once at her sixteenth birthday party and the night he took her home from the theater." He hefted his beer mug and took a swig before adding, "According to Anne, Caroline was at the theater that night because she had gone to see one of the actors, one of the male leads. Anne also told me that Caroline and the Shakespearean actor had been secretly meeting for weeks and that they had shared several romantic trysts. Apparently Caroline saw herself as a modern day Juliet to the actor's Romeo. They met in secret because Caroline knew her father wouldn't consider an actor as a possible son-in-law: It was out of the question."

"How does Caroline's friend know all of this?" Lee asked.

"Caroline confided in her."

"How does she know Caroline didn't make this up—that it wasn't just the romantic fancy of a sixteen-year-old girl imagining herself in love with a handsome actor?" Lee asked.

Willis grinned. "Caroline kept a journal and she entrusted it to Anne for safekeeping."

"Have you seen the journal?"

"No," Willis said. "But I believe it exists."

"Does anyone else about the journal?"

"According to Anne, Mrs. Millen knew Caroline kept a daily journal. Caroline gave the book to Anne so her mother wouldn't be able to find and read it."

"But Anne Greenberry knows David Alexander isn't Lily Catherine's father," Lee said.

"Yes."

Lee smiled. He took another drink of his Irish coffee. "If Caroline Millen told her best friend about her actor lover, then it's possible someone else knew about him. Someone like Senator or Mrs. Millen, or . . ."

"James Sarrazin," Willis continued David's train of thought. "The senator's personal secretary. And Sarrazin was in a position to know exactly how much embarrassment and political damage Lily Catherine's existence could cause the senator if the word got out that his daughter was carrying the illegitimate child of an actor and that Senator Millen had deliberately destroyed David Alexander's Washington career because Alexander refused to marry Caroline."

"But we have to prove James Sarrazin was blackmailing the senator. You've followed him to Pennsylvania and to Mrs. Millen's Georgetown home following the senator's death. What can we prove?" Lee asked.

"Word is that Senator Millen was spending rather large sums of money on a regular basis, but I haven't been able to prove it," Willis said.

"If we could tie the money to Sarrazin and to the Millens, I'm sure I could get an audience with Mrs. Millen." Lee finished his coffee.

"I've tried to call on her twice," Willis said, "to offer my condolences, but she's refusing all visitors."

"Except James Sarrazin," Lee mused aloud.

Willis drained his beer mug. "But Sarrazin was the senator's secretary. He may have had a very legitimate reason for calling on Mrs. Millen."

"Keep an eye on Sarrazin just the same," Lee instructed. "See if he's spending more money than usual, and find out where he banks. If he's not spending it, he must be depositing the money somewhere—either in Washington or in Philadelphia. Oh, and find out if any other members of the Senator's staff have visited Philadelphia or the surrounding area since the distinguished gentleman's demise. Find out if any little girls Lily's age have been left in any of the orphanages in the vicinity of Philadelphia."

Willis groaned. "Do you know how many two-year-old female orphans there could be?"

Lee thought of Maddy. She was just a bit older than Lily Catherine, and orphaned, too. Maddy had him and Mary to love her and to take care of her. Lily Catherine might be alone. Lee shook his head. "I only know that if we work hard enough, there might be one less orphaned little girl."

Willis nodded. "What are you going to do while I'm visiting foundling homes?"

"I thought I might pay a visit to Mrs. Warner Millen."

"She won't see you," Willis warned.

"I think she might," Lee said. "If she thinks I've come about her husband's account at the bank. But first, I have to contact a friend of mine," Lee said, "at the Treasury Department."

Willis smiled. Lee Kincaid had his own impressive connections.

Chapter Eighteen

The morning after Lee left the house, Mary began a frenzy of activity. While Louisa kept an eye on Maddy and Judah, Mary made a trip down Main Street to Sherman's General Store.

A big, broad-chested man came around the counter to greet her as she entered the store and Mary noticed he walked with a pronounced limp.

"Hello, welcome to Sherman's General Store. I'm Jed Buford, owner and operator." He extended his hand. "And you must be Miz Gray's sister-in-law." He repeated Louisa's earlier greeting in a slow, southern drawl.

"I'm Mary Kincaid." Mary stepped forward to shake hands with him. And as her eyes adjusted to the dimly lit interior of the store, she discovered Jed Buford was much younger than she thought. Mary had been expecting an older man, but found Jed Buford to be around her own age. He had bright red hair that was thinning on top and a neatly trimmed beard. His eyes were bright blue and they seemed to radiate with humor and intelligence. Mary liked him immediately.

"We've—" He stopped and smiled. "I mean the people here in town have been expecting you for a while now, Miz Kincaid. Tabitha said you would come to take care of the little one and old Mr. Crane. We were a bit worried about your leaving once you learned the mine was closed, so you can imagine how happy this whole town is that you and your husband have decided to stay and make Utopia your home."

"Thank you," Mary said. "We're glad to be here." She made the polite response even if it might not be the entire truth. Mary opened her purse. "I've come to settle the Ettinger House account and to order a few things."

Jed shook his head. "The only bill I've got for Ettinger House is the one for the groceries Lou picked up yesterday. And that comes to three dollars and sixty-eight cents."

Mary handed Jed three dollars and the change. "What about Tabitha's account?"

"I closed it out when Tabitha passed away," he told Mary. "There wasn't much outstanding—only ten dollars or so—and I'll gladly absorb the loss. Tabitha did so much for me and the people of Utopia."

"I'm sure she was a paragon."

Jed laughed. "Oh no, she wasn't. She had a temper and faults just like the rest of us. She enjoyed having money while the mine was open, but she didn't like the way her uncle treated the mine families."

"Her uncle?"

"Arthur Ettinger," Jed explained. "He built Utopia and Ettinger House and owned the silver mine."

Mary smiled. "Arthur. I should have guessed."

"Yes, ma'am," Jed agreed. "Old man Arthur practically worshiped King Arthur and the knights of the round table. Too bad he didn't treat his subjects as well as King Arthur treated his."

"I don't understand."

"Up until Miz Gray, Tabitha, moved here, Utopia didn't have a general store. The mining company operated the store and the miners could only buy from the company store—at outrageously inflated prices. I had opened my store, but I could barely support myself on what I made off sales to the other residents of Utopia. When Art died, Tabitha inherited everything." He paused and scratched his beard. "I don't know why old Art didn't leave everything to your husband, ma'am, what with him being Tabitha's only brother and all."

"You might say my husband was something of a loner before we married," Mary told him. "I don't believe he had much contact with his family after the war."

Jed nodded. "I can surely understand that. I lost most of my family and everything I owned in the war." He reached down and rapped his knuckles on his right leg above his knee. "Even lost my leg at Vicksburg."

"I'm sorry."

"Don't be, ma'am," Jed said. "It turned out to be one of the best things that ever happened to me. My father owned a string of businesses back home and I was studying business. But I was a wild one before the war, hell-bent on destruction. I hated being confined. I hated the university. I didn't want to be a shopkeeper, I wanted to be a hero. I couldn't wait to enlist and fight for the South. I had to learn things the hard way. I saw enough destruction during the war to last me a lifetime. And after I lost everything, I decided to come west. I knew I couldn't work as a miner with a wooden leg, but I had sense enough to know that miners needed equipment and supplies. I scraped together some cash and came west.

"I settled in Utopia because the name and the location appealed to me. But I nearly starved the first year. I couldn't compete with the company store. Anyway, after Art died, Tabitha closed the store and allowed me to buy the contents. You could say she saved my business, and all she asked in return was that I treat the mine employees fairly. I agreed, and we did business together until she died."

Mary sighed. It was impossible to stay angry at a dead

woman. Especially when the dead woman was someone she admired—someone she was sure she would have liked if they had met before Lee Kincaid came along. "I know about Tabitha's arrangement with the wives of the miners," Mary said. "How have you managed since the mine closed?"

"I managed because Tabitha used her savings to buy food and goods from me." Jed shook his head and scratched his beard again. "I don't know how she survived. She must have exhausted her money. Supporting a whole town is expensive. Kids always need shoes and clothes and even if they're thrifty, women have to buy things once in a while."

"That's what I want to talk to you about." Mary saw her opening and seized it. "I want to keep the arrangement with the miner's wives. I would like for you to continue to supply them with the necessary food and household goods and whatever school supplies they need—books, slates, pencils, pens, ink."

"The children in this town don't need school supplies, ma'am," Jed told her. "Utopia doesn't have a school or a schoolteacher."

Mary frowned. "What do the children do all day?"

"Most of them work or keep house and take care of the younger ones while their mothers work."

"But they should be in school!"

Jed shrugged. "Like I said, Utopia doesn't have a schoolhouse or a teacher."

Mary's face seemed to light up. "They do now!"

"Ma'am?"

"I'm a teacher, Mr. Buford," Mary answered. "The town needs a teacher and I need pupils. Please order a case each of elementary grade spellers, readers, and arithmetic books, to start. And slates and chalk, and a standing slate board for me as well as pencils, pens, and ink." Mary thought for a moment. "Oh, and desks. About twenty of them."

"I'll be glad to order any supplies you need, Miz

Kincaid," Jed said. "But have you thought where you're going to put this school? We don't have any vacant buildings left in town except the jail, and even if it was suitable, it wouldn't be big enough."

"What about one of the saloons?" Mary suggested.

Jed shook his head. "The Ajax already doubles as the assayer's office and the bank and the Silver Bear—well, the Silver Bear has an upstairs business the children ought not to see."

"The servant's kitchen at Ettinger House is plenty big enough," Mary said. "But we need the seating space for meals."

"What about after breakfast and dinner?" Jed suggested. "You could have school in the afternoon between dinner and supper."

"That would only give us two or three hours of school, and the children will need more time than that."

"A little schooling a day is better than none," Jed reminded her.

"Yes, I know," Mary admitted. "But there must be a way. Some place—" Suddenly, she knew where she could start the school. "The *ballroom*."

"What?"

"The third floor of the Ettinger House has complete servants quarters and a ballroom." Mary was excited. "The ballroom is more than big enough, and with the servant's quarters, we could even house students from outlying farms and towns. And I won't even have to leave my home. I can be there to take care of Judah and Maddy. Order the supplies, Mr. Buford, Utopia is about to get a school!"

Although enthusiastic about the school and the sales for his store, Jed Buford was also practical. He figured it was bad enough having nearly everyone in town going in and out of Ettinger House for meals. Adding a school would be adding more inside traffic and a lot less privacy for the residents. "Maybe we ought to wait to order the school supplies, Miz Kincaid, until after your husband gets back."

"Why?" Mary asked, still carried away by the idea of founding Utopia's first school.

"Maybe you ought to discuss this over with your husband first. He might not think it's such a good idea . . ." Just this morning, Louisa Shockley had mentioned to Jed, when he delivered fresh eggs and milk, that it was a shame that Lee Kincaid had to leave Utopia to take care of a business matter when he and his sweet wife were still honeymooning. Jed wouldn't like leaving a woman like Mary Kincaid home alone on her honeymoon. And he certainly wouldn't enjoy having a town full of strangers traipsing through his house at all hours. Mealtimes would be bad enough, but having the town's child population underfoot all day long monopolizing his wife's time. . . . After hearing about the passionate kiss between Kincaid and his wife in the middle of Main Street yesterday afternoon, Jed didn't imagine Lee Kincaid would be thrilled with the idea either.

"There isn't any need to discuss this with my husband." Mary gritted her teeth at Jed's suggestion. "I'm the teacher. It's my decision. Besides, my husband is a very well-educated man and I'm sure he'll be delighted by the idea of having a school that the children in town can attend." At least, she hoped Lee would be delighted. She'd been so excited by the idea of starting a school that she hadn't given any thought to Lee's reaction. What would he say when he discovered that not only did she plan to redecorate most of Ettinger House, but open a school too? Still, Mary told herself, Madeline needed the company of other children, and what better way to get it than to have the other children go to school upstairs in her home? Mary bit her bottom lip. Jed Buford was right—she probably should consult with Lee. But he might be gone for weeks and she really wanted to get started on the project immediately.

"Anything else you need, Miz Kincaid?" Jed asked.

Mary handed him her list of paints, wallpaper patterns, and fabric selections. "And now that we've decided to open a school, I think I should add a dozen or so blankets, sheets, and pillows to the list in case we get boarders. And several bolts of white cotton, navy blue serge, and navy blue wool for school uniforms."

"Anything else?" he asked as he added the other items to Mary's list.

"Can you tell me where I can find a telegraph office?" she asked.

"At the depot," Jed answered.

"Thank you, Mr. Buford, thank you very much." Mary waved good-bye as she left Sherman's General Store and practically skipped down Main Street until she reached the Denver Pacific Railroad depot.

"I need to send a wire," she announced as she entered the railroad office.

"Right this way, ma'am." Carl Baker, the manager of the depot and the telegraph operator, escorted Mary over to the opposite side of the depot where a high counter and the sign proclaimed the existence of an official Western Union telegraph office. He handed Mary a pencil and a slip of paper. "If you'll be so kind as to write the message out for me."

Mary took the pencil and paper and wrote:

Mr. Reese Jordan,
Trail T Ranch, Cheyenne, Wyoming Territory.

Dear Reese, I am starting a school in Utopia. Need funds for renovations. Please send enough capital to equip and supply a school of approximately twenty students, plus extra to cover the cost of turning a ballroom into a schoolroom and for emergencies. I am opening an account at—

Mary looked up at the telegrapher. "Can you tell me the correct name of the bank here in town?"

"It's called the Ajax Saloon, Bank, and Assayer's Office of Utopia, Colorado Territory," he told her. "And it's the only bank in town."

—the Ajax Saloon, Bank, and Assayer's Office of Utopia, Colorado Territory. Need funds as soon as possible as Lee is in Washington on business. Thank you. All my love to the family. Yours, Mary. P.S. Do not wire Lee for approval as this is meant as a surprise. Also, as we do not have a newspaper office in Utopia, please place advertisements announcing the opening of the Utopia School for summer term in the area papers.

She finished writing out her message and handed it to the telegrapher.

"That will be one dollar and forty-three cents," Carl told her. "Will you want to wait for a reply or have it delivered? It's an extra two bits for delivery."

Mary took the money out of her purse and added the extra twenty-five cents. "Thank you, Mr. . . ."

"Baker, ma'am. Carl Baker."

"Thank you, Mr. Baker. I'm Mary Kincaid. I'm new to Utopia. I have several more errands to run this morning." She glanced at the watch pinned to the bodice of her walking dress. "I don't expect to get an answer before I return home, so please have the reply delivered to Ettinger House as soon as you receive it."

"Yes, ma'am."

"Now, can you please tell me if the Ajax Saloon, Bank, and Assayer's Office is open this time of morning?"

The bell over the front door to the depot jangled merrily. Carl Baker looked over at his latest customer. "I'll be with you in a moment, Miss Delight, as soon as I finish with this lady."

Mary glanced over her shoulder at Mr. Baker's customer. Miss Delight was a stunningly attractive woman in her late thirties or early forties. Her blond hair shimmered beneath her bright blue feathered hat and she wore a dress fashioned after the latest Paris styles in a matching shade of blue. Mary noticed that her eyes were the same bright blue.

Carl Baker turned his attention back to Mary, but took a moment longer than necessary to reply. "Yes, ma'am, it's open."

Mary sensed something was wrong. "What's the matter? Aren't ladies allowed in the saloon to conduct banking business?"

"Yes, ma'am," Mr. Baker continued to hesitate. "Hugh Morton, that's the owner of the Ajax, allows ladies inside the saloon."

"But . . ." Mary prompted.

"Ma'am," Mr. Baker said with a rush, "he don't allow no Indians or half-breeds."

Mary recoiled as if he had slapped her. Everyone in Utopia had been so kind. Most of the town had appeared at Ettinger House for breakfast, had sat down at the table and eaten with her, yet no one had even remarked on her heritage—or refused the meal she provided, although she was sure Louisa had enlightened the townspeople about their new benefactress's bloodlines. Besides, Mary sighed, there was no sense trying to hide her heritage. Anyone could see she carried Indian blood in her veins.

She had been sheltered by her family for so long and protected and accepted into Cheyenne society, because of her family's influence and wealth, that she had forgotten how prejudiced and narrow-minded some people could be. She had related the incident that had happened to her years before at school to Lee and told him she had never forgotten it. And Mary realized she hadn't forgotten the viciousness of her classmates, the attempted rape, or her unjust dismissal from school, but she had forgotten the reason for it. She had been accepted by her close-knit family and circle of friends for so many years that she had forgotten there were people who, unlike Lee, and Maddy, and Judah, refused to accept her as a human being with thoughts, feelings, needs, and desires just like their own.

"Ma'am," Carl Baker was saying, "I didn't mean to hurt your feelings, but I thought you ought to know before you tried to go to the Ajax."

"Does he refuse admittance to all Indians and half-breeds or only poor ones?"

"He don't allow no Indians. Period. He lost a brother and his father in a massacre down in Texas before the war."

"I see." Mary turned to leave.

"Miz Kincaid, ma'am, we have cash on hand here at the Western Union office. We might be able to meet your needs."

Mary tried to smile. "Does Western Union provide banking services?"

"No, ma'am."

"I appreciate the offer, Mr. Baker, but I'm quite certain I'll need to open a bank account. I won't be able to conduct my business without access to my funds."

"What about your husband?" Carl asked. "Can't he open an account for you? He's not—" He broke off.

"No, he's Scots-Irish," Mary answered. "Or are *Irish* barred from the saloon as well?"

"No, ma'am. Some of the Ajax's best customers are Irish. Why don't you ask your husband to take care of your banking business for you?"

Mary gritted her teeth once again. She hadn't realized that the state of matrimony came with so many give-and-takes. She had given up her name and independent status when she married Lee, but she'd been given a certain amount of social freedom in return. She could, for instance, walk down the street without constant supervision or an escort with the knowledge that the wedding band on her finger protected her from some of the unwanted attention she had been subjected to as a single woman. She was also aware that Lee's name provided a certain amount of protection and status, but she hadn't known she would be considered by most men and some women to be lacking in intelligence and abilities, and required to ask permission of her husband or gain his approval simply because she was married. The Cherokee were a matriarchal society, and the men in the Jordan-Alexander family always treated the women with love, admiration, and respect. "My husband is away on business," Mary answered finally. "And I can't ask a stranger to open a bank account for me."

"You won't have to ask." The woman in the doorway stepped forward. "I apologize for eavesdropping, but I couldn't help but overhear part of your conversation. My name is Silver Delight. I have a business here in town and I would be pleased to go to the Ajax and open a bank account on your behalf."

Carl Baker moved to stand between Silver Delight and Mary. "Miss Delight, you ought not to approach a lady like Miz Kincaid in a public place. People might get the wrong idea about her."

Silver fixed Carl with an icy blue stare. "Some people already have the wrong idea about her," Silver replied. "*Some* people thinks she's a savage Indian, when anyone can see she's a lady."

"Of mixed blood," Carl said.

"But a lady nonetheless," Silver told him. "And I would be proud to help her out—or even loan her the money she needs myself."

"Thank you, Miss Delight." Mary walked around Mr.

Baker, stood before Silver Delight, and offered her hand. "I don't think a loan will be necessary, but I would greatly appreciate your help in opening a bank account."

Silver shook Mary's hand. "Fine. I'll go down to the Ajax right now."

"Oh, but you have business with Mr. Baker," Mary protested.

"No, I don't," Silver answered, as she took Mary by the arm and ushered her away from the Western Union office and Carl Baker's hearing, and out the front door of the depot. "I came here looking for you."

"Why?" Mary asked.

"I left Sherman's a few minutes ago. But while I was there, Jed Buford mentioned you were going to start a school over at the Ettinger House."

"Yes, I am," Mary answered.

"Well, Mrs. Kincaid, I'd like to talk to you about taking on a few of my girls as students."

"Your girls? You mean your daughters?"

"No, ma'am," Silver replied, "I mean my girls . . . my employees. You see, I own and operate the Silver Bear Saloon."

"The Silver Bear?" Mary thought for a moment. "That's where Judah said the young unmarried men go for—for companionship." She blushed.

"That's right," Silver said. "Look, Mrs. Kincaid, I'll be frank with you. I'm what some people call a madam. I employ young women who provide sexual services for the men in town."

"I see." Mary felt her face turn even redder as she struggled to pretend a sophistication she didn't feel.

"Business is off at the saloon," Silver continued. "It's like Mr. Crane said, except that there aren't enough young unmarried men in Utopia anymore. Or *any* men—young, old, married, or unmarried."

"Why have you stayed?" Mary asked as they walked down the street toward the Ajax Saloon.

"It's my home," Silver replied honestly. "The Silver Bear isn't much, but it's mine. I worked hard and saved my money and I bought it. I thought about moving on, but it isn't as easy as one would think for a woman like me to start over in another town. At least in Utopia, I know my customers. I know what to expect and how to protect my girls. In another town . . ." She shrugged her shoulders. "If it was just me, I might leave, but I've got the girls to consider."

"How?"

"Let's just say that in another town things would be different. My business can be dangerous if you don't know who you're dealing with, and if I left Utopia, I'd be starting from scratch, building my clientele, learning my customers' likes and dislikes along with the girls. When I heard that the late Mrs. Gray's brother and his wife had come to take over the mine, I decided to stick it out and see if there was any chance of the mine reopening."

"I don't know," Mary answered honestly. "I haven't been to the mine yet and neither has my husband. We haven't yet spoken to the mine engineers about the possibility of reopening."

"Would you consider it?" Silver asked.

"Of course, we'll consider it," Mary told her. "The mine is Madeline's inheritance, and we would like to have it operating and earning income not only for Maddy but for Utopia."

"That's all I'll ask," Silver promised. "You see, Mrs. Kincaid, I really want to stay in Utopia and so do most of the girls. But we don't have very many customers these days. I'm lucky. I've been operating the Silver Bear long enough to have made my fortune, but the girls haven't. They're bored with nothing to do and no money to spend. And if Utopia dies, so does my business: I won't be able to keep the girls on. That's the problem, because most of my employees can't read or write. Farming and ranching and the kind of work they're doing is the only thing they know how to do. But none of them are likely to meet a farmer or a rancher in Utopia. So, when Jed mentioned that you were starting a school, I realized it might be a solution to my problem. If the girls had an education, they could find other work in other towns and wouldn't be dependent on places like mine."

"So, you're asking me to enroll your girls in school so they can have an opportunity to better themselves."

"That's it. Exactly." Silver nodded, the blue feathers on her hat bobbing up and down. "I'm asking you to clear the way so the miners' wives won't raise an outcry if my girls show up at your school."

"How many girls are we talking about?" Mary asked, already making a mental list to see if she needed to order more desks and more supplies.

"Three or four," Silver answered. "I have two seventeen-year-olds, one eighteen-year-old, and one who swears she's sixteen, but I suspect she's younger—thirteen or fourteen."

Mary stared at the madam, a stern schoolteacher expression on her face.

"I didn't recruit them into the business, Mrs. Kincaid," Silver said quickly. "One's pa left her on my doorstep and rode away, two are orphans I found starving on the streets in Denver, and one came begging me for a job and food and shelter. I couldn't turn them out any more than you could discontinue Tabitha's Gray's practice of feeding the town." She came to a stop outside the door to the Ajax Saloon, Bank, and Assayer's Office.

"No, I guess you couldn't," Mary agreed.

"Will you take them on?"

"I plan to have uniforms made for all the students—two dresses of navy serge for warm weather and two dresses of navy wool for cold weather and trousers and shirts for the boys—so the mothers don't have to worry about providing decent school clothes. Your girls are accustomed to wearing . . . different kinds of clothes. Will they agree to the uniforms and the rules?"

"Yes, ma'am," Silver said. "And since I'm quite a good seamstress, I'll help you make the uniforms. I'll make certain the girls are in school every day and on time and scrubbed clean like the other girls. And I'll see that they do their homework and go to bed early."

"What about their jobs?" Mary asked. "How will they earn money?"

Silver laughed. "We haven't had enough upstairs customers lately for it to matter. Just saloon business. But I've already thought about the money and I decided to pay the girls to go to school, at a reduced rate of course, but at least they'll be making something."

"Can you afford to do that?"

"Yes, ma'am. Like I said, I've put aside some money for my old age." Silver extended her hand. "I'll take care of opening your bank account for you whether you take the girls on or not, but I'd like to know if we have a deal so I can go home and tell the girls about it. Have we or haven't we?"

Mary reached out and shook the other woman's hand. "It's a deal, Miss Delight."

Silver pumped Mary's hand several times. "Call me Silver. No, never mind that, call me Syl. My real name's Sylvia."

Mary laughed. "Call me Mary," she said. "I think we're about to become friends as well as business associates."

"Who would have ever thought it?" Silver asked. "A madam and a schoolteacher becoming friends." She laughed along with Mary, then turned and entered the Ajax Saloon.

Minutes later, Mary Alexander Kincaid became the first half-breed Indian to have an account at Hugh Morton's Ajax Saloon bank.

Chapter
Nineteen

"Hello, Edwin," Lee said as he entered the Pennsylvania Avenue office of Edwin Carraway, Comptroller of the Currency of the United States.

A tall, spare man with graying hair and spectacles, Edwin Carraway came from very wealthy Maryland family—a family that had managed to stay loyal to the Union during the war. And Edwin Carraway had lived to see his loyalty rewarded by receiving a coveted Cabinet post from President Grant.

"Hello, my boy." Edwin rushed over to Lee, gripped his hand in a firm handshake, then embraced him.

"It's been a long time," Lee said as Edwin released him.

"It has indeed." A sheen of tears sparkled in Edwin's brown eyes. He walked back to his desk and sat down. "I've kept up with your career through the years, up until recently. I know a lot about you, Lee. I know you travel a great deal, that you take needless risks at times, and that you've barely touched the money. I know almost everything about your career. My friends have kept me informed. Allan Pinkerton kept me informed. You're looking very well, my boy. Very well."

"So are you." Lee continued to stand in the doorway, awkwardly gripping the brim of his hat. He hadn't realized until this moment how much he liked and trusted Edwin

Carraway and how much he had missed his companionship.

Edwin motioned him forward to a chair. "Now, come in, my boy. Come in and sit down and tell me what brings you to see me after all these years."

Lee sat down on the chair across from the desk and stared at Edwin. For four brief months, from April to July, back in sixty-one, Edwin Carraway had been his father-in-law. And in the twelve years since that time, Lee Kincaid had been ashamed to face his father-in-law. "I've come on business, Edwin. And I've come to ask a favor."

"I see." Edwin sat back in his chair, rested his elbows on the chair arms, and steepled his fingers in front of his face. "I'll do my best to help you, Lee, you know that. Are you still with Pinkerton?"

"Yes," Lee said. "But I'll be retiring soon. I'm working on my last case."

"Tying up loose ends before you move on again?" Edwin asked, probing but not pushing for answers.

Lee took a deep breath. "No, Edwin, this time I'm tying up loose ends before settling down."

Edwin nodded silently.

"What do you know about Senator Warner Millen?" Lee asked.

Carraway smiled. "I heard someone had been asking questions about the late senator, but I had no idea you were in town doing the asking."

"I was asking questions before the senator's death," Lee informed him. "Someone else has been asking questions since his death. But it's nice to know the Washington grapevine is fairly accurate."

"I'd met the man many times," Edwin said. "Socially and once or twice on business. But I can't say I ever actually knew or liked him."

"What do you know about his business dealings?"

"I heard he had become involved with some rather

questionable individuals and made several questionable business deals. I heard he was losing rather large amounts of money at the gaming tables."

"Losing or paying out?" Lee asked.

"I heard he was losing money at the tables," Edwin answered. "But I remember thinking it rather odd, as I had never heard anyone mention seeing the Senator at the usual gambling dens in and around Washington."

Lee knew that his former father-in-law knew just about everybody in Washington. Carraway was respected and well-liked, reliable, and a man of impeccable reputation. People trusted Edwin Carraway and they tended to say things in his presence, things they would ordinarily keep to themselves. Carraway was the type of man Pinkerton loved, the type of man Pinkerton tried to recruit. And Lee was aware that Edwin would never betray a confidence—that he was only talking to Lee now because they were old friends, and because they had once been family. Almost father and son.

"And what have you heard about a man named Sarrazin? James Sarrazin?"

"Millen's secretary?"

Lee nodded.

"Not much, although I personally find him to be rather repulsive." Edwin made a face. "He rather reminds me of a snake, always slithering around, doing his best to blend into the background. He's the sort of fellow the average person would choose as a spy. Not at all like the real thing, of course." Edwin winked at Lee.

"Have you heard of Sarrazin going on any spending sprees lately?" Lee asked.

"Not at all. But then, I confess I haven't been paying much attention to the likes of James Sarrazin. I've been busy with this cabinet appointment and the rash of counterfeit bills we've been getting in."

"Counterfeit bills?"

"Aaha!" Edwin exclaimed, "Now I can ask *you* a favor. I understand you're something of an expert in the field. At least Pinkerton thinks so." He opened his top desk drawer, removed a small stack of bills, leaned forward and handed them to Lee along with a large magnifying glass. "What do you think of those?"

Lee studied the bills under the magnifying glass. "They're very good. Damn near perfect. But he has a little problem with the eyes. They're not quite right. I've seen bills like this before." Lee put down the magnifying glass and looked at Edwin. "Where did you get these?"

"From the western territories. They were in circulation in Denver, Cheyenne, Omaha, and Council Bluffs."

"Cheyenne and Omaha are on the Union Pacific main line. Council Bluffs is at the intersection of the Chicago Rock Island, Sioux City and Pacific, and Kansas City St. Joseph railroad lines. Denver is located on the spur line Denver Pacific which joins the Union Pacific at Cheyenne." Lee paused and thought for a moment. "My guess is that your counterfeiters are working in or around Cheyenne or Denver. Probably Cheyenne."

"That's what Pinkerton said when I contacted him," Edwin told him. "Are you interested in taking on the case?"

Lee shook his head. "I'll do what I can to help you, Edwin, while I'm with the Agency, but I plan to resign in less than ninety days. After that, someone else will have to take over."

"Fair enough," Edwin agreed. "Do you have a replacement in mind? I want the best and I need to know for whom to ask."

Lee grinned at the older man and his mustache tilted to one side. "Willis. Daniel Willis."

"Thank you," Edwin replied, quickly jotting down the

name. "Now, is there anything else you want to ask me? Any other gossip you can pry out of me?"

"Just one more thing," Lee admitted. "Have you heard anyone mention David Alexander's name lately?"

"David Alexander . . . Alexander . . . where did I hear that name?" Edwin snapped his fingers. "I've got it! David Alexander was the name of Senator Millen's attorney. The attorney the senator practically ran out of Washington. What's it been? A year or two ago?"

"That's right. Have you heard anyone talking about him during the last couple of weeks? Since Senator Millen died?"

"No." Edwin shook his head. "Nothing except the usual gossip. Rumors of an intimate relationship between Alexander and the senator's daughter. I doubt that there was any truth to the rumors, though. The majority of the stories came from the senator and his cronies. And I can't give much credence to the truth of such rumors when a man is dragging his own daughter's reputation through the mud."

Lee nodded.

"Is this Alexander fellow a client of yours?" Edwin asked.

"Yes," Lee answered. "A client and a very good friend." He paused, gathering his thoughts, trying to decide how to break the news to Edwin. Lee took another deep breath and slowly let it out, then plunged ahead. "There's a reason for my sudden retirement from the agency. The truth of the matter is that David Alexander is not only a client and a good friend, he's my brother-in-law. I remarried a little over a week ago."

Edwin stared at his desk blotter for a few moments, then looked up at Lee. Tears shimmered in his eyes once again. "It's time, my boy. It's past time. Twelve years." He nodded. "Twelve long years. Congratulations, Lee, I'm sure your bride is a fine young woman."

"Thank you, Edwin." Lee felt awkward, and yet he felt Edwin Carraway deserved an explanation. "I felt it was time to settle down—again."

Edwin stood up and walked around his desk to stand beside Lee's chair. "I have a meeting with the Secretary of Treasury in—" He took out his pocket watch, snapped open the lid, and checked the time. "About fifteen minutes. I hate to cut this short, my boy, but you know where to find me if you need to ask me more questions. It's good to see you again, Lee. I've missed you. Promise me you won't wait another twelve years before coming to see me again."

Lee didn't respond. His gaze was fixed on the twin photographs in the cover of Edwin's watch. Jeannie Carraway and her mother, Joan. Jeannie Carraway, the girl he had promised to love, honor, and protect. Edwin's only child, his only daughter. But Lee had failed in his duty. He had loved her and honored her, even honored her memory, but he had failed to protect Jeannie—failed to protect her from herself, and that headstrong willfulness of youth.

Edwin quietly snapped the lid of his watch closed, then placed his hand on Lee's shoulder. "It wasn't your fault, Lee. And God knows, you've never done anything to disappoint me. I'm as proud of you now, of the man you've become, as I was the day Jeannie married you."

"If I hadn't left her at the house with Patrick . . . he was supposed to look out for her. But I should have known he wouldn't stand firm around her. She could always twist him around her fingers. If I had insisted she go stay with you, then maybe . . ." Lee closed his eyes. It had been twelve years since he had last seen Jeannie Carraway. Twelve years since he'd dared to look at a picture of her because he had been haunted by his memories of her. But now, when he closed his eyes, all he saw was Mary. Mary pulling a gun on him the first time he met her. Mary dancing with him at David and Tessa's wedding. Mary standing at the altar in a white dress, solemnly repeating her wedding vows. Mary dressed in a white ruffled nightgown. Mary running down Utopia's Main Street to tie a red ribbon around his upper arm. Mary. Lee raked his fingers through his hair. After deliberately omitting a huge chunk of his personal history, how the hell was he ever going to work up the courage to tell Mary he had been married before? After telling her about Tabby and seeing her reaction to Tabby's ultimatum, how could he break the news about Jeannie Carraway? He glanced at Edwin and realized his former father-in-law was speaking. Remembering.

"Jeannie was a strong-willed young woman. She had a mind of her own. She loved everyone and everyone loved her. We spoiled her, Lee. You and I, and even your father, Patrick. After you left for the war, she got it in her mind to ride out and watch the first battle. Patrick and I thought we had convinced her how dangerous it could be, that the battle to come wouldn't be an afternoon picnic. But she didn't believe that. She played along, Lee. She led us to believe she had forgotten all about riding out to watch the battle, then that morning, she did exactly what she wanted to do. She saddled her horse and rode out to watch her husband—her hero—whip the rebels. But it didn't turn out that way." Edwin wiped at the tears rolling down his face. "The Union forces lost that battle, and Jeannie was killed by a stray bullet."

"It shouldn't have happened," Lee insisted. "If only she had listened to me, listened to you. If only Patrick had done what he promised to do."

Edwin tightened his grip on Lee's shoulder. "You're right, it shouldn't have happened, but it did. And Jeannie's dead because she did something utterly foolish. She disobeyed you and me and Patrick. She got *herself* killed, my boy. We had nothing to do with it." Carraway sighed. "You waited long enough. It was time for you to remarry, Lee. Now, it's time for you to forgive Jeannie for being young and foolish and terribly in love with you, and to forgive me . . ."

"I never blamed you, Edwin."

"No," Edwin agreed. "You blamed yourself and you blamed Patrick for something he couldn't prevent. Lee, your father did his best to keep his promise. That's all any man can do. Forgive him, Lee. Forgive yourself."

Lee listened to Edwin's words and braced himself against the gut-wrenching pain that always came to him at the thought of Jeannie, at the mention of her name. But the pain and guilt that had torn him apart, that had ripped at his heart for so many years, was gone. Today, there was only sorrow and, for the first time in twelve years, Lee Kincaid felt at peace. Now, he could remember Jeannie—remember *loving* Jeannie Carraway—and smile.

Lee got to his feet and extended his hand in farewell. "Thank you again, Edwin."

"You're welcome, my boy," Edwin grasped Lee's hand once again and squeezed it hard. "Don't stay away so long next time. I'm here and you're always welcome. You're family, Lee, the only family I have left. It's time you accepted that. When Jeannie married you, you became my son. And she may have died, but you remained my son. Come back to see me, my boy. Bring your bride and your little girl."

A look of astonishment appeared on Lee's face as he stared at his former father-in-law.

Edwin opened his desk drawer once again, removed several papers, and handed them to Lee.

Lee recognized the stationery. The Agency's logo, the "Pinkerton Eye," stared back at him.

"Like I said," Edwin winked, "my friends keep me informed. I knew all about Tabitha Gray. And I'm looking forward to meeting Mary and Madeline."

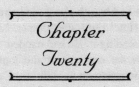

Chapter
Twenty

"My name is Lee Gordon," Lee announced to the very proper British butler who opened the door to the late Senator Millen's Georgetown house two days later. "And I'm here to see Mrs. Millen."

"Mrs. Millen isn't receiving visitors."

"I think she'll see me," Lee told him.

"The lady isn't seeing anyone." The butler attempted to close the door in Lee's face, but Lee anticipated the move and stopped him.

"Tell her I'm a representative from her late husband's bank. Tell her I've come to talk to her about some very large withdrawals made before and immediately after the senator's death." Lee reached into his suit pocket and pulled out a crisp white calling card with the words: Lee M. Gordon, Representative, Washington National Bank, printed on the front and handed it to the butler. "Oh, and be sure to tell her that if she refuses to see me, there will be a Senate investigation into alleged wrongdoings by the late Senator Warner Millen."

"Very good, sir. Wait here." The butler accepted Lee's calling card and withdrew into the interior of the house, leaving Lee standing on the stoop with the front door wide open. He patted the pocket of his canvas duster. Inside the pocket was a red leather-bound journal—Caroline Millen's journal. Anne Greenbery had given it to Willis at dinner last night, and Willis had had the book delivered to Lee's room at the Madison Hotel right after dinner. Lee had spent the rest of the night reading it. He had napped, breakfasted with Willis to discuss the contents of the journal, and finally ridden out to Georgetown to talk to Caroline's mother. Willis was waiting in a carriage down the block in case Sarrazin made an appearance.

Now, he stood listening as the British butler approached Mrs. Millen.

"I refuse to see anyone, Powell. Send him away."

"But, Madame, the gentleman says if you refuse to see him you will face a Senate investigation into your husband's, the late senator's, business and financial dealings."

"Who is this man?" Mrs. Millen asked.

"He says his name is Lee Gordon and that he's a representative from your husband's bank."

"The bank? Don't keep him waiting, Powell. Send him in."

Powell returned to the foyer and stiffly ushered Lee inside. "Madame will see you now."

"So I heard," Lee replied with a grin as he removed his hat and followed the butler into the sitting room. Powell announced Lee, then retreated, as Mrs. Millen dismissed him.

The butler left the sitting room doors open, but Lee took it upon himself to close them.

"Mr. Gordon." Mrs. Millen rose from her chair behind her writing desk. She slipped her hand out of her skirt pocket and approached Lee as he finished pulling the doors closed.

He turned to face her. He had seen Mrs. Millen from a distance at the senator's funeral but he hadn't gotten close enough to discern her features. And she wasn't at all what Lee expected. She was younger than he imagined and tiny, less than five feet tall, with blond hair and blue-green eyes.

Dressed completely in black mourning and veil, Mrs. Millen resembled a younger, slimmer Queen Victoria. She was small in build and stature, but her voice was impressive. It was deep, well-modulated, and regal, and with a hint of Great Britain about it. Lee had the feeling she practiced her speech in front of her mirror, practiced ordering lesser beings around. She came to a halt in front of him and extended her hand for him to kiss. "I'm Cassandra Millen."

Lee stared at her fingers shrouded in her black lace half-gloves and declined the role of subject. He didn't lift her hand to his lips, but shook it instead. "Lee Gordon."

Cassandra Millen shot him a dirty look, turned, and walked back to her chair and seated herself. "I understand you've come from the bank about my late husband's account."

"No, ma'am." Lee smiled his most charming smile.

"But Powell said . . ."

"I confess to misleading your butler, Mrs. Millen, in order to gain an audience with you."

"What are you?" Mrs. Millen jumped to her feet. "Some reporter for some scandal sheet? Have you come here looking for a story?"

"No, ma'am, I've come to tell you that I already know the story. I work for the Pinkerton National Detective Agency, and David Alexander retained me to—"

"Get out! How dare come into my house under false pretenses and mention that man's name?"

"I dare because I know the truth about David Alexander and your daughter, Caroline. I know that there was nothing between them. I know that your daughter died giving birth to your grandchild—a daughter whose name was legally recorded as Lily Catherine Alexander on the seventh day of January, eighteen hundred seventy-one in a courthouse in a little town on the outskirts of Philadelphia. I know Lily's real father was a married Shakespearean actor named

Tristan Darrow, and that Tristan Darrow had intimate relations with your daughter, Caroline, while he was traveling with a London touring company. I even know the times and places."

"Don't be lewd," she snapped.

"I'm not being lewd, Mrs. Millen," Lee explained. "I'm being honest."

"I don't know what you're talking about," she said. "I don't know anything about a Shakespearean actor. I only know that David Alexander took advantage of my child. Where did you come by this sordid information? Who told you this pack of lies?"

"Caroline," Lee answered softly.

"That's impossible. Caroline is dead."

Lee pulled the journal out of his pocket.

Mrs. Millen gasped.

"Recognize this?" Lee asked. "It belonged to your daughter, Caroline. According to the inscription, you gave it to her for Christmas in the year of our Lord, eighteen hundred and seventy. She recorded her thoughts and deeds every single day until the first week of June when you and Senator Millen sent her to stay with an acquaintance in that little town outside of Philadelphia."

"Oh, my God," Cassandra breathed. "Where did you get that? And what do you plan to do with it? Blackmail me too?"

"Caroline gave her journal to a friend for safekeeping. Your daughter recorded all the intimate details of her romance with Darrow and she was afraid you might come across the journal and read it."

"I would never!"

"She didn't feel she could take the chance. And her friend only agreed to part with the journal after your husband"— Lee chose his next words deliberately—"killed himself."

"You must be mistaken," Cassandra Millen insisted. "My husband died of heart failure."

"No, he didn't," Lee corrected her. "He died in his office of a self-inflicted gunshot wound to the head. And we have people who will testify to having heard the shot and seen your husband's body."

"Are you planning to smear the senator's good name and blackmail me with that information, as well?"

"I don't intend to blackmail you at all, Mrs. Millen. I'm here to find the man who is blackmailing you, have him arrested, and locate your granddaughter."

"Don't call her that!"

"Why not?" Lee asked. "Lily Catherine is your grand-daughter."

"That child is a half-breed Indian." Cassandra replied derisively. "And no kin of mine."

"Lily Catherine may bear David Alexander's last name, but she is not his child. Tristan Darrow is her father and your daughter was her mother," Lee pointed out. "That makes you her grandmother whether you choose to accept it or not."

"I choose not to accept it," Mrs. Millen said. "I choose not to recognize that illegitimate spawn as part of my family."

"I'm relieved to hear it," Lee answered. "Because I think an innocent child deserves better than to have an embittered, narrow-minded old woman for a grandmother."

"I am not old."

Lee thought it telling that the only insult Mrs. Millen reacted to was the reference to her age. "Then you refuse to claim Lily Catherine? Refuse to recognize her?"

"Of course I do. And what business is it of yours anyway? Why do you want to know?"

Lee smiled. "I'm asking on behalf of David Alexander

and his wife, Tessa Roarke Alexander. They wish to adopt Lily Catherine as their own."

"Whyever would they want to do that?" Cassandra Millen couldn't contain her curiosity. "Why does he want the child now? She won't inherit any of my money."

"David Alexander isn't interested in your money. He's only interested in the welfare of the child that legally bears his name."

"If he's so interested, why didn't he marry my daughter when the senator th . . ."

"Threatened to ruin him?" Lee smiled at Mrs. Millen once again. "David didn't think he should be forced to pay for another man's sins. He didn't love your daughter. He barely knew her. And unlike you and the senator, David and Tessa don't care about Lily Catherine's origins. They only care about her welfare. David hates the idea that a child with his name will one day grow up to think her father abandoned her. He and Tessa feel Lily Catherine shouldn't be made to suffer for her parents' sins any more than David should have had to pay for Darrow's. They want her, and they'll give her a good home and a loving family." Lee paused, trying to gauge Cassandra Millen's reaction. Her face remained impassive. He couldn't tell if his appeal had made any impression at all.

"I don't know where she is," Cassandra lied.

"I think you do," Lee countered. "The senator paid his secretary, James Sarrazin, to provide a home for Lily. But Sarrazin got greedy and demanded more money than the senator was willing to pay. I think the senator stopped paying and Sarrazin threatened to reveal what he knew about the whole affair between Tristan Darrow and Caroline and how your husband had used his power and influence to defame David Alexander, to ruin his political aspirations and his Washington practice—and all because David Alexander refused to marry Caroline to prevent a scandal."

"But Caroline named her child Lily Catherine Alexander anyway. We had the name recorded. As far as the law is concerned, it's her legal name."

"But there was no marriage."

"The marriage didn't matter. Caroline knew she was dying. She begged us to record the last name as Alexander. The only thing that mattered was that her child not be branded a bastard." Cassandra began to cry. "Caroline wanted to name her little girl Lily Cassandra after me, but I refused. She named her Lily Catherine instead. The senator didn't want to put Alexander down. He was afraid someone would find out that he had paid to have a marriage license between David and Caroline forged and legally recorded, so the birth would be legitimate."

"There is a forged marriage certificate?" Lee hadn't known that. "Who did it?"

"I don't know. Mr. Sarrazin hired someone to do it."

"Who has it?"

"My husband did have it, but it disappeared from his safe," Mrs. Millen told him. "Sarrazin took it. He used it to blackmail the senator for money, and when my husband died, Sarrazin used it to blackmail me."

"And you have no idea who forged the marriage document?"

"No. Only that Mr. Sarrazin had known the man for years. He said they worked together on occasion," Cassandra admitted.

"Thank you." Lee grabbed his hat.

"What are you going to do now that I've told you?" she asked.

"I'm going to go get Lily Catherine if you'll tell me where she is—which orphanage she's in."

"She's not in an orphanage. She never was. Lily Catherine has been living with James Sarrazin's mother in a row house in Philadelphia since the day of her birth. Mr.

Sarrazin arranged everything. That's one of the reasons he felt he could blackmail us."

"But David Alexander thought . . ."

"The story about the orphanage was a ruse my husband told Mr. Alexander to discourage him from trying to find the little girl."

Lee took a sheaf of papers out of his suit pocket. "This is a legal document drawn up by David Alexander stating that you agree to relinquish all claim to the child known as Lily Catherine Alexander."

"I don't think that will be necessary," Cassandra Millen said softly.

"David asked me to have you sign it."

She nodded, then stood up, drew herself up to her full height, took the papers from Lee, walked over to her writing desk and opened the lid. She retrieved a pen from inside the desk, then signed her name to the papers with a flourish. She handed the papers back to Lee. "What now? What are you going to do to me? What about the possibility of a senate investigation?"

"I don't know, Mrs. Millen. That's up to your late husband's colleagues."

"Can't you make sure the Senate doesn't start probing into Warner's business? Can't you use your influence?"

"I don't have any influence, Mrs. Millen. I'm just a detective." Lee turned to leave. Cassandra Millen followed him out of the room, down the hall, through the foyer to the front door.

"If a senate committee should investigate, and if you're called to testify, what will you tell the committee about the senator's role in all this? What about our good name and our reputation? What will you tell them about me?"

"I don't think there is anything I could tell the good people of Washington about you and the senator that they don't already know," Lee said. "But if I'm called to testify,

Mrs. Millen, I'll tell the truth. The pure, unadulterated truth about this whole sordid affair." Lee tipped his hat to her and turned away. He made it down five steps before she spoke.

"I was afraid you'd say that."

Something in her tone of voice warned him. Lee turned back to face her. The glow of the porch lamps beside the front door glinted off the silver gun barrel.

Seconds later, he felt a burning pain in his side as Cassandra Millen shot him. Lee pressed a hand to his side and staggered backward down the last step. Closing his eyes against the pain, he flinched at the sound of another shot and waited for more pain. It never came.

Lee opened his eyes.

Cassandra Millen lay dead on the porch with the gun still clutched in her hand.

Chapter
Twenty-one

"Lee!" Willis jumped out of the carriage at the sound of the shot and ran the half block to the Millen house. He found Lee lying on the bottom step.

Mrs. Millen was lying on the stoop. The butler stood in the open doorway. "She's dead, sir," he said as Willis started toward the senator's wife.

Willis turned back to Lee and half-lifted him from the step. "Christ," Willis muttered beneath his breath as he felt Lee's warm blood seeping through the layers of his clothing. Willis pressed his ear to Lee's chest, then breathed a sigh of relief when he heard the steady thump of his heart. He tore open Lee's jacket, waistcoat, and shirt, trying to locate and gauge the severity of Lee's wound. "You were just supposed to talk to her. What happened?"

Lee opened his eyes and gritted his teeth against the pain. "She shot me."

Willis glanced over his shoulder at the butler, silently asking for confirmation.

Powell nodded his head. "It happened just as Mr. Gordon said. Madame shot him, then turned the gun on herself."

Lee sucked in a breath as he tried to look down at the wound. "How bad is it?"

"I can't tell," Willis answered. "You're bleeding like a stuck pig. We've got to get you to a hospital."

"No hospital," Lee said. He had seen enough army hospitals during the war to have a permanent loathing of the stench and suffering of the surgeon's workplace. "Take me to the hotel." He struggled to get to his feet.

"What about Mrs. Millen?" the butler asked.

"Police." Lee bit out. "Send someone for the police."

"But there will be scandal," the butler replied, appalled by the idea.

"What does it matter?" Willis asked. "She's dead, Millen's dead, and their daughter is dead—there is nobody left to be affected by a scandal." He turned his attention back to Lee. "Can you make it to the carriage?"

Lee shook his head.

"Then wait here. I'll be right back."

"Lily Catherine," Lee whispered, grabbing at Willis's coat. "I know where she is. We've got to go after her."

Willis shook his head. "You're not going anywhere except to a doctor."

Lee woke up three days later in the Washington Hospital ward. Daniel Willis sat in a chair by his side. "I *told* you no hospitals."

"Yeah, well, the Madison Hotel has a no-admittance policy for gunshot victims. It seems they can't run the risk of having people die in their establishment."

"What day is it?" Lee rubbed his aching head. There was a knot the size of a hen's egg at the base of his skull.

"Tuesday, the sixth," Willis answered.

"I slept for three days?" Damn! Mary's birthday was the tenth of May and Lee didn't intend to miss it. He had big plans for her twenty-ninth birthday celebration and he still had to pick up the presents he'd ordered. But he had to finish his business with Willis before he could get Mary's gifts.

"You hit your head on the steps when you fell. You

suffered a concussion, but the doctor says that with plenty of rest, you'll be fine."

"What about Mrs. Millen?"

Willis shook his head. "Suicide."

Lee winced. "The journal?" It had been in the pocket of his duster when he fell. He could only hope his blood hadn't made it illegible.

"It's fine. Most of your blood was absorbed by the drawers." Willis chuckled. "And I've been waiting for three days to ask you what you were doing with a pair of ladies' underwear and two hair ribbons in your coat pocket!"

"My wife's," Lee replied as if his explanation answered Willis's question or satisfied the younger man's curiosity. He hated the thought that Mary's lacy drawers and his two favors had been stained by his blood.

"Oh. I didn't know you were married." Willis shrugged his shoulders. "Well, the sisters managed to get out most of the blood. They're not as white as they once were, but your wife's under . . . clothing . . . is serviceable once again."

"Ribbons?" He grunted the question as he pushed himself up against the pillows and flipped back the covers.

"They were laundered as well. They turned out fine. I think the sisters put everything back where they found it."

"Sarrazin?"

Willis shook his head again. "No sign of him yet, but we have men watching the Millen House and the senator's office. And I still have men checking the orphanages in and around Philadelphia for Lily Catherine."

"Forget the orphanages." Lee struggled out of bed.

"You shouldn't be up. You lost a lot of blood," Willis told him. "And you're damn lucky to be alive. A few inches higher or lower and she might have killed you."

Lee glanced down at the neatly bandaged place in his side. He was stiff and sore and his muscles ached from three days of inactivity, but the burning pain in his side had faded to a dull ache and Lee figured that meant that the bullet hadn't lodged in his body or done serious damage. "Did they get the bullet out?"

"It passed right through and out the other side. That's why you bled so much."

Lee nodded. "Millen lied to David about the orphanage. Lily Catherine is with Sarrazin's mother. She lives in a row house in Philadelphia."

"I know."

"You know? How?"

"You must have told me a thousand times over the past three days while you were unconscious. I had agents in Philadelphia canvassing the neighborhoods. They're gone, Lee. The neighbors say Sarrazin moved his mother and the little girl to New York."

"Damn him to hell and back!" Lee leaned against the bedpost and gasped for breath. "Hand me my pants, would you?"

Willis did as Lee asked and calmly handed over the trousers. "Where do you think you're going?"

"New York."

"You're in no condition to travel to New York. Besides, you've been relieved of duty. I telegraphed Robert Pinkerton in New York. He has men searching for Lily Catherine now. Your orders are to stay in bed and rest until further notice."

"Can't." Lee managed the one word as he struggled into his trousers.

"Why not?"

"I promised myself I'd find Lily Catherine before I go home. And I've got to be home before May tenth."

"We've got a dozen men searching for Lily Catherine. Right now, you'd just be in the way. Rest up, Lee, so you can go home. I promise to send word to you when we locate

Sarrazin and the little girl. Besides, what's so important about May tenth?" Willis wanted to know.

"It's Mary's birthday."

Willis looked blank.

"My wife, Mary. I'm missing our honeymoon now, but I sure as hell don't intend to miss her birthday."

"You've got four days left."

Lee shook his head. "It takes two and a half days to get there. And I need to pick up the gifts I ordered for my wife. And there's the gift I'm having delivered to my hotel room."

"You rest," Willis suggested. "Tell me what you need to have done. I'll do it."

"You serious?" Lee asked amazed.

"If surprising your wife with a birthday present means this much to you, I'll be happy to pick up your gifts for you. Besides"—Willis grinned—"Robert Pinkerton sent word that he would have my head and my job if I let you out of bed before the doctor says you can go." He pulled a little notebook and a pencil out of his coat pocket. "So give me your list."

Lee took a deep breath, then began to list everything he had ordered for Mary's birthday. Well, almost everything. There were some presents money just couldn't buy.

Lee's wound healed very nicely, and a day and a half later he walked out of the hospital and boarded a train headed west. He managed to sleep during most of the journey so he was well rested when the special mail train chugged into the Utopia depot after eleven on Friday evening, May ninth. Lee was the only passenger.

"You need any help, Mr. Kincaid?" Ned Sampson had been awakened by the train whistle. Ned could see that Lee had his hands full, so he hurried forward to help with his leather satchel and the brown paper-wrapped bundles Lee gripped by their strings.

Lee dropped his satchel on the platform, then nudged it with his foot. "Bring that by the house in the morning, Ned, and leave it on the front porch." His satchel contained several changes of clothes and his little tool kit, but nothing vital.

"What's that you've got in the front of your shirt, Mr. Kincaid?"

Lee glanced down to see a black and gray furry little head sticking out from the vee of his waistcoat. He reached up and patted the puppy. "A birthday present."

"For Maddy?"

"No," Lee said with a smile. "For Mary." The terrier pup was only one of the presents Lee had for Mary and, like the others, he had carried it with him. Lee flipped a coin to the porter. "Thanks, Ned."

Lee walked down Main Street. The soft glow of the street lights barely penetrated the darkness. Fortunately, he was accustomed to the darkness, accustomed to negotiating muddy streets and sidewalks, unfriendly dogs, and frightened neighbors. A dog barked in the distance. The puppy whimpered and Lee reached up again to soothe him. "We're almost home, fella. We'll have you settled into a nice warm bed by the fire in no time." Lee had to admit that he was looking forward to settling into a nice warm bed himself—and lighting a fire—with Mary.

He reached the fence surrounding Camelot, as he had dubbed Ettinger House, unlatched the wrought-iron front gate and stepped inside the yard. Lee took the puppy out of his shirt and put him down on the ground, and while he waited to the puppy to tend to nature, Lee stared up at the outside of the house. It was dark except for the dim light glowing at the window of a second story bedroom. Lee smiled. His bedroom.

Minutes later, Lee located the terrier pup, picked him up

and put him back into his shirtfront. Lee stepped up onto the porch and reached out to open the front door.

It was locked. Lee patted his coat pockets, then his trouser pockets, searching for his key, but it wasn't there. He checked the pockets of his duster, but except for Mary's drawers and the two hair ribbons, his duster pockets were empty as well. Never mind, Lee told himself, he was a master at breaking and entering. He could easily pick the lock. He reached for his ever-present leather satchel before he remembered that he had left it with Ned Sampson at the depot. So Lee reached into his duster pocket for Mary's unmentionables. He wrapped the muslin around his hand and stared at the stained glass panel of King Arthur beside the front door. The stained glass picture was a work of art. Lee couldn't bring himself to break it. That left the windows.

Moving as quietly as possible along the porch, Lee walked over to the floor to ceiling windows of the red parlor and found the wooden shutters were locked. He couldn't get to the window without breaking the shutters. He checked the windows along the front porch. They were all shuttered and locked. Lee stroked one side of his mustache absentmindedly. Hell's bells! Mary had the place sealed as tight as a fortress. He could yell for Mary to come downstairs, but he didn't want to risk waking Maddy or Judah. This was the night he planned to make love to his wife. To show Mary, once and for all, how he felt about her, and he didn't want Judah or Maddy interrupting it. But yelling for Mary was better than scaling the walls to the second floor and Lee knew he might have to resort to yelling. While he felt he was perfectly able to make love with his wife, he doubted he could climb to the second story to do it. And if by some miracle, he gained entrance to Mary's bedroom, Lee knew he'd be too tired to do anything about it. For now, the only other place he could try on the ground floor was the door to the kitchen.

Lee gritted his teeth and jumped off the porch. He grunted in pain as his hard landing from the high porch jarred the wound in his side. The puppy whimpered sympathetically. Using the exterior walls of the house as a guide, Lee found his way through the darkness to the kitchen door. It was also locked. But this time, Lee knew he could break in because half of the back door was paned with glass. Lee selected a window pane close to the door lock, then placed the heel of his muslin wrapped hand against the glass and pushed. Hard. His efforts were rewarded by the muffled sound of glass giving way to pressure and the satisfying sound of it shattering against the brick floor. Grinning at his success, Lee reached through the empty window frame, quickly unlocked the door, and pushed it open. Once inside the kitchen, he quietly closed the door. The broken window glass crunched beneath his booted feet.

Lee took off his hat and tossed it onto the kitchen table as a signal to Louisa. Do not disturb. The head of the household was home once again and was upstairs making love to his wife. For the very first time. Lee's pulse quickened and his heart began to pound in anticipation as he negotiated the hallways leading from the kitchen to the main staircase.

"Stop right there and put your hands in the air!" Mary's voice broke through the quiet as Lee climbed the last stair to reach the landing. "I have a gun and I'll shoot."

"Don't! Please," Lee said, raising his hands slowly over his head. "Judas Priest, Mary, I've already been shot once this week."

"Lee!"

Suddenly Mary was in his arms.

Lee groaned and the puppy squirmed.

"What's this?" Mary stepped back, then placed her hand

on Lee's chest and felt the fuzzy little head. "You seem to be a little furrier than I remember," she teased.

"Come into the bedroom and find out." Lee took Mary's hand and walked down the short hallway, and through the open doorway of his bedroom.

A lamp burned low on the night table, and the quilts and sheets on the bed were thrown back and rumpled. Lee glanced over at the bed, then smiled at his wife. "Who's been sleeping in my bed?" he teased, a gruff voice.

"Me," Mary admitted.

"Have you been waiting for me? Keeping my place warm?"

"Uh huh." She nodded.

"Then close and lock the door, and come stand beside the bed by the night table," Lee ordered gently. "And close your eyes."

She did as she was bidden. "I don't like surprises," Mary said.

"You'll like this one." Lee set the terrier pup on the floor, then stood up and leaned against the bedroom door, soaking in the sight of Mary silhouetted by the light of the lamp. Her silky black hair was loose and hung nearly to her waist. He had dreamed of her this way, in her white nightgown with her hair unbound, her body exposed by the transparency of her nightgown, yet shadowed and mysterious. His body tightened in reaction.

The puppy waddled over to Mary and licked her bare toes. Lee ached to do the same. She giggled. "May I open my eyes now?"

"Not yet." Lee hurried took off his duster, his suit coat, shirt, and waistcoat. He unbuttoned his trousers, then pushed the fabric down over his lean hips. He balanced first on one foot and then the other as he removed his boots and socks.

Mary heard the whisper of fabric and the barely discernible sounds of clothing falling to the floor, following by the thump, thump of his boots. She felt herself flushing. "Lee?"

"Not yet."

When he was completely undressed except for the bandage covering his gunshot wound, Lee walked over to Mary and gently nudged her back against the bed. She reached out to him, but Lee kept his distance and didn't allow her to touch him. "Climb in bed, love."

Again Mary did as he asked without protest, but her ears picked up on Lee's casual endearment and she pressed it to her heart like a floral love token pressed in a book.

"Mary?" Lee asked softly.

"Yes?"

"Did you mean what you said about granting me your favor when I returned from Washington?"

"Yes."

"Will you trust me?"

"Yes."

"Good." With that, Lee bent at the waist, cupped his hand around the chimney of the oil lamp, and blew out the flame.

Mary smelled the kerosene smoke and came halfway out of bed. "No! Lee! The dark!"

Lee put his hands on her shoulders and gently pressed her back against the mattress. He could feel the rapid pounding of her heart beneath him and could almost taste her fear. "It's all right, Mary. We'll light the lamp again in a few minutes. I promise. But for now, open your eyes."

Mary opened her eyes.

"What do you see?" Lee asked, looming over her.

"You. Leaning over me."

"Describe me."

"You're big. Your shoulders are broad and muscular. Your arms are strong. Your face is shadowed. I can't see it clearly."

"Then how do you know it's me?"

Mary chuckled, relaxing. "Because you're the only man in the room."

"How do you know?"

"I followed you inside. There was no one else here. Besides," Mary told him. "I know you. I recognize the sound of your voice. And your scent. I know you don't mean me any harm. I know you won't hurt me. I sense it."

"The same way you sensed danger when you woke up in a dark room and discovered the two young men standing over you?"

"Yes."

Lee let go of her and lit the lamp once again. "What about now?" He took a couple of steps away from the bed so Mary could see him fully.

Her eyes widened at the sight of him. She had seen him naked before, but not like this. Mary stared. He was beautiful. He was all male. And all hers. Mary knew he was capable of hurting her physically and emotionally, but at this moment, she also knew he only wanted to give and receive pleasure. And so did she. "You were right," she said, "I do like this surprise." She smiled at him. "I like it very much. I don't think I'll ever be frightened by the sight of a man standing by my bed again, as long as it's always you."

Her reaction surprised him. He leaned over her then, trapping her against the mattress, framing her face with his hands as he climbed onto the bed and straddled her. "Even now?"

Mary reached up and touched his cheek, then traced the corner of his mustache. "Especially now. I think I like this even better because now I can touch you." She put her arms around his neck and pulled him down to kiss her.

"Please do," Lee murmured before her lips met his.

His kiss was hot and sweet enough to tempt an angel. But Mary was no angel and she didn't need temptation. She pulled him down to her until she could press herself against him. She flattened herself against his chest, feeling the heat of his flesh as she deepened the kiss. The twin points of her breasts pressed into him. Lee groaned. Encouraged by his response Mary allowed her hands to roam over his shoulders, and down his back. Lee groaned again. He pulled his mouth away from hers and began to trail hot wet kisses on her face, her neck, her throat, and over to her earlobes.

"Aah, Mary," Lee whispered close to her ear, "I want to feel you against me and I want to bury myself inside you." His arms began to shake. "I just want you so badly."

"You've got me," Mary whispered back. "I'm not going anywhere."

Lee pushed himself up on his elbows so he could see the expression on her face. "Are you sure?"

Mary smiled. "Make love to me, Lee," she said simply. "Make me your wife in more than name only."

That was all the encouragement he needed. Sitting back on his heels, he reached down and untied the neat satin bow at the neck of her white ruffled nightgown, and worked the tiny pearl buttons loose from their braided silk loops. He opened the bodice and spread the sides wide so he could feast on the sight of Mary's rounded breasts. "You're beautiful," he breathed.

Mary saw the look of admiration in Lee's eyes and knew that he meant it.

He leaned forward, cupped one smooth satiny globe in his hand, and touched his lips to the dark center.

Mary sucked in a breath at the wonderful sensation his kiss evoked. Desire gripped her. Eager for more, Mary tangled her fingers in Lee's thick blond hair and held his head to her breasts. "Again," she ordered.

Lee obliged. He touched and tasted and gently nipped at her. And then, he suckled her and Mary thought she might die of the pleasure.

"Touch me," he told her.

Mary rushed to obey. Her untutored hands aroused him to such an extent, he finally had to stop her.

"No more," he muttered, against her breast.

"More?" she asked, stroking him gently.

"No!" Lee reached between them and grabbed hold of her wrist to make her stop the exquisite torture.

"Don't you like it?"

"I *love* it," he groaned. "But I can only take so much. Christ, Two-shot, I want to make love to you."

"Then get on with it, Lee," Mary said. "Don't keep me waiting any longer." She felt hot and achy and almost delirious with need.

Lee didn't need any more convincing. He let go of her wrist, and grabbed her ruffled nightgown by the hem and whisked it up around her waist, pushed it up, and over her head. Mary sighed with relief. At last she was naked against him.

Lee kissed his way down her body and his tongue seemed to light little bonfires wherever he touched her. Although his lips were otherwise occupied, his hands eagerly roamed where they would, finally coming to rest on her inner thigh.

Mary reacted immediately, opening her legs ever so slightly to allow him greater access. She couldn't seem to get close enough to him. Her anticipation rose to a fever pitch. Her excitement made Lee feel crazy. He had to have her. He had to feel himself inside her, feel her surrounding him, feel them joined together the way husbands and wives were meant to be joined.

Lee placed his hands under Mary's hips, lifting her slightly as he leaned forward and positioned himself to enter her in one fluid motion. "Slow or fast?" He offered her the choice, although he seriously doubted whether or not he could go slow even if she asked him too. "Hard or soft?"

"Now, Lee," Mary answered as she locked her long legs around his waist, "Please. Now."

By the time Lee felt the barrier, it was too late. "I'm sorry," he said as he surged forward and buried himself in her depths.

Mary cried out as he pushed into her, then sank her teeth into the flesh of his shoulder. She unlocked her legs and tried to move away from the pain, but Lee held her fast.

"Lie still, Two-shot, and the pain will lessen." He kissed her cheek, then her eyelids, and finally, her mouth. He kissed her gently, tenderly, reverently, and held her as if she were precious and fragile.

She shifted her hips experimentally, then moaned as the feverish pleasure-pain began to build once again.

"Ssh, ssh, sweetheart, I promise it will get better."

Mary lifted her hips again, and this time Lee understood. He fought to go slowly, fought to maintain control, and his body strained with the effort. Mary tightened her hold on him. She put her arms around his neck, then locked her legs around his waist once again. She held on as he supported her hips with his hands as he began to move within her. Gently, slowly at first, then faster.

The dull aching pain gradually disappeared and a different kind of ache took its place. Mary followed Lee's lead, matching her movements to his until they developed a rhythm uniquely their own. She kissed him as they moved together—kissed his arms, his shoulders, his neck, his chin, the corner of his mustache. And she trusted him to lead her to that place that seemed just beyond her reach, the place where she became him and he became her, the place where the two of them became one. And then suddenly, she felt him shudder uncontrollably, heard him yell her name, and Mary let herself go with him. The real world seemed to slip away, there was only Lee and the almost unbearable feeling of pleasure spiraling inside her. She called out his name. In wonder. In joy. And in gratitude.

Chapter
Twenty-two

Mary awoke later to find her head cradled on Lee's shoulder, her hair fanned out across the pillow, and one of her arms wrapped around his waist. Her hand rested atop the cotton dressing covering his wound. She sighed, then snuggled closer to him and pressed her lips against the side of his chest. "Thank you," she whispered.

"You're welcome," Lee answered in a husky voice as he tightened his arm around her. "It appears that I don't have the willpower to refuse a woman when she says please and thank-you so nicely."

"A woman?" Mary asked.

"Did I say woman?" Lee asked innocently. "I meant to say my wife. And not in name only, I might add."

"Not anymore." Mary stretched lazily.

"Happy birthday," he said softly.

"Was this my birthday present?" she asked, cuddling closer.

"Part of it. What's the matter? Don't you think it's appropriate for a twenty-nine-year old?" He turned to his side and propped up one elbow so he could look at her.

"Oh, I think it's very appropriate." Mary rolled over to face him. "Especially for a twenty-nine-year old who's wearing her birthday suit."

"And what a pretty birthday suit it is!"

"Yours isn't so bad either," Mary told him. "Except that

it appears to have a hole in it. And I don't remember pulling the trigger."

Lee glanced down. "What, this?" He tried to make light of his gunshot wound. "It's nothing. Just a flesh wound."

"It's bleeding." She touched the stained bandage very gently.

"Probably from all the exertion. I didn't expect to have to break into the house just to be here in time to give you your birthday gifts." He watched as Mary's brown eyes widened in shock and her face paled at the memory of their confrontation on the stairs.

"I thought you were a burglar. Oh, dear Lord, Lee, I nearly shot you."

He leaned over to kiss her, gently. "But you didn't."

"I could have. I could have killed you." Mary began to shake and her voice quivered.

"But you didn't. And, except for a previous hole in my handsome birthday suit, I'm fine. See?" He took her hand and placed it on his chest over his heart.

Suddenly overcome by emotion, Mary wrapped her arms around his neck and began to cry.

Her tears alarmed him. "Ssh, ssh." Lee smoothed the stray strands of silky black hair away from her face, rubbed her back, and kissed first her cheek, and then her mouth. "Twenty-nine-year olds aren't allowed to cry on their birthdays," he told her.

"But I could have lost you, Lee," Mary sobbed, "and then, I would never have known about . . . this."

Lee couldn't help himself. He burst out laughing. "Oh, I'm pretty sure you could have talked someone else into showing you all this."

"It's not funny!"

"Sure it is," he teased. "What man wouldn't be thrilled by the prospect of teaching Mary Alexander all about lovemaking?"

"Mary Kincaid," she corrected, drying her tears on the top of the sheet. "Did you teach me everything?"

Lee shook his head. "No, but you sure taught me something." His voice was husky and low and sent shivers of anticipation running down Mary's spine.

"What was that?"

"How lucky I am. If you had shot me, we definitely wouldn't be doing this right now."

A teasing light appeared in Mary's brown eyes. "But we aren't doing anything."

"Oh yes we are." Lee leaned closer and covered her mouth with his. He wrapped his arms around Mary and hugged her tightly, then rolled to his back so that she lay sprawled atop him. "Time for another lesson, teacher," he told her when he finally let go of her mouth. "And this time, in deference to my wound, I'm going to let you do the work." He lifted her then, and carefully eased her down to cover him.

Mary almost purred. "I think I'm going to like this lesson," she said. "Teach me."

Lee taught her the motion, then lay back and allowed her to practice until she got it right.

They awoke a second time to the sound of a high pitched bark coming from the pile of clothing Lee had dropped on the floor as the terrier puppy reminded them of his presence.

"What was that?" Mary asked, coming slowly awake.

"Your other birthday present." Lee rolled to his side, then leaned over, and lifted the puppy onto the bed. "I think he's lonely."

The terrier pup waddled over the bed clothes, across Lee and over to Mary, where he promptly licked her face. "Lee, he's wonderful." Mary hugged the little fellow.

"I thought he might make a nice companion for you. Something to bark at would-be thieves and housebreakers whenever I'm away. Something to guard you while you sleep whenever you're alone." Lee's voice took on that husky quality Mary loved, the one that made her heart race and her body quiver with anticipation.

"Only when you're away?"

"You won't need him to guard you when I'm here," Lee told her. "Because I plan to be right in bed beside you from now on."

"Good," she told him. "Because that's where I want you from now on."

They watched in companionable silence as the puppy amused himself leaping at the bed clothes, barking, and tugging at the sheets, until he finally curled up into a tight little ball of black and gray fur and fell asleep between the two of them.

"What are you gong to call him?" Lee asked.

"Barker," Mary decided.

"It fits." Lee reached out to scratch one of the puppy's ears.

"Thank you," Mary said, staring at him with all of her love for him shining in her dark brown eyes.

"You're welcome."

"I don't just mean for the puppy. I mean for everything. You altered the course of my life, Lee, and have given me all the things I wanted so desperately. I can't tell you how much that means to me."

Lee squeezed his eyes shut. "You could have had all these things with someone else. Maybe not Cosgrove, but with someone else."

"I don't think so." Mary shook her head. "Who else would have taught me not to be afraid of the night like you did? Who else would have given me a puppy for my birthday?"

"Among other things," Lee interjected.

"Among other things," Mary agreed. "And who but you could have given me this town? This house? Or Judah? Or most importantly, Maddy?"

Lee took a deep breath, then slowly let it out. The

moment of truth had come. It was time to tell her all he knew about Madeline. "Mary," he began, "there's something I think you should know about Maddy."

"What?"

"Well, remember when you asked about my personal relationship with Tabby?"

"Yes." Mary knew where the conversation was heading but she wouldn't make it easier for him. He had to tell her the truth, not the Pinkerton truth, but the real truth—all of it. And he had to do it in his own way.

"And I avoided the question by telling you that I didn't remember saying anything about a personal relationship between Tabby and me."

"I remember."

"Well, there was one," Lee said at last. "A very brief one."

"How brief?" Mary couldn't keep herself from asking the question.

"Four weeks."

"I see." Mary bit her bottom lip.

"No, you don't," Lee told her. "It wasn't like this. It wasn't what you and I shared. It was something else. We were working together, pretending to be lovers, practically living together as we worked—going to parties, dances, the opera, and midnight buffets." Lee exhaled and raked his fingers through his hair. "Anyway, it all started on New Year's Eve. Tabby and I went to a party. We danced and drank champagne and, well, one thing led to another and pretty soon we were in bed together. I think I knew it was a mistake almost from the first moment. It felt dishonest somehow. I felt guilty afterward, as if I'd taken advantage of her. I mean, I *liked* Tabby. I really liked her. I admired her ability and her courage."

Mary was very still and very quiet.

"But I didn't love her. I wasn't in love with her."

"Then how could you . . . ." Mary broke off.

"It was passion, Mary. And lust. And loneliness. And need.

The kind of need we all have that makes us want to be sure we're still alive, that we can still feel things for other people. I think Tabitha must have felt the same way. We drifted into an affair. We were adults with healthy appetites. I don't apologize for that. I just want you to understand that what I shared with Tabitha was not the same as what you and I shared tonight. It was different. It ran its course and at the end of the four weeks, we were friends but no longer lovers. I left Denver for Chicago and I never saw Tabitha again. I thought everything ended when we said good-bye at the depot, but I was wrong."

Mary watched as Lee rolled gracefully out of bed, and taking the sleeping puppy with him, walked unashamedly naked across the room to the pile of clothes he had dropped on the floor. He bent down and lifted his waistcoat from the pile before he placed Barker on the bundle of clothes for the night. Lee removed his gold watch from out of his waistcoat pocket, let the garment fall to the floor, and returned to the bed with the watch in his hand.

He handed the watch to Mary. Mary studied the ornate gold design on the lid and the initials engraved in the center: L.G.M.K. The gold pocketwatch hung on a fancy gold rope chain and a small portrait watch fob hung beside it.

"Open the watch," he said.

Mary lifted the lid and found herself staring at a miniature of a woman—a woman with dark brown hair and bright blue eyes—a woman who was the grown-up version of Madeline. Mary turned to look at Lee.

He nodded. "This is what Maddy will look like in thirty years."

"Who is she?" She already knew the answer. There could only be one reason for the unmistakable resemblance to Maddy. The woman in the watch was family—Lee's family.

"My mother," Lee answered softly. "Jane Alice McIntyre Kincaid, aged thirty-two. It was painted shortly before she died. She gave me the watch with her portrait inside for my eleventh birthday so I wouldn't forget her." Lee managed a little laugh. "As if I ever could. She meant everything to me."

"And now you have Madeline, who's the spitting image of her grandmother."

Lee smiled. "Yeah. Now, I have Maddy. I didn't know about her until I arrived in Denver the day before you and I got married." He shook his head. "I had no idea. But the minute I saw her, I knew. And Tabby never told me, never sent word."

"Maybe she didn't know how to reach you or what to say."

"She knew," Lee said. "She knew how to reach me before she died."

"Look at the situation from her point of view," Mary suggested, "would knowing about Maddy have made a difference between the two of you? Would it have changed your relationship?"

"Of course," Lee said. "I would have gone back to Denver and married her."

"Even though you didn't love her?"

"Yes."

"That's why she didn't tell you. Tabitha would rather have lived her life alone with Maddy, than to have you marry her on those terms. You may not have loved her, but I think she loved you very much." And so do I, Mary wanted to add, so do I.

Lee cleared his throat. "Now that you and I are married in every sense of the word, I thought I should tell you the truth. I don't want any lies or 'Pinkerton truths' between us, Two-shot." He paused for a moment before continuing. "I don't regret tonight. I don't apologize for it. I wanted you. I still want you. And I think there's a very good chance that I'll always want you. But you have to be sure, Two-shot. You have to be able to live with my past."

"I love Maddy," she said simply. "I loved her before I was

certain she was your daughter and I love her even more now that I know she is."

"You knew?" Lee stared at her.

"I had a fairly good idea."

"You had a fairly good idea, and yet you let me go through this—*torture*—of trying to tell you and wondering how you would react? Wondering what you would say or do?"

"Yep."

"Why?" he asked.

"Because confession, Liam Gordon McIntyre Kincaid"— Mary accentuated each of his given names with a kiss—"is supposed to be good for your soul. And, now that I'm your wife in more than name only, looking after the welfare of your soul is part of my business. Have you any more confessions to make?"

Lee shook his head.

"Not even one?"

"No. Why?"

"Aren't you even going to tell me who put that hole in your birthday suit?"

Lee shook his head again. "You wouldn't believe it."

"Try me," she invited.

And he did. Lee told her all about his trip to Washington and his confrontation with Cassandra Millen. He didn't omit a single detail and when he finished telling Mary about that, he told her all about Jeannie Carraway, her father, Edwin, and his own father, Patrick.

Mary held him while he cried. And when Lee finished telling her everything in his past, Mary Alexander Kincaid helped her husband put it behind him. She helped him lay his ghosts to rest by giving him three little words.

"I love you," she said. "I love you."

And then she showed him just how much.

Chapter
Twenty-three

Mary gave Lee her little silver two-shot derringer as they dressed for breakfast the following day.

"What's this for?" Lee asked.

"I won't be needing it anymore," she told him, as she slipped on her chemise. "I can protect myself without it. I have you now and I have Barker too."

"But it was a birthday gift from your uncle."

Mary nodded. "I got it for my fifteenth birthday and I'm giving it to you for my twenty-ninth. I don't want to run the risk of accidentally shooting you ever again."

"Are you certain about this?" Lee tucked his shirt into the waistband of his trousers.

"Completely. I'm not afraid of the dark anymore."

"I'll keep it for you," Lee said as he walked over to the bedpost and dropped the little gun into the pocket of the canvas duster hanging there. "But if you ever want it back, all you have to do is ask."

"Thank you," she said. "But I don't think I'll be needing it again. Let's save it for Maddy or our other daughters."

"Are we going to have more daughters?" Lee asked.

"Most definitely," Mary teased. "My husband and I have been working on it."

"You'll let me know when this comes about, won't you?"

"You'll be the very first to know." She sidled up to him

and kissed his chin before entering the dressing room to get her lingerie.

"What are you doing in there?" Lee asked.

"Getting dressed."

"Not fair," he protested. "Come out where I can see you. Come out where I can watch you." He hurried out of the bedroom to the landing and retrieved the brown paper-wrapped packages he'd dropped last night when Mary had stopped him at gunpoint.

She returned to the bedroom with a corset and a pair of muslin drawers.

"Happy birthday," Lee announced, presenting her with one of the packages.

"What's this?" Mary asked. "First you, then Barker, now this?"

"Yep. Open it." Lee sat down on the side of the bed to watch her.

Mary tore into the package and discovered several pairs of white silk and satin drawers. She held one pair up and realized they were *much* shorter than she was accustomed to wearing. In fact, all they covered was her bottom. They stopped above the thigh and didn't conceal her legs at all. They were soft and smooth—the silk ones nearly transparent and the satin ones, luxurious and delightfully sinful. She looked at Lee. "Why? How? Where?"

Lee chuckled. "The why should be obvious after last night and this morning," he reminded her. "As to how and where; remember when we arrived in Utopia? When you took Maddy to the necessary?"

"Yes."

"And you handed me your jacket with clothes bundled up inside?"

"Yes."

"Well, I dropped it and a pair of your drawers fell out. I stuck them in the pocket of my duster, then watched as you tripped over your skirt a half a dozen times on the way to the house because you had taken off all your underthings to keep Maddy from being embarrassed about wetting hers and going without."

"You knew all along?"

"Yeah," he confessed. "And I spent the hours on the train from here to Washington wondering how you looked and felt without them. I ordered those"—he nodded toward the lingerie she held in her hand—"from a French modiste in Washington. She said they were all the rage in the more wicked places in Paris."

"I can't believe you knew about that day and didn't let on."

"I should have," he said. "Because I almost went crazy just thinking about prim and oh-so-proper schoolteacher, Mary Alexander, walking through the streets of Utopia for all to see in broad daylight with nothing on beneath her skirts."

"The streets of Utopia were deserted," she reminded him. "Nobody saw and nobody knew."

"*I* knew." Lee raised an eyebrow at her. "And I did everything I could think of to try to catch a glimpse of your long luscious legs after that." He leered at her. "By the way, Two-shot, did you know those prim white ruffled night-gowns of yours are practically transparent?"

Mary thought of the times Lee had seen her in her ruffled gown—how he had placed her in front of the lamp last night. "You didn't!"

"Every chance I got."

Mary reached over, placed her palms against his chest and shoved him back onto the bed.

"You can't do that! I just gave you a birthday present," Lee reminded her.

"And because it's my birthday, I can do anything I want," she answered, loftily.

Lee stretched out on the bed, then rolled to his side, and propped up on one elbow. "Well, do you think you might want to try on those fancy underthings I bought you? Do you think you might like to show them to your husband and maybe get his approval?"

She did, and Lee approved. And the two of them were very late for breakfast.

She received a present from Lee every day for a week following her birthday. He said it was to make up for the honeymoon he'd missed, but Mary suspected he showered her with gifts to keep from having to say what he felt. She loved the gifts, but more than anything, she wanted the words.

But except for the fact that the words didn't come, she and Lee lived the life of newlyweds who are hopelessly in love.

Mary told him of her plans for the school and Lee eagerly pitched in to help with the preparations. He papered and painted, arranged furniture, and carted the cast-offs up to the attic. He unloaded the desks and supplies, the books and slates, and even gave his opinion on the style of the school uniforms.

Mary helped Nan and Birdie get the house back in order. She helped Louisa to cook and Syl to sew the uniforms. She admitted to Lee that Syl was, in fact, a madam and that three of the upstairs girls from the Silver Bear would be starting school come summer term. They also discussed the state of affairs in town—that unless the mine reopened, Utopia was dead.

Lee understood that they couldn't let that happen. He set out to find a way to make the mine productive once again.

Their only disagreement came late one afternoon when Lee, Mary, Judah, and Maddy sat on the edge of a small pond. Lee and Judah had spent the afternoon fishing.

Actually, Judah spent the afternoon fishing. Lee spent most of his time patiently baiting Judah's hook, unsnarling the line, and removing the catch. Mary sat on a blanket nearby keeping a close eye on Barker and Maddy, who occasionally ran to Lee and fished for a while before returning to the blanket and the pretend tea party she, Barker, Mama, and Mary were having.

"Have you ordered everything you need for the school?" Lee asked, baiting yet another one of Judah's hooks and carefully casting the line into the pond before he handed the pole back to Judah. Maddy stood watching, Barker at her heels.

"I think so."

"And have you paid for everything?" came his casual question.

"Why do you ask?"

"I just wondered where the money was coming from."

"If you must know," Mary said. "I wired Reese and asked him to send me the money."

"That's what I thought."

"What's wrong with asking Reese to send money? It's ours."

"It's yours. And I don't mind you spending your money to supply the school if that's what you want to do with it, but I don't want you spending your money on this house," Lee reminded her.

"But the school's in the house."

"Yes, but all this redecorating is expensive. You'll run through your annual allowance in no time flat."

"But Lee, I want to contribute. It's not my money, it's our money and our house."

"You do contribute. And besides," he said, "I've got money, loads of it, just sitting in bank accounts drawing interest. I need someone to spend it on. And I'll be happy if you'll oblige me by letting me pay the bills."

"You're welcome to pay the bills, my love," Mary told him. "Believe me, I'm relieved to know you're loaded with cash. I didn't know how we were going to make ends meet on your Pinkerton pay and after you quit. . . . The mine still isn't open and frankly, I wasn't sure how much longer I could afford to support the town. I've been worrying about it for months."

"Mary Two-shot, all you had to do was go to the bank and get a draft on my account."

"I didn't know you had an account."

"I opened one the day after your birthday."

"All this time I've been worrying, wondering if I should telegraph Reese again, and you had money sitting in the bank?"

"Yes. And all you have to do from now on is walk into the bank and sign a draft for however much you need."

Mary snorted. "Easier said than done."

"What do you mean?"

Mary sighed, knowing she'd said too much, yet also knowing Lee would not stop asking questions until he got an answer. "I'm not allowed to enter the Ajax Saloon, Bank, and Assayer's Office of Utopia, Colorado Territory."

"Who told you that?" Lee said. "I see ladies going in and out of there every single day."

"You don't see half-breed Indians going in the bank *ever*."

"You can't go in because . . . ?"

"Because I'm part Indian and Hugh Morton hates Indians." Mary smiled at him. "Fortunately for us, he has nothing against handsome Irishmen."

Lee was confused. "But I thought you have an account there. I've seen you pay bills with Ajax bank drafts."

"I do have an account there. I can keep my money in his bank, I just can't go in to use it. He doesn't have anything against money, just certain people."

"Then how did you open an account? How do you do your banking?"

"Syl does it. That's how we met and became friends. I couldn't go into the Ajax to open an account and Syl offered to do it for me."

"Silver Delight?"

"Sylvia," Mary corrected. "Sylvia Delight."

Lee laughed. "Does Morton know the town madam does your banking for you?"

Mary shrugged her shoulders. "I doubt it. Syl banks for several other women as well."

"Syl banks for her girls, Mary. I'd be willing to bet that the only woman Syl banks for besides herself and her girls is you."

"Maybe so, but that doesn't matter to me," Mary said, "as long as I have access to our money. Wait, what are you doing?" She watched as Lee quickly rolled up the line on his fishing pole.

"Keep an eye on Judah and Maddy for me," he instructed. "I'll be back in a little while."

"Lee? Where are you going?" Mary's voice rose a bit higher when she realized exactly where Lee was headed and what he might do when he got there. "Hugh Morton's prejudice doesn't matter."

"The hell it doesn't!"

Mary jumped up to follow. "Lee!" She placed her hands on her hips and stomped her foot for emphasis as she shouted his name.

"I'll be back before you know it," he promised as he headed toward the path leading into town and the Ajax Saloon.

"Poppy!" Maddy squealed. "Go wid Poppy!" She ran toward Lee.

"No, sweetheart." Lee squatted down to Maddy's level. "You can't go with me."

"Why not?"

"Because Poppy has to take care of some business in town. Grown-up business," Lee explained.

"What bidness?" Maddy demanded.

Lee glanced up and met Mary's somber gaze. "I'm going to defend Mary's rights against the town bigot," he answered carefully.

"Poppy do what?" his daughter asked.

Lee thought for a moment, then studied the earnest expression on his little daughter's face. "I'm not really sure," he admitted. "But I think I'll start with a punch in the nose and go on from there."

"Lee," Mary said. "Please, don't cause any trouble."

"I'm not going to *cause* it," he answered. "He caused it. I'm going to put an end to it." He stood up, then walked over and kissed Mary on the forehead while Maddy scampered off, satisfied with Lee's answer and bored with the lack of attention.

Lee reached up and traced the frown lines on Mary's face with the tip of his finger. "Don't worry, Two-shot. I know what I'm doing."

Mary started to reply but Judah's cry of triumph stopped her. She turned in time to see the older man, with Maddy standing close by, pull another fish from the water.

Judah swung the fishing pole toward the bank and Maddy clapped her hands in delight as she reached for the fish. "Maddy help Zhudah!" she exclaimed.

"Madeline! No!" Mary yelled a warning just moments before Maddy grabbed hold of the slippery trout.

She came away screaming and holding her hand.

"It's all right." Lee hurried to his daughter's side, dropped down to his knees, and began wiping Maddy's hand with his handkerchief, inspecting the damage.

"She was pricked by the trout's fins," Lee called to Mary. "But she's all right. See, Maddy?" Lee held her hand to his lips, "Poppy will make it all better." He kissed his daughter's tiny hand.

Maddy stopped crying and hugged him, then glanced at

her hand and ran calling to Mary. "Mama! Mama! Mama make better."

Mary grabbed the doll as Maddy ran onto the blanket and into her arms. Maddy held out her hand. "Mama kiss make better," she ordered.

Mary took Mama and carefully touched the doll's painted lips to Maddy's almost invisible wound. "There," she said when she finished. "Mama made it all better."

Madeline stared at Mary, then pushed the doll away. "Not want doll," she said very clearly as she threw herself into Mary's arms. "Want Mama."

Mary hugged Maddy, kissed her tiny fish prick, and all her other fingers as well. Lee stood for a moment and watched. His dreams had come true—he had a family at last.

Then he waved to Mary, Madeline, and Judah, and hurried down the path toward Utopia and a long overdue confrontation with the owner of the Ajax Saloon, Bank, and Assayer's Office of Utopia, Colorado Territory.

And at supper, later that evening, if anyone noticed the bruised knuckles on Lee's right hand, nobody commented on them.

In the days that followed, Mary found that the daylight hours she spent in Lee's company were limited. Her days were filled with the ordinary demands of Maddy and Judah and Louisa and Syl and the families of the miners, friends who shared a part of their lives, and the town of Utopia itself. His were spent interviewing the men left in town about the mine conditions and inspecting the site. But their nights belongs to each other. And she and Lee made the most of those nights—making love until the wee hours of the mornings, sleeping, then waking to start the day. The time they had together was special, and both of them understood that the days were ticking away. Nearly two and a half months had passed since their wedding, and Mary knew that the life she shared in Utopia with Lee and Madeline could come to an end if Lily Catherine wasn't found very soon.

"I sent a letter to David last week asking about the legalities of Tabitha's will in view of the fact that Maddy is my little girl," Lee said. "And I got an answer this morning. It seems we're in practically the same situation as David and Tessa, except that David isn't Lily's natural father but is legally recorded as such. And although I'm Maddy's natural father, I don't have a legal record of it."

"Too bad we don't have a forged marriage certificate for you and Tabitha like the one Senator Millen paid to have made for Caroline and David," Mary said, thinking aloud.

"Now, there's a thought," Lee teased. "We'll hire a forger."

"If it will guarantee we get to keep our daughter, I'll gladly pay for it."

"Oh no, you won't," Lee said. "We have to do this legally."

Mary sighed. "If only Tabitha had tied this loose end a bit tighter. If only she had named you as Madeline's father. There has to be a way. If only we can find it in time."

Two days later, Ned Sampson delivered a telegram to Lee. It read:

HAVE FOUND LILY CATHERINE STOP SAFE AND SOUND STOP SARRAZIN IN CUSTODY STOP SHALL I BRING OR WOULD YOU PREFER TO COME GET HER STOP REPLY IMMEDIATELY STOP DANIEL WILLIS.

Lee turned to Mary. "It's up to you."

You've waited a long time for this day," Mary said. "I think you should go get her."

"How do we tell David and Tessa?" Lee asked. "They've waited even longer than I have. Should we send a telegram or a letter, or go in person?"

Mary thought about it for a moment. "You go get Lily

Catherine and I'll take Maddy and Judah to the ranch and tell them in person."

"Okay," Lee agreed.

"I'll help you pack."

Lee issued last minute instructions as he stood waiting for the Denver Pacific. Once again Mary, Judah, and Maddy were dressed in their Sunday best to see him off. And once again Lee had ribbon favors from his ladies tied to his arm. "Don't forget that, even with us traveling light and fast, it's going to take a week to get back."

"I know."

"You remember how to reach me."

Mary nodded. "Who are you this time?"

Lee thought for a moment. "I'm Jones again. L.K. Jones."

"All right, Mr. Jones, I'll telegraph you if I think I might be delayed."

"Delayed? Why would you be delayed?" Lee wanted to know.

"When I'll be trying to open a school and settle in the new students who are going to be boarding with us, helping cook meals three times a day for an entire town, interviewing the mining engineers in your absence, keeping track of an active two-and-a-half-year-old girl like Maddy and a dog like Barker, *and* also making sure Judah doesn't get into any danger during the day, there are any number of things that might detain me." She stared up at Lee. "Especially when I suspect I might be in the family way."

Lee hugged his wife, then kissed her right there on the platform for all to see. "Good Lord, Two-shot, what a time to tell me!"

"I only suspected it this morning when I lost my breakfast. And I did promise that you'd be the first to know."

"I can't go to New York," he said. "I'll just have to

telegraph Willis and tell him to bring her here." He raked his fingers through his hair.

"And make David and Tessa wait another day or two? Make us wait another day or two when you know that time is running out? Oh no, Mr. Jones, you're getting on that train and going to New York to retrieve your niece, then you're going to march into Robert Pinkerton's New York office and resign before the ninety days are out. And then, Mr. L.K. Jones is going to become my husband, Lee Kincaid, once again. And that's an order."

"Yes, ma'am." Lee saluted her.

The train whistle sounded its last warning for passengers to board.

"You'd better go," Mary said in a repeat of their last parting.

"This is the last time," he promised. "You'll be okay while I'm gone?"

"Don't worry about us," Mary said. "Just bring your birthday suit home without any holes this time."

"I'll do my best."

"That's all I ask."

Lee stared at his wife. She was beautiful, warm, wise, loving, passionate, and courageous. All the things that he had wanted in a wife but had never thought he would find again. And he loved her more than life. "Mary, I . . ." He stopped abruptly. It wasn't the time or the place. She deserved to hear him say the words over a romantic breakfast, or late at night when she lay in his arms. She deserved a better setting than a crowded railroad platform.

"What is it?" She looked up at him, recognized the warmth in his gray eyes and thought for a moment that he might be on the verge of telling her how he felt.

"Take care of yourself," he replied hurriedly. "I'll see you in Cheyenne in a few days."

Chapter
Twenty-four

Lee had only been in New York half a day and already he was tired of it and eager to get home. And in a few minutes, when his interview with Robert Pinkerton—Allan's younger son and head of the New York office—was over, he could take Lily Catherine Alexander and go back home to Mary and Maddy and Judah. But for now he sat in the Pinkerton office, with Lily on his lap, her head pillowed against his chest, and waited.

Lily had come as a surprise. Even though Lee knew David wasn't her father, he had been expecting her to look a bit like Mary or even Maddy, but Lily was aptly named. She was tiny and fragile-looking, with skin so fair the network of blue veins showed through. She had curly white-blond hair and big blue eyes. Though only a few months younger than Madeline, Lily weighed far less. But like Madeline, Lily Catherine favored her grandmother. And Lily Catherine was as quiet, well-mannered, and polite as Maddy was outgoing. When she spoke, it was in a whisper, almost as if she were afraid to make any noise. But she was affectionate. She clung to Lee, and he realized that she needed his nearness. She was going to a new home and to parents and a family that loved her already, but at the moment, she felt lost. A little girl surrounded by strangers who had been taken away from the only home she'd ever known.

"Good to see you again, Lee." Robert Pinkerton stepped out of his office and walked over to shake his hand. Lee didn't stand up.

"I see you've made Lily's acquaintance."

"Yes."

"She's a precious little girl," Robert said. "And we're lucky to have found her in all this mass of humanity." He waved an arm toward the window and the crowded streets below.

"How did you find her?"

"We waited until Sarrazin wired money from Washington to a bank here in New York, then watched to see who picked it up. Luckily for us, Mrs. Sarrazin did. Easy as pie once we knew where to look and for whom to look," Pinkerton pronounced. "Now, how about you, Lee? How are you feeling?"

"Fine."

"No ill effects from the gunshot wound?"

"No," Lee said.

"Daniel Willis filed a report. I'm sorry about Mrs. Millen. It was tragic, but it wasn't your fault."

"Yes, it was tragic," Lee said. "And if I had had any idea that my visit would provoke such an action, I wouldn't have gone alone. But I didn't anticipate her reaction. Having met her, I realized I should have recognized that Cassandra Millen couldn't face another family scandal—that she wouldn't allow the senator's name, her name, to be tarnished."

"The senator's name was bound to be tarnished, Lee, whether she liked it or not. She couldn't prevent it and neither could anyone else." Robert paused. "Sarrazin has come clean. Senator Millen was more corrupt than any of us imagined. Not only did he try to force David Alexander to marry his daughter, Caroline, he paid to have a marriage license forged and bribed a clerk to record it. And still, he set out to ruin David. Senator Warner Millen even financed that counterfeiting ring in Denver—the one you and Tabitha investigated two or three years ago."

"What?!" Lee was clearly surprised.

Robert nodded. "I guess that's why he was able to get an expert forger to create a marriage license for David and Caroline."

"Then Sarrazin wasn't blackmailing the senator with the scandal involving Caroline or even L-I-L-Y." He spelled Lily's name because, over the past few weeks, Lee had learned that little girls had very big ears. "But something even bigger and uglier."

"The scandal involving Caroline would have definitely damaged the senator's reputation and might even have hurt his re-election, but let's face it, people talk and gossip travels fast, and almost everybody in Washington knew about it in some way or another. What Senator Millen couldn't allow to come to light was that he was responsible for financing the ring of counterfeiters and had used his influence to have the counterfeit bills circulated. But the unfinished business with David bothered him enough that he had a man keep track on the Jordan-Alexander clan."

"Who?" Lee demanded.

"We don't know," Pinkerton admitted. "But we know he was very close to the family. Sarrazin confessed that up until a few weeks ago this man, whoever he was, was close enough to know David's every move—and had been for several months."

"Then why didn't he just tell David where"—Lee nodded toward Lily—"she was."

"We don't know. Maybe he thought David would continue the investigation even after he located the little girl."

"Adoption," Lee said suddenly. "He was afraid of the adoption proceedings. Because in most states and in the territories a legal adoption requires an act of the legislature.

Senator Millen was afraid that if David adopted L-I-L-Y, the forged marriage license might surface and David, of course, knew he hadn't married Caroline Millen. Most of Washington knew he hadn't married Caroline. There would have been no reason for the senator to ruin his own son-in-law."

"But David's name was already legally recorded as the little girl's father."

Lee grinned. "Yes. But Tessa wouldn't be satisfied with that. She wants to adopt L-I-L-Y as their own, the way they adopted Coalie—to become L-I-L-Y's legal guardian right along with David."

"But women can't be the legal guardians of their children." Pinkerton pointed out.

"That's correct in just about every state in the Union, but Wyoming is an exception. In Wyoming, woman can and do vote, sit on juries, and hold public office. In Wyoming, women are recognized as having the same rights as men."

"And David and Tessa Alexander reside in Peaceable, Wyoming Territory."

Lee nodded. "So if Senator Millen couldn't stop David from trying to locate L-I-L-Y, or hiring us to do it, then David posed a threat and had to be watched. But by whom?" Lee thought for a moment. "Did Sarrazin tell you anything about this man?"

"Only that he received his share of the money for his work in the counterfeiting operation and left Denver before the others were arrested."

"But Sarrazin doesn't know who he is."

"Sarrazin doesn't know the man's real name. Only how to contact him when he needs a job done. But I suspect Sarrazin may have contacted the man before he was arrested. I suspect he may be aware that we're on his trail."

Lee thought back. "The only man in the Denver ring who didn't get caught was the pen man. The forger. So that's how he escaped capture. He was paid early. He probably banked his money and ran. Money . . . bank. Banker!" The tiny hairs at the back of Lee's neck stood on end and he jumped to his feet, startling Lily, who was napping. "Holy Mary, Mother of God! I've got to go!" Lee started for the door.

"Wait! What is it?"

"Just a hunch. But I've got to go."

"Don't forget to send me a full detailed report," Pinkerton demanded, sounding just like his father, Allan.

"I resigned." Holding Lily tightly, Lee hurried out the front door and down the stairs.

"Send me a report anyway!" Robert yelled after him.

Lee had been gone five days. He and Lily Catherine would be arriving in Cheyenne on the morning train and Mary knew she wouldn't be there to greet them because she knew she would never make it to the train on time. And there didn't seem to be anything she could do to prevent it. She listened helplessly as the last train whistle blew one last time. The day had been a disaster from start to finish and appeared to be getting worse by the minute. Mary felt like crying when she realized she wouldn't be able to get to Cheyenne by early evening as she'd planned. Louisa had stayed home to take care of two of her children who had come down with the chicken pox. And although Mary had help from Nan and Birdie and Sylvia, the brunt of the work of preparing the meals fell to her. Breakfast was late. So was dinner. And Mary was trying desperately to salvage supper. She had sent one of the boys down to the depot to send a telegram to the Trail T to tell them she would be delayed. She wouldn't be able to leave Utopia until Sylvia arrived in the morning, and that was only if Madeline and Barker were feeling better. Maddy and Barker didn't have the chicken pox, but were suffering from the upset stomach they got when the two of them shared a plate of strawberry tarts when Mary was called upstairs to the schoolroom to help one of the new boarding students unpack and settle in.

After being gone for five days, Lee was scheduled to arrive with Lily at eight the following morning. David and Tessa and Coalie and Reese and Faith were waiting on the platform to greet him, but there was no sign of Mary, Judah, or Madeline. The train chugged into the station right on time and Lee held Lily in his arms as he exited the train. David and Tessa surrounded him almost as soon as his feet hit the platform. Once again Lily clung to him.

"Oh, David." Tessa turned to her husband. "She's so tiny and so pretty."

"And she's finally ours." David smiled at his new daughter.

But Lily buried her face in Lee's collar.

"It's all right, sweetheart," Lee soothed. "These are the people I was telling you about. This is your daddy and this is your mama. And this is your big brother, Coalie." He carefully introduced the little girl to David, Tessa, and Coalie.

"May I hold her?" Tessa asked.

Lee glanced at Lily. She looked to Lee.

"This is your new mama," Lee repeated. "And she'll take very good care of you."

Lily looked as if she wasn't going to let go of Lee, then suddenly, she changed her mind and reached, not for Tessa or David, but for ten-year-old-Coalie.

Coalie turned to Tessa. "What do I do?"

"Hold her," Tessa said, with tears in her eyes. "She trusts you."

Lily slipped into Coalie's arms.

"Why, she's light as a feather!" Coalie exclaimed, bouncing her up and down in his arms. "See?" Coalie showed David how he could lift her.

Lily began to laugh.

David moved closer and Lily reached out for him. He lifted her high into the air. She laughed again.

Tessa stood watching as tears rolled down her face, then suddenly Lily reached for her.

Tessa hugged the little girl to her breast and cried even harder. "Oh, Lily, Lily, we've waited such a long time for you."

Lee stepped back out of the way so that David, Tessa, and Coalie could get acquainted with the newest member of their family.

Reese moved forward and clapped Lee on the back. "Good work, Lee. Thanks for bringing Lily to her family."

Lee nodded absentmindedly, as he searched the crowd for a sign of Mary before he finally turned to Reese. "Where's Mary? She was supposed to meet me here this morning."

"She was delayed yesterday. She sent a telegram to tell us that there had been an outbreak of chicken pox among Louisa's children and that Maddy had a stomachache. She said she wouldn't be able to get here until this morning," Faith answered.

"Mary isn't here? She's not in Cheyenne?"

"She didn't mention being ill herself," Faith told him. "Only that Maddy had a stomachache. She said she couldn't get here until the evening train."

"Come on, Lee, I'll help you get your bags and we'll ride on out to the ranch."

"I don't have any bags, just my case." Lee lifted the leather satchel for Reese to see. "And Lily's things, what there are of them, are in here. Are you sure Mary's all right?"

"Mary's fine. She'll be on the late train." Reese clamped his hand on Lee's shoulder. "We came in two carriages. Ours is parked in front of the depot. Is there anywhere you would like to go before we leave town?"

Lee stared at Reese as if he didn't comprehend the simple question before he answered. "The bank." Lee didn't wait for a response, he simply started walking away from the depot in the direction of the bank.

Reese glanced at Faith. "I'd better go with him," he said.

And Faith quickly agreed. "I'll wait here with David and Tessa."

Reese waved to his wife, then hurried after Lee.

"Which carriage is yours?" Lee asked abruptly as they passed the row of buggies and carriages parked in front of the depot.

"That one," Reese pointed.

Lee walked over to it and tossed his satchel inside, before he continued his march toward the bank.

Reese lengthened his stride to keep up with Lee. "Do you mind if I ask why you're in such a damned hurry to get to the bank?"

"Pelham Everhardt Cosgrove III."

"What?"

"I think Pelham Cosgrove III may be involved in the counterfeiting and forgery ring that operated out of Denver three years ago."

"Mary's . . . I mean . . . *our* . . . Pelham Cosgrove III?" Reese was stunned.

"The same," Lee said. "When I saw him at the wedding, I knew I had seen him somewhere before. And while I was in New York talking to Robert Pinkerton, I finally remembered where. In Denver, three years ago."

"Why are we going to the bank instead of the police?" Reese asked.

"If Cosgrove's at the bank, we'll send for the police. If he's not at the bank, Mary may be in trouble."

"Mary? Why?"

Lee stared at Reese. "I remembered where I'd seen him before, and he's bound to remember where he saw me. And it's no secret—at least it's not a family secret—that you and David and I were all Pinkerton men. And Robert Pinkerton learned from one of the suspects in the current counterfeiting incident that Senator Warner Millen had a man very close to the Jordan-Alexander clan and that the late senator paid that man to watch every move David Alexander made with regard to locating Lily Catherine."

"Damn!" Reese muttered, picking up his pace. "We'd better pray he's at the bank."

But he wasn't. The bank president informed them that Mr. Cosgrove had resigned his position at the bank and left town the previous evening without giving sufficient notice.

"Any idea where he was heading?" Reese asked.

"I think he mentioned Denver," the bank officer replied.

Lee practically ran out of the bank and all the way back to the depot where he immediately got into a discussion with the station manager. "I need to get to Utopia, Colorado. When's the next train?"

"This afternoon."

"What about that one?" Lee pointed to the train he had just exited.

"We've got to unload the cars and back them up on a sidetrack, then turn the engine around before that train can go east or south."

"Forget the cars. What about an engine? Can you get an engine on the track to Denver?" Lee asked.

"Yeah, we can do that, but I need authorization."

"How soon?"

"Forty-five minutes. But I can't do it without authorization," the stationmaster insisted.

"What do you need as authorization?" Reese asked.

"A Union Pacific official, a stockholder, or a federal marshal," the stationmaster replied.

"I'm a stockholder in the U.P. and so is he." Reese

pointed to Lee. "He's also a Pinkerton detective. Is that good enough?"

"I don't know."

"Turn an engine around," Lee ordered. "In forty-five minutes, I'll have authorization from President Grant himself, if that's what it takes."

"Yessir."

"I'm going with you," Reese announced.

"No, stay here. Get the damned authorization. But don't let on to David and Tessa that anything's wrong. They've waited a long time to get their daughter and we don't want anything to spoil Lily Catherine's homecoming."

"Where are you going?" Reese demanded.

"I'm going to wire the Denver police to be on the lookout for Cosgrove, and wire Mary, and then I'm going to check every hotel and boardinghouse in this town just to make certain he's not hiding out. Do whatever you have to do, but get that damned train turned around. I'll be back in twenty minutes and I want to be ready to go."

Darkness had settled over the tiny town of Utopia. The last meal of the day was over and everyone had made their way back to their own homes. Maddy and Barker were asleep upstairs, as were the three boarding students, and Mary and Sylvia were sitting in the kitchen savoring a pot of hot tea before Syl had to return to the Silver Bear for the evening crowd.

"I never thought we'd finish these darned uniforms you're so set on having the students wear," Syl announced. "I should have remembered how much I hated sewing my own clothes before I volunteered to make all these dresses and pants."

"We could have hired a seamstress and a tailor from Denver," Mary reminded her. "But we would have missed out on all this fun." She smiled at Sylvia. "And it has been fun, hasn't it, Syl? Go on, admit it. You've enjoyed being a part of this project and working with the other women in town as much as I have."

"Yes, it has been nice," Sylvia agreed. "I've forgotten what it was like to be accepted into town society. To have women friends who aren't in the business, so to speak. But I've enjoyed it. I never really minded doing what I do for a living until now. But suddenly I find the normal life appeals to me lately. Besides, I hate being an outcast."

"I know what you mean," Mary said. "The only other people who've ever fully accepted me for what and who I am is my family and Lee."

"And now, the town of Utopia," Sylvia added.

"Except for Hugh Morton at the Ajax."

"Yes, well, I don't know why he thinks he can look down his nose at other people. He's not as much of a prize as he thinks he is! Trust me," Syl told her. "I know."

"I'll bet you do."

"Oh, the things I could tell you if you weren't a lady!" Sylvia laughed. "Sometimes, it's all I can do to keep a straight face."

"Tell me anyway," Mary invited. "I may be a lady, but I'm old enough to learn about the sinful side of life. Besides," she reminded Sylvia, "I'm married."

They spent a few minutes swapping stories about their past, with Sylvia sharing the most colorful stories, while Mary related the antics of Reese and Faith's and David and Tessa's courtships. She finally concluding with the story of how Lee had burst into the church in Cheyenne and interrupted her wedding to Pelham Cosgrove III.

Finally Mary looked down at the watch pinned to her dress. "You'd better be going, Syl, or you won't have time to transform yourself into Silver Delight."

Sylvia chuckled. "I know. And believe me, it's taking a lot longer to do it these days. I had forgotten about the early mornings when I volunteered to help you. At the time, I didn't have as many customers, and I wasn't staying up until all hours of the morning."

"So business is improving?"

"Yes. Word has gotten out about you and Lee hiring those engineers to come back to work at the silver mine, and that they've discovered newer and bigger veins of silver. The miners are beginning to trickle back into town. You might say the saloon business is booming."

"What about the other?"

"That's one of the things I wanted to talk to you about. I was thinking of letting one of the other girls take over the running of the upstairs business until she earns enough to buy me out."

"What will you do?"

"I'd like to invest in the mine and—" Syl looked down at her teacup and actually blushed. "I'd really like to help you teach here at the school. I think I'd make a good teacher. I'm educated, I read, my penmanship is very good, and I know my arithmetic, spelling, history, and literature. I even went to a ladies' finishing school." She looked over at Mary. "You don't have to give me an answer now. Just say you'll think about it."

"I'd be pleased to have you teach in my school, Syl. Very pleased."

"Thank you," Sylvia said. "I'm . . . thank you." She stopped abruptly when the words she tried to say stuck in her throat. She put her hand out and reached across the table.

"You're welcome." Mary clasped Sylvia's hand and gave it a gentle squeeze. "I know. Now go before you make me cry or you're counted tardy. Or both."

Sylvia got up from the table and gave Mary a quick hug.

Mary rose and walked with her out the kitchen door and down the back steps.

"You know, Mary," Sylvia managed at last. "It's lucky for us that Lee Kincaid burst in on your wedding. I'm real glad he carried you off and brought you to Utopia."

"So am I," Mary said. "And I can laugh about it now, because everything worked out for the best. But I was furious at the time. I thought Lee had ruined all my beautiful plans."

Sylvia nodded in understanding, then turned and walked around the house. Mary stood in the darkness of the backyard watching until she saw Syl pass beneath the street lights halfway down Main Street, then she went back into the house. Mary removed the cups and saucers from the kitchen table and carried them to the sink, then went back to the table to retrieve the china teapot.

"He did ruin all my beautiful plans."

Mary looked up from the table at the sound of a man's voice and discovered Pelham Cosgrove III standing in the doorway of her kitchen.

"Pelham, this is a surprise." The tiny hairs at the back of her neck stood on end and Mary fought to keep from sounding frightened. She lifted the teapot from the table and held it in her left hand. "What are you doing here? And why didn't you let me know you were coming?"

"I came to see you, Mary," Pelham said. "Because there's no place left for me to go. And I didn't send a message ahead because I really didn't want to spoil the surprise." Pelham stepped into the room.

He was Pelham, Mary told herself, just Pelham. She thought she had no reason to be afraid of him, but her instincts told her otherwise. Pelham was different. He had changed in the weeks since she'd last seen him. He looked older. Colder. And desperate.

"What do you want with me?" Mary asked.

"I'm not sure," he admitted, "but since your Pinkerton detective husband has made it impossible for me to show my face in Cheyenne or Denver any longer, I decided to come here."

"Why would Lee do anything to you? Did you leave Cheyenne? And why can't you show your face in Denver?" Keep him talking, Mary told herself. Keep him talking until she found out what he wanted, and why he was in Utopia.

"I've just come from Denver." Pelham sneered at her. "And I barely managed to escape arrest. The police are searching for me."

"Whatever for?" Mary truly couldn't imagine her former fiancé doing anything even remotely illegal. He was always so controlled.

" 'Whatever for?' " he mimicked. "You really don't know, do you? You had no idea that the only reason I was courting you was to keep an eye on your precious brother, David, and to get my hands on all that lovely money your family possesses."

"You're wrong about that," Mary told him. "I knew you only wanted to marry me for my money, but I didn't know why. You have money of your own." The kitchen table was between them and Mary couldn't see Pelham's hands.

"I *had* money of my own," Pelham told her. "Until my father found out that I was creating my own money upon occasion. I guess he didn't appreciate my artistic talent. He disowned me. Cut me off without a penny."

"But you always had cash," Mary insisted. "I've seen you with lots of money. You live very well. Too well for a bank clerk—unless that clerk has money behind him."

"And so I did until your husband"—he sneered the word—"intervened. Until he caused the death of the source of all my money."

"Lee didn't *cause* anyone's death!" Mary defended her husband.

"Tell that to Senator Warner Millen. Tell that to his wife."

"Judas Priest!" Mary exclaimed, using Lee's favorite oath. "You worked with the senator."

"So you do know," Pelham said. "I wondered."

"I don't know what you did for the senator, but I know it couldn't have been good." Mary eased back from the table. She could see through the window of the back door from where she stood and she almost let out a scream as someone tiptoed up onto the back porch. She stifled a sigh of relief as Lee passed by the window behind Pelham.

"I see you do appreciate my talent," Pelham said as he watched Mary's brown eyes widen. "Before I moved to Cheyenne, I created currency for Senator Millen. And a few stocks and bonds and legal documents when he needed them. But once I settled in Cheyenne, the senator hired me to watch David. And look how dedicated I was! Why, I was even willing to marry his half-breed sister to be close to him."

"You—you—snake!"

Pelham took another step forward. "It took me a while to recognize your husband, but I finally placed him. You see, we ran into each other in Denver a few years back."

"You're the forger." Mary watched as Lee raised a finger to his lips and shook his head. "The pen man." Lee frowned at her.

"He told you about that, too? That's too bad, Mary. Now, you know all my secrets. And I don't like having people know my secrets." Pelham stepped around the table. He had a gun in his hand and it was pointed at Mary.

"Don't come any closer," Mary warned. "I'll shoot." She reached into her right pocket for the silver derringer. But her pocket was empty. Lee had her gun. She'd given it to him.

"It appears we're at a standoff. But I don't think you'll shoot me, Mary. After all, I was your beloved intended." Pelham took another step.

"You're wrong," she bluffed. "I will shoot you."

"No, you won't," he replied confidently as he raised his gun to fire.

"She might not," Lee announced from behind him, "But I will, you sorry son of a bitch!" Lee held the silver two-shot derringer in his hand.

When Pelham saw that Lee held the derringer, he smiled. "I'll kill her," he warned.

"No, you won't!" Mary screamed as she flung the teapot at his head, then dropped to the floor behind the kitchen table.

Pelham fired, but the shot went wide, missing its mark.

Lee fired back.

Pelham clutched his shoulder and fell back against the table.

Lee grabbed Crosgrove by his shirtfront, lifted him off the furniture, clipped him on the chin with a vicious uppercut, and let him fall to the floor.

In seconds, Lee was around the table kneeling beside Mary. "Mary, are you all right? Where did he hit you? Christ, Two-Shot, are you bleeding anywhere?" He ran his hands over her body feeling for blood, searching for the wound.

She sat up. "I'm fine, Lee. He didn't shoot me."

Lee grabbed her and lifted her to her feet. He hugged her tightly, kissed her hard on the mouth, then released her to cover her whole face with kisses before releasing her again. "Why in the hell did you do such a stupid thing? You could have been killed! Whoever heard of throwing a damned teapot at a man holding a gun. Are you crazy?"

"I was afraid he'd shoot you!"

"I had a gun," Lee reminded her.

"A gun that's not very accurate from a distance."

"You're right," he said, momentarily distracted. "It shoots high."

"You hit him in the shoulder."

"Hell, I was aiming for his black heart!"

"Oh, Lee." Mary threw herself in his arms. "I was so scared!"

"I know, my love," he soothed. "Me, too. I swear you scared ten years off my life. And if you ever do anything like that again, I'll kill you myself! Jesus, Mary, I thought I had lost you! And I don't know what I would do if something happened to you. Christ, woman, I love you."

Mary pushed back from his chest and stared up at his face. "You do?"

"Of course, I do."

"Since when?" she demanded.

Lee reached out, took her by the shoulders, and looked her straight in the eyes. "I think I fell in love with you the day you took your drawers and petticoats off to please Maddy."

"What?"

"I was always attracted to you, Two-shot, right from the beginning in Peaceable. And when I walked into the church in Cheyenne that day and saw you standing at the altar with Cosgrove, my life—my *empty* life—seemed to flash before my eyes. I wanted you for myself. I looked at you that day, and I thought you were the most beautiful woman I'd ever seen. But I was wrong. You grew more beautiful the day you took off your drawers to make Maddy happy and you continue to grow more beautiful. You become more precious to me every day. I love you, Mary Alexander Kincaid. I have from the beginning and I intend to spend every day showing you how much—right up until the end of my life."

"Oh, Lee . . ." She wrapped her arms around his neck and kissed him, until they both forgot their fright and remembered only their love for each other.

Epilogue

Two weeks later, Lee sat relaxing in a big leather easy chair in the red parlor of Ettinger House. Reese, David and Judah sat with him. Each man had a snifter of brandy and a fine Havana cigar by his side. Judah hadn't spoken a word and Lee had had to snip his cigar for him, and light it, but after spending much of his time in the company of women, Judah seemed to enjoy the male camaraderie.

Mary had redecorated the entire house, stripping the walls and floors of their dark coverings, but she had left the red parlor inviolate.

Lee leaned back in his chair. "I'm sure glad Mary didn't change this room. It's gaudy as hell, but I like it."

"Yeah," Reese agreed, "It must be nice having a billiard table and a bar and a roulette wheel in the comfort of your home—having a room with all of your favorite vices in it."

"You have a room like that, too, Reese," David teased. "It's called the bedroom."

Reese grinned. "Yes, so it is."

The three of them laughed.

"Well, Lee, what are you going to do now that you've finally resigned from the Agency and Sarrazin and Cosgrove are behind bars?" David Alexander asked. "Become a silver baron?"

"From what I've seen," Reese added. "He's well on his way."

"And so are you," Lee reminded him. "As stockholders in the Ettinger Silver Mine."

"So what are you planning to do?" David repeated his earlier question, then took a sip of his brandy.

Lee stretched his long legs out in front of him. "I've decided to build a bank."

David swallowed his brandy in one gulp, then coughed and nearly choked on it.

"We heard about that incident at the Ajax Saloon, Bank, and Assayer's office," Reese told him. "We heard how you marched into the saloon and punched Hugh Morton right in the eye and told him that since your wife was supporting the whole damned town of Utopia, and since she had enough money deposited in his bank to own the damn thing, Morton had better get down on his hands and knees and welcome her into the Ajax. In fact, he'd better get down on his hands and knees and beg her apologies. Because if Mary Alexander Kincaid was welcomed everywhere else in town, she'd sure as hell better be welcomed in a miserable excuse for a business like the Ajax."

David laughed. "We thought the incident was settled after he apologized."

"Well," Lee began, "it was as far as Mary is concerned. But you know, the more I think about it, the more I hate having to go to a miserable son of a bitch like Hugh Morton every time I need to deposit or withdraw money. I think I'd be much happier in my own bank. Besides, I'm going to need a bank now that Mary's decided to turn the teaching of the school over to Sylvia for a while."

David sat forward in his chair. "Mary's giving up teaching?"

"Yep." Lee grinned with satisfaction.

"What's she going to do?" Reese asked. "Stay home and run the house?"

"Are you kidding?" Lee teased. "Mary's got the running of Ettinger House and Utopia School down to a fine art. She needs a bigger challenge."

"What now?" David couldn't believe how his sister had blossomed since her marriage to Lee.

"She's decided to run the mine."

"What?" Reese and David asked in unison.

"I think it's a wonderful idea. The mine doesn't belong to me. It belongs to Maddy. And one day, Maddy will be in charge. Mary thinks the miners and the businessmen around Utopia ought to have the opportunity to become accustomed to the idea of a woman running things. She's going to learn the business so she can teach Madeline. Mary's convinced it's what Tabby had in mind all along."

"And what do you think?" Reese asked.

"I think she's right. I think Tabby had a reason for every one of her demands and I think they had everything to do with what she hoped the town could be."

"She did, young man," Judah said suddenly. "And that's why she sent for you. Tabitha wanted Madeline to know her father and be part of a family, but most of all, Tabitha needed you—and a woman like Mary—to rescue the people and the town she loved. Tabitha trusted your judgment. She knew that with the right incentive, you would pick the perfect woman for the job."

Outside on the front porch, Mary sat with Tessa and Faith watching as their children—Joy, Hope, Coalie, Maddy, and Lily Catherine—played a game of tag in the front yard. Lily had come a long way in two weeks. She was running and playing and talking and laughing right along with the others.

The town of Utopia was shaping up nicely, too. The mine would reopen soon and the miners would go back to work.

The children had a school, and the women who wanted jobs had them.

Mary sat in her rocker and beamed with pride. She and Lee had each other, and Maddy and Judah, Louisa, and Syl and a whole town full of good friends. She patted her stomach; they also had an addition to the family on the way. Another Kincaid to carry on the family traditions she and Lee were establishing.

David and Tessa had Coalie and Lily and a thriving law practice in Peaceable. Reese and Faith had Joy and Hope and the responsibilities of running the Trail T.

Life was good. Life was very good. And Mary knew she owed everything to Tabitha Gray—to her foresight and wisdom—to her selfish determination to make things right, but especially to the love Tabitha had felt for Lee Kincaid and the love she had left to them all.